Samurai Cat
Goes to the Movies

Written and Illustrated
by
Mark E. Rogers
(With An Assist From Don Rash and Joe Serrada)

Infinity Publishing
December 2005

ISBN 0-7414-3000-2

Published by:

PUBLISHING.COM

Infinity Publishing.com
1094 New DeHaven Street, Suite 100
West Conshohocken, PA 19428-2713
Info@buybooksontheweb.com
www.buybooksontheweb.com
Toll-free (877) BUY BOOK
Local Phone (610) 941-9999
Fax (610) 941-9959

Printed in the United States of America

Printed on Recycled Paper

Published February-2006

To Steve.

Have a Nice Day

THE TERMINATIONER

If the robot assassin had been capable of astonishment, he would've been astonished.

As it was, he was amazed.

His circuits struggled to make sense of what he was seeing, finally coming up with three explanations:

MALFUNCTION

INCORRECT INFORMATION

ACTUALLY JUST LIKE THOSE MOVIES

He'd seen a lot of Japanese giant monster flicks when he was a little Terminationer, and even then, the special effects had struck him as pretty cheesy; it had never occurred to him that they weren't FX at all. But here he was, standing on the outskirts of Tokyo, and if any of those buildings were an inch over four feet tall, he was badly mistaken.

Rubbery looking dinosaurs were hopping around among the miniatures, being attacked by toy tanks and planes; recording the action with four cameras, the movie folks were all normal size--- the Terminationer guessed they must be from other parts of Japan.

"You, you there!" cried the director through a bullhorn. "Get out of my shot!"

The robot considered blowing the man away. Instead he asked:

"Ze Hello Dere Kitty Building. Vhere?"

Filming halted. The dinosaurs squinted at the robot, one crying:

"Arnold Schwarzenegger!"

"Oh!" another shouted. "Please show us your red-glowing eyes!"

The robot had no idea who Arnold Schwarzenegger was, but lowered his shades nonetheless, gave out a bunch of "Best wishes, Arnie" autographs, then got his directions and strode off.

Miniscule tanks and planes assailed him; he paid them little heed, soon arriving at the building. Standing nearly twice as tall as the structure, he could've easily kicked it to pieces, killing everyone inside, but his computer brain rejected that approach as far too efficient.

GET SMALL, he thought, and, taking out his Temporal Plot-Device, one very handy little time machine, he projected himself into Tinyspace, utilizing the principle that time and space are manifestations of each other, or some such bullshit for those of you who require explanations. Thoroughly little, he entered the building and took an elevator to the boss's office.

Wearing a Hello There Kitty baseball cap, a secretary looked up at the robot as he entered. Behind her red, white, and blue Kitty desk, Hello There Kitty merchandise crammed a glass case. The office's walls were covered with framed Kitty art, all the figures bright primary colors against flat white backgrounds; strange Kitty-faces with dots for eyes and noses and mouths stared inexpressively at the Terminationer. The robot was glad he wasn't a human being, as he was quite sure all this exceedingly Japanese Japanese culture would've wierded him right out....as he approached the desk, Kitty mobiles trailed across his bristle brush crewcut.

"May I help you?" the secretary asked.

"I'm here to see Mr. Miaovara Shiro," the robot answered.

"Do you have an appointment?"

He pondered a list of options:

WALK ON IN

SHOOT HER

SHOOT HER AND WALK ON IN

SAY YOU'RE THAT SCHWARZENEGGER GUY

"I'm dot Schvarzenegger guy," he said.

"*Arnold* Schwarzenegger?" she asked delightedly.

He dipped his sunglasses. Immediately she hit a button on her speaker phone, saying:

"Arnold Schvarzenegger to see you, sir!"

"To what do I owe the honor?" the boss answered.

The robot replied: "I vass in town, just tought I'd drop in."

"What a pleasure!" said Mister Miaowara Shiro.

The secretary ushered the robot into the inner sanctum. A stout middle-aged Japanese man rushed to greet him.

"Miaovara Shiro?" the Terminationer asked.

The Kitty King bowed.

NOT A CAT, the robot thought.

"Schwarzenegger-*san*?" the other said. "Is something wrong?"

"You're not ze Miaovara Shiro I'm looking for," the robot answered.

"Sorry," Mister Miaowara said.

The robot stared at him, weighing his choices:

WAX HIM ANYWAY

TURN AND GO

TELL HIM HE'S A LUCKY BASTARD

ASK HIM IF HE INVENTED ALL THIS KITTY JUNK

"Did you invent Hello Dere Kitty?" the robot inquired.

Miaowara-*san* nodded.

Instantly a new thought flashed into the Terminator's brain:

REMEMBER PEARL HARBOR

The robot reached into his jacket, pulling out a longslide Colt .45 automatic with a laser sight.

"Mercy!" said Mister Miaowara.

"For ze man who invented Hello Dere Kitty?"

Miaowara seemed dumbfounded, as though he'd never really considered how he'd abused his free will; then his face became the very picture of agonized remorse.

"You've got a point," he said, produced a Hello There Kitty Pistol, and popped himself through the head.

The robot strode from the inner office, ignoring cries from the secretary. Re-entering the elevator, he hit the button for the lobby, holstered his automatic, and opened his copy of the Donnelly Nipponese Person Directory. Besides the Shiro that had just been accounted for, there were two more listings; one on the Island of Peleliu in 1944, the other in sixteenth-century Japan.

PELELIU, the robot thought.

Pocketting the directory, he took out his Plot-Device.

Located in the Palau archipelago, some five hundred miles east of the Philippines, Peleliu was a small hunk of coral rock which had, in autumn 1944, become the scene of a ferocious battle between the First U.S. Marines and a desperate Japanese garrison dug deep into the Umurbrogol, a jagged hogback which had been nicknamed "Bloody Nose Ridge" by the Americans. Day after day the slaughter had gone on, and the artillery-denuded slope was awash in blood under the broiling equatorial sun, except at night, that is; the Marines were just marshalling their forces for a fresh assault on the heights when the Terminationer appeared among them, looking most out of place in his 1990's leather-punk outfit.

"And just who the hell are you?" cried a leatherneck colonel.

"Ahnult Schvarzenegger," the robot replied.

The Marines didn't seem familiar with the name.

"Sounds German," the colonel said. "Come to think of it, that's some kraut accent you've got there."

"He's a spy, sir," said a lieutenant. "Must be working for the Japs."

"Are you a kraut, boy?" the colonel asked the robot.

"Ja," said the Terminationer. "I'm viss Von Steuben's volunteers."

"Von Steuben fought in the *Revolutionary* War," the lieutenant said.

"Isn't ziss war about ze the very same ideals?" the robot asked.

"Damn if we aren't, boy!" the colonel cried. "What's the capital of Idaho?"

"Trenton," the robot answered.

"What can we do for you?" the colonel asked.

4

"Chust keep out of my vay," the robot said.

"You got it," the colonel promised.

Cocking his Johnson M1941 automatic rifle, the Terminationer stood up in full view of the Japanese, calling:

"Candy-Gram for Miaovara Shiro!"

"Oh!" a multitude of voices answered. "Candy-Gram!" Thousands of Japanese soldiers appeared from out of every hole and crevice on the Umurbrogol, waving. "I'm Shiro! That's me!"

The robot barely had time to determine that none of them were cats before the Americans opened up. The slope erupted in dusty bullet-impacts; blood squirting from their mustard-colored uniforms, the Japanese crumpled, one rolling to the Terminationer's feet.

"What kind of candy was that?" he gasped.

The American colonel looked at the lieutenant.

"Let's remember this for Iwo Jima," he said.

The Terminationer slung the Johnson over his shoulder and took out his directory once more, wondering when he was going to get to kill someone.

The address for the third Shiro was Thirty-Four Shakespeare Lane, Oxford Mews, Omi Province, Japan; the date, 1579. He punched the information into the Plot Device. The Marines stepped back, startled as he disappeared in a blaze of NPBTBFL, which, as I'm sure you all know, is short for No-Purpose-But-To-Be-Flashy-Lightning.

"Where'd he go, sir?" the lieutenant asked the colonel.

"Perhaps he time-travelled into the past," the colonel theorized.

"Not the future? *I'd* rather visit a world full of perfect political institutions and flying cars."

"He could go there *after* visiting the past. And then, return to the present."

"So why isn't he here?"

"Let's ask him when he comes back," the colonel said.

The Plot-Device got the robot to his destination before he even used it; there was no one in the house, but a family portrait showing a group of unmistakable cats proved he'd come to the right place. Going to their answering machine, he hit playback.

"Hi, papa-*san*," the machine said. "Shiro here, as if you didn't know. Just thought I'd tell you that me and uncle Tomokato are all right. We're in America; it's April 3rd, 1993, and I'm helping Uncle-*san* track down Hasdrubal "The Horrible" Lectern---you know, the guy who ate Nobunaga's liver. Say hello to mama-*san* and my rat brothers, please. If you want to reach us, we're staying at the Hyatt in downtown Baltimore. *Sayonara.*"

The Terminationer clicked off the machine.

"There," said Dr. Lectern to Shiro. "All nicely trussed up."

The kitten was tied to a chair in the basement of Lectern's current hideout. Hasdrubal the Horrible pulled up a seat opposite.

"Where'd you learn to tie knots like this?" Shiro asked.

"Johns Hopkins," Lectern said.

"Didn't they fire you?"

"After they found the Dean's head in my freezer."

"People can be so narrow-minded, Doc," Shiro commiserated.

"Don't call me that."

"What then?"

"Doc*tor*. But if you *must* get familiar, you can call me---" Pausing for effect, the murderer leaned forward, shone a flashlight up under his face, and leered: "---Hasdrubie."

"Hasdrubie?" Shiro said, put off by the sheer silliness of it. "I think I'd rather call you Doctor."

"Most people would."

Shiro had to admire the madman's cunning.

"Personally, I'd rather be called Hasdrubers," Lectern continued. "But other people would rather call me that too, and they'd be getting right chummy with me after a while. If only my parents had named me Hamilcar! Now then---" He pulled the seat closer to Shiro's.

"So," he said. "You and your uncle actually thought you'd get the better of *me!*"

"No, we were trying to kill you," said Shiro. "Which is more like getting the *best* of you, I think---"

"Where *is* your uncle?"

"Wouldn't you like to know?"

"That's why I asked," Lectern snapped.

"What was the question?" Shiro asked.

"Where is your uncle?"

"Wouldn't you like to know?"

"How long do you expect to keep this up?"

"If you want to find out, just keep asking me where Uncle is," Shiro said.

Lectern pondered this.

"No," he said after a time, with a triumphant sneer.

Damn, Shiro thought.

"Now then," Lectern said. "I've heard some very nasty things about you. If you relate some of the more pathological episodes in your life, I'll kill you less painfully."

"That's certainly something," Shiro answered, and gave him an account of his stint in Chicago, pointing out that he'd rubbed out more people during that brief period than Lectern had in his whole career.

"You only murdered thirteen, right?" he asked.

"Yes, but in particularly repellent ways," Lectern said irritably. "And then I *ate* them."

"Well certainly, if we're going on points, each of your killings scored higher than mine."

7

"Every one was a Ten."

"I'd say mine were Threes," Shiro said. "Would you agree that was fair?"

Lectern nodded. "What are you driving at?"

"I've still got you beat on points. I'm way out ahead, as a matter of fact. Quality is all very well and good, but sheer overwhelming *quantity* is nothing to be sneered at..."

"I'm much more evil than you are," Lectern insisted.

"So you say. But the numbers just don't add up. And when you consider that I was involved in a plot to sell nuclear weapons to Quebecois terrorists... Hell, *that* was irresponsible, even by my standards..."

Plainly flustered, Lectern said: "I don't believe you."

"Didn't you see those hearings?" Shiro asked. "When I went up before the Senate and turned state's evidence---"

Suddenly the door opened, and in strode Tomokato, paw on hilt.

"That didn't happen, Shiro,"he said. "Remember? It was all a dream. Someone *else's* dream, as a matter of fact..."

"No wonder I don't remember dreaming it," Shiro said.

Lectern rose slowly from his chair, facing Tomokato.

"Do you know what I'm going to do to you?" he asked, grinning as he advanced. "I'm going to bite the nose clean off your face and spit it in your eyes. And when you scream, I'm going to sink my teeth into your tongue and snap it off and swallow it..."

Shiro was deeply grossed out. He hated tongue.

"...Then I'm going to strip your face from your skull with my bare hands and bind a book on *cats* with it, and blow up your intestines and bladder with my very own breath and twist them together to make balloon-animals, and--- Oh." Lectern halted. "Pardon me, but is that a *sword* you have there?"

Tomokato gave him a dozen very good reasons to think so. Hasdrubal the Horrible's severed head came to rest next to a glistening mass of his own viscera.

"And me without a spoon," he sighed.

8

Tomokato freed Shiro.

"Were you listening at the door, unc?" Shiro asked.

"Yes," Tomokato answered angrily. "I never knew that you actually *murdered* anyone in Chicago."

"Before or *after* you got there?"

"Before. The men you killed afterwards were dealt with justly, in my opinion."

"Set your mind at ease, unc," Shiro replied. "I never did any hits. I was just trying to psych Lectern out."

Tomokato looked at him sidelong.

"You don't believe me?"

"Would you if you were me?"

"Well," Shiro said, "Seeing as how I *know* I'm telling the truth, I guess we *both* would. Now, *my* question is, if I were you, would there only be one of us? Or if there still were two of us, would they both be me, or would they both be you?"

Tomokato elected to press him no further.

"Let's go," he said.

They went up from the basement and out of the house. A dozen or so police cars were parked in the street.

"You are surrounded!" a cop cried. "Drop the sword and put your hands up! Also, take those stupid cat-heads off!"

"Fight 'em?" Shiro asked Tomokato.

"No," Tomokato said, then called to the police: "Are you here for Lectern?"

"Yes!" the cop replied. "Now put down that sword."

Tomokato complied, over Shiro's protests.

"These men are not evildoers, nephew," the cat said. "Perhaps we can reason with them. After all, we've saved them some work."

The police rushed forward.

That evening as he was cleaning his Gatling gun, the Terminationer sat watching the news in Shiro's suite at the Baltimore Hyatt, waiting for the kitten to return. The big story was the death of Dr. Lectern.

"At this moment, the alleged slayers, who are said to be two guys in really good cat costumes, are in the custody of the Hunt Valley

Police---"

Gatling in hand, the robot marched to the door.

"So," said the police psychiatrist, "Why was it necessary to slice Lectern into so *many* pieces?"

"To cover as much of the carpet as possible with his body," Tomokato answered.

"Wasn't that a bit excessive?"

"It was a very ugly carpet."

The psychiatrist made a notation, then asked: "You say he ate your Lord's liver?"

"With a little sprig of parsley."

"Why parsley?"

"Don't ask me. Garnishes leave me cold. Moreover, I wouldn't have eaten my Lord's liver under any circumstances."

"What if you'd been very hungry?"

"A true samurai wouldn't get so hungry. Also, I would've needed my Lord's permission, and he'd never have given it."

"What if he were already dead?"

"He'd have been be even *less* likely to have given it. These are silly questions. May we go now?"

"That's not up to me," said the shrink, standing, clipboard under one arm.

"You think we're crazy, don't you?" Shiro asked.

"I don't use that word. However, I *would* say you're nutty as a fruitcake.

"Don't you mean nutty as *two* fruitcakes?"

"No, that's how nutty you are."

The shrink rapped on the door. A cop let him out.

"I say we make a break," said Shiro.

"Let's see if they charge us with anything," Tomokato replied.

The cop at the front counter looked up to see a huge jut-jawed fellow in a leather outfit looming over him, red lights glowing dimly behind his shades.

"I vant to see ze guys who killed Dr. Lectern," the giant said.

"Who are you?"

"Dere lawyer."

Overhearing this claim, another policeman stepped up behind the first.

"They haven't made their phone call," he said.

"I saw ze story on ze TV."

"How do you know those two are your clients?" the second cop.

"Dere alvays dressink up as cats," the giant said.

"Not good enough," the first answered. "This is Hunt Valley, Maryland, pal. Half the prisoners we get are dressed that way. Why do you think we knew they *weren't* cats?"

The Terminationer switched to another tack. "Zey contacted me telepathically."

"Well, that's another story, isn't it?" both cops said, beaming. "Do you have any firearms you'd like to bring in with you?"

"My Gatling," the robot said. "But it's out in ze car."

"Better go get it, then, hey?"

"I'll be back," he replied, and left.

"Doesn't he blend right in with that physique and that German accent?" said the first cop to the second.

The other answered: "Wouldn't *we* be surprised if he turned out to be a robot assassin from the future?"

The first looked out through the glass double doors and said:

"He wasn't kidding about that Gatling."

The second looked as well---the giant was marching toward the entrance lugging a .42 caliber army Gatling mounted on a field carriage, complete with a drum magazine and a crank.

They rushed out from behind the desk to open the doors.

"Don't bozzer," boomed his voice from outside, reflections on the glass vibrating as the sound passed through.

The cops stepped back from the doors.

He began to crank.

The doors exploded in a blizzard of glass splinters. The police flew back across the lobby, each with a slug in the shoulder and/or leg.

"Why didn't you kill us?" they gasped to the robot.

"I'm programmed only to kill Miaowara Shiro, or Hello Dere Kitty creators," the Terminationer replied, lifting his gun way up as he passed through the gap in the counter.

"Damn!" the first cop said. "He *is* a robot assassin from the future!"

"Aren't we surprised!" his companion replied.

As the gunfire erupted, Shiro cocked an ear and said: "U.S. Army Gatling....42 caliber...drum magazine...mounted on a field carriage..."

"When was it made?" Tomokato asked.

Shiro cupped a paw to his ear. "July 2nd through the 3rd, 1874."

"Where?"

"The Colt Factory in New Haven, Connecticut."

"Who was the foreman on that particular line?"

Shiro listened hard. "A Mr. William S. Tunney."

"And where did he live?"

"22 Buttles Lane. New Haven, of course."

"What was his wife's name?"

"Sarah."

"Was he faithful to her?"

"No."

"Why did she put up with it?"

"She really loved him."

"You certainly know your guns, Shiro," Tomokato said, just as three sweating, panting cops came rushing in, all of them furiously reloading their shotguns. As luck would have it, One of them happened to have Tomokato's sword tucked into his belt.

A great dark silhouette appeared beyond the threshold, aiming a smoking Gatling into the room. A twist of the crank, and the cops were on the floor, moaning and clutching their bloodied thighs and/or shoulders.

Tomokato grabbed his sword as the giant relented.

"Miaovara Shiro?" the intruder asked.

"Do I know you?" Shiro replied, grabbing up one of the fallen shotguns.

The other marched into the room, the Gatling's wheels ripping out the doorframe on either side.

Shiro fired first. Most of the pellets missed, but several caught the giant's brow and cheek. Bits of flesh leaped off, revealing patches of gleaming steel skull.

"A robot, unc!" Shiro cried.

Something went *boing!* inside the metal head; the robot loosed the crank and banged himself on the temple twice. A spring sprang out of his ear.

"Now zen," he said. "Vhere ver ve?"

Tomokato stepped past the Gatling's barrel, slicing. His sword bounced harmlessly from the robot's endoskeleton.

14

The robot lashed out with a fist. Tomokato sailed back with Shiro, who'd picked up one of the shotguns; before the robot could grab the crank again, Shiro salted him down with three more doses of buckshot, pump-BLAST, Pump-BLAST, pump Buh-LAST!!!! Taking the first burst, the robot dropped the Gatling, and catching the second, slapped flat up against the wall of the corridor outside; at the third, he went clean through, punching a tremendous cutout in the barrier, Schwarzenegger-shaped right down to (or right up to) the flattop.

Yet much to the annoyance of the two felines, the robot quickly righted himself, stepping back out into the hallway. Sheathing his sword, Tomokato picked up a shotgun, and asked:

"If we shoot you again, will you get right back up?"

"Ja," said the robot, entering the room once more, climbing over the fallen Gatling.

The cat and Shiro potted him just as he stepped down. One foot straight out, the robot sailed back over the gun in a beautiful reverse hurdle, hit the linoleum---- and proved he was as good as his word, immediately rising behind the weapon.

Shiro said: "If we shoot you *again*---"

"I'll chust get up---"

"That's been established. But would you be able to do a hundred push-ups too?"

"Ja."

"Two hundred?"

"Vatch me," said the Terminationer, beckoning them to shoot.

"One-handed?"

"Shoot, shoot, shoot."

They blasted him once more. He fell.

Tomokato looked under the Gatling. The robot turned over onto his stomach and started counting off a series of deep, perfect one-handed push-ups, sounding for all the world like a huge malevolent Lawrence Welk.

"A vun! A two! A tree! A four..!"

15

The cat and his nephew slipped out the door, racing along the hallway. A crowd of cops stood at the far end, watching the robot do his pushups in perfect awestruck silence. Tomokato and Shiro simply thrust on through. They spotted a Harley parked outside the station and took off on it, heading back towards Baltimore.

But it wasn't long before they heard shots, and looking back, saw another motorcycle in hot pursuit.

The robot was making do with a pistol now, trailing the Gatling behind his chopper. Tomokato guessed the machine-gun must be out of ammo. He wondered how the robot could be gaining, seeing as how he was pulling such a heavy load. But the cat knew from long experience that the individual details of his adventures, let alone whole plots, rarely made any sense.

Quite in keeping with that, the robot kept missing them, even though he'd shown earlier that he was a fearsomely good shot, even with a weapon as cumbersome as the Gatling.

Entering a cutting beneath a railroad trestle, Tomokato swung round a corner on the far side, steering directly towards an oncoming semi.

"A thousand situps?" he cried over his shoulder to the robot, then swerved out of the truck's path.

"No sveat," the Terminationer answered.

And crashed head-on into the truck.

"Nephew," Tomokato said, "Why is that robot trying to kill you?"

"Beats me, unc," Shiro replied.

"You don't have the slightest idea?"

"Not a clue."

"You don't have any irritated business partners that I should know about?"

"No!"

A likely story, Tomokato thought.

Standing beside the crumpled ruin of his cab, the trucker watched the Terminationer grind through his situps.

"Man, are you in shape!" said the driver.

Finally the robot stood.

"They should make you the head of the President's Physical Fitness Council!" the driver declared.

"Zey vouldn't take me," the robot answered.

"Why not?"

"Ife used shteroids."

The robot strode back along the trailer, which had overturned. It was full of Volkswagen Jettas.

"Hey!" the driver cried, coming up beside him. "You're some kind of Kraut, right? Just what does *Fahrvergnugen* mean, anyway?"

The Terminationer searched his language files. "Ve vant to take offer your country, and ve'll shoot your muzzer if you try to shtop us."

"That's what I thought it meant," the driver said.

The robot pried an intact Jetta out of the trailer.

"What are you doing?" the driver asked.

"Shtealing ziss car," the Terminationer replied.

"You can't do that!" the driver shouted.

The robot grabbed him by the throat, lifted him clear off the ground and answered: "Press charges."

"Why bother?" the driver gasped. "Can't legalize morality."

After chucking him up into a nearby tree, the robot hitched his Gatling to the back of the Jetta, and took off for Baltimore.

"After all that," the driver cried. "Don't you want your car?"

The Terminationer returned, looking a trifle sheepish in an impassive roboty sort of way.

"Sanks," he said, crammed himself into the VW, and lit out.

Reaching Baltimore's Inner Harbor, Tomokato and Shiro parked their motorcycle in the Hyatt's garage, then went into the lobby. They hadn't been back to the hotel for several days, and a Science-Fiction convention had begun in the interim.

WELCOME HEFTYCON read an event board.

"Heftycon?" Shiro wondered aloud.

"It's a convention for overweight science-fiction fans," Tomokato said. "I've heard it's the most heavily attended in the country."

Like the Argonauts negotiating the Symplegades, or some such pretentious metaphor, they threaded their way through the various beanied fatties to the elevator and went on up to their suite, which had plainly been visited by the robot.

"Look at those robot-butt prints on my bed," Shiro said.

"Well, at least he didn't eat our mints," Tomokato answered, tossing one to Shiro.

"Thank Buddha," Shiro said, unwrapping it and popping it into his mouth.

"They *are* wafer-thin," Tomokato said.. "Let's get our toothbrushes and go."

They packed up their bathroom-gear.

"You know," Shiro said, "He'll probably come back here as soon as he finishes his sit-ups."

"No," Tomokato answered. "It's my guess he'll try to find some ammunition for that Gatling. And bullets for such an old gun won't be easy to come by."

"But what if you're wrong, Uncle-San? What if he found a drive-through Gatling ammunition store that was right on the way here?"

"That we didn't see?"

"What if he knew a shorter route back, and the store was along *that* road?"

Tomokato looked at his watch. "Then I expect he'd be here right about..."

"Knock knock," called a Teutonic voice from out in the hall.

"Who's *they*-er?" Shiro asked, doing his best Bugs Bunny.

"Maid service."

"Yeah, right," Shiro whispered to Tomokato. Pulling up a chair, he looked out through the peephole. "Hey, Uncle-*san*! It really *is* the maid!"

"Does she have a Gatling?"

"Yes..."

Tomokato went to the door.

"You know," he cried, "The idea that you could just change shape like that is thoroughly ludicrous."

The robot was silent for a while, then said: "Liquid metal---"

But Tomokato wouldn't have any of that, saying: "A concept which comes precariously close to magic in an ostensible science-fiction story."

"Liquid metal," said the robot again, rather more weakly this time.

Tomokato replied: "If you were *really* liquid metal, you could've just come sliding under the door..."

"I couldn't bring my gun."

"What would you need a gun for?" Tomokato demanded. "You could kill us in any number of other ways. And anyway, if we can imagine a liquid robot assassin, why couldn't we imagine a liquid robot Gatling? Why can't you just stick to the level of technology that was established earlier in the story---?"

Shiro tugged at Tomokato. "Uncle-*san*!" Shiro cried. "You're losing it! Calm down!"

Tomokato took several deep breaths. "It's really quite out of character for me."

"Yes," Shiro said.

"So then," Tomokato resumed. "What's it going to be?"

"I'll try not to be so shtupid," the robot replied.

The cat looked out through the peephole to see the automaton back in his original form.

"Very good," Tomokato said, ducking, pulling Shiro down from the seat.

Wood-chips flew as a line of bullets chewed across the door.

Tomokato and the kitten rushed to an adjoining door, which the cat kicked open, the pair dashing through just as the Terminationer smashed his way into their suite. Reaching the corridor, they saw the robot backing out into the hall, wheeling his Gatling round.

"Before you shoot," the cat said, "will you at least explain why you're trying to kill my nephew?"

"Certainly not," the Terminationer replied. "It vould be a vaste of time and qvuite contrary to my programming for me to tell you zat I must kill him before he becomes ze Maleffolent God-Emperor of ze Universe."

"Who sent you?"

"Ze Rebel High Command," the Terminationer answered, "But I can't tell you zat eizzer."

"Ah."

The robot opened up.

"Squat thrusts!" Tomokato cried, retreating slowly, sword whirling, deflecting the slugs, sending at least half but perhaps as many as two-thirds back into the giant.

"How many?" the Terminationer asked, leather suit already reduced to bloody tatters, large sections of his shining endoskeleton laid bare.

"Ten thousand?" Tomokato answered.

"Five!" the robot answered, still cranking furiously.

"Done!" Tomokato answered.

Drum magazine emptied at last, the robot commenced squatting and thrusting.

Tomokato and Shiro dashed into the nearest stairwell, where a thick clot of porky filkers soon retarded their downward progress. By the time they neared the bottom, they could hear---amid many screams, yelps, and oinks--- the robot and his Gatling banging down behind them.

The felines pelted out into the lobby, where Tomokato noticed a harpoon gun on a bellman's cart. Balancing on a white peg-leg, a tall nautical type in a stovepipe hat was checking in.

"Excuse me," said the cat. "Aren't you Captain Ahab?"

"Aye," Ahab replied.

"What are you doing at Heftycon?"

"'Tis a good place to find a white whale."

"Could we borrow your harpoon gun?"

"Certainly."

The Terminationer charged out of the stairwell; Tomokato fired the gun at him. The robot dodged to the right, placing himself directly in front of the shaft of the scenic elevator. The harpoon ripped through the stairwell door.

But Shiro had already loaded another missile into the gun; Tomokato caught the Terminationer square in the chest with the spear, bashing him back into the elevator door, which flattened beneath him.

Above, the elevator had begun to descend.

"Any reqvuests?" the robot asked, pulling the harpoon out of his chest.

"Bench-press the elevator?" Tomokato inquired.

"How many times?"

"Just once."

"Piece uff cake," the robot replied.

But the Terminationer hadn't reckoned on a lift full of SF fatties, and despite his best efforts, the elevator kept descending, the robot disappearing beneath it to the sound of crumpling metal.

The fans stepped out. The elevator rose again, groaning with relief.

Tomokato and Shiro went to look at the remains of the robot.

"I guess *he's* finished," Shiro said.

Tomokato turned; eyeing the robot-crushers waddling off towards the hotel's revolving door, he winced to think of the nightmare that was about to develop there.

"He *must* be," the cat said.

"Well," said Shiro, "Now that that's wrapped up---"

"Yes?"

"I'm considering going home to visit my folks."

"What have they done to deserve that?" Tomokato asked.

"They *had* me, unc," Shiro replied. "By the way, what did you make of that God-Emperor stuff?"

"I don't know."

"Sounded great, didn't it?" Shiro said.

"The whole universe ruled by *you*? After you were trying to sell nuclear weapons to terrorists?"

"If I was God-Emperor of the universe," Shiro answered, "I wouldn't *have* to sell them nuclear weapons. *They'd* have to buy them---from me."

"Works out to the same thing," Tomokato replied.

"Then I could just *give* them nuclear weapons."

"Shiro, you don't sound very repentant to me."

"Unc, the story where I *really* repented, turned state's evidence, was that dream sequence one. The one I didn't dream..."

Tomokato shook his head. "Sometimes, Shiro, your lack of moral progress depresses me so much that I wish I'd never been born."

Shiro laughed. "Don't do anything rash, unc. The issue's still in doubt. And actually, I suspect I'm teetering towards the side of the angels. That spanking in that next-to-last story was no dream after all."

Tomokato gave him a hard look. "Let's get out of here. The police are going to descend on this place any second, and they might pick us up over that Lectern business again."

Going into the garage, they hopped on their motorcycle, but before Tomokato could start it up, Shiro asked:

"How are you going to manage without me, unc?"

"Just fine," Tomokato answered. The thought that he was going to be off on his own was beginning to sink in; hunting down his next victim would almost seem like a vacation. "There's no chance that you'll *stay* in Japan, is there?"

"And leave you all alone?" Shiro asked. "Certainly not, Uncle-san. I need Lessons in Life. You're always telling me so. And you're just the cat to give them to me. Besides, my parents *may* deserve a visit from me. But they *don't* deserve having me around indefinitely."

"And I do?"

"No. But I like you too much to worry about it."

Tomokato groaned and kick-started the cycle.

After a suitable interval, the Terminationer's electronic brain clicked back on.

WHAT THE FUCK WAS IN THAT ELEVATOR? he thought.

Men in white lab coats were looking down at him.

GOVERNMENT TECHNICIANS. BUG OUT BEFORE THEY EXAMINE YOU.

He lifted an arm from the flattened bloody wreckage of his chassis, the men in the white coats gasping and leaping away. Ignoring them, he jerked his hand over his face and inserted his thumb in his mouth.

INITIATE REINFLATION SEQUENCE, he thought, and commenced to blow with all his might.

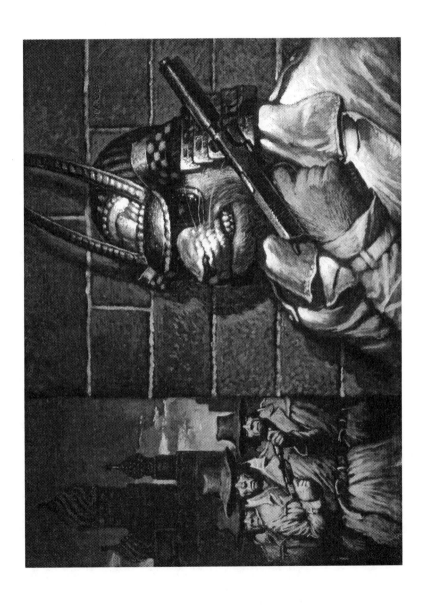

THE YELLOW BRICK ROAD WARRIOR

Shiro's seat at Gate 22 faced a huge window that looked out over the landing-field and a vast expanse of dreary flat Kansas beyond. The sky was grey, the land was grey, *he* was grey; of course, he was normally grey, but even his kimono, which was generally blue, had gone quite the color of ash, and very dispirited ash, at that.

If I didn't know better, he thought, *I'd swear this whole Kansas place was black and white.*

Yet that merely raised another question--- if indeed Kansas was entirely   black and white, how did that explain all the grey? Whatever the case, the colorlessness even extended to the shows on the little coin-op TV beside his seat, including several movies he knew *for a fact* were in color, such as *Miracle on 34th St.* and *The Maltese Falcon.*

A chicken bobbed past him, pecking at kernels of corn that some farmer had strewn over the floor. Kansas was a very rustic place, or so it seemed. The terminal was full of guys in overalls and straw hats. There were also considerable numbers of hogs, goats, and ducks, some of whom appeared to be unchaperoned. The corridors echoed with snuffles and baas and quacks.

Shiro flipped the TV's channel-changer full-circle one more time, then decided to clean his weapons, two Micro-Uzis. He'd traded his Remington 870 in at the gunshop at Baltimore-Washington International; the pump-action and a thousand dollars had bought him the Uzis, which, the owner had assured him, had only been used in a single drive-by down in D.C. Proceeding to the phony document stand, Shiro had picked up full FBI credentials, and just in case those failed to pass muster when he tried to bring the guns aboard the plane, he'd also bought a card identifying him as the Speaker of the U.S. House of Representatives. Good thing, too--- the folks at security had proved way too smart to fall for that FBI scam.

He unzipped his flight bag and took out the guns and his cleaning kit. He'd capped off several hundred rounds since Baltimore; looking for all the world like a future starship captain--- training toupee and all--- a fellow next to him on the plane had noticed that the wing was crawling with gremlins, not little rubber green ones, but the *scary* kind---that is to say, Looney Tunes Gremlins. In characteristic Shiro fashion, the kitten had carried the fight to the enemy, depressurizing the cabin in the process---hence this layover in Topeka. And undoubtedly, his barrels required a thorough swabbing.

He stripped both guns and cleaned them, lubing the parts with a light film of high-grade machine oil. Reassembling the Uzis, he'd just put them back into the carry-on when a news flash pre-empted *The Maltese Falcon*, declaring a tornado watch in effect.

He looked out over the tarmac again. The sky sure had darkened.

"This just in," said the announcer. "The National Weather Service has just upgraded the tornado watch to a tornado warning. A twister has touched down in the region of the Topeka airport, and is making directly towards Gate 22."

"Don't see it," Shiro muttered.

"What do you mean?" the announcer asked.

"I don't see a tornado," Shiro answered. "Look for yourself."

He swivelled the TV to face the window.

"Damn," said the announcer. "Where do you think it is?"

"You're the weatherman," Shiro replied.

"No, I just read the copy. Hey, wait---what's that over there, on the right?"

Shiro squinted. A dark finger was extending earthwards from the lowering greenish cloud-ceiling.

"That's it," Shiro said. "What should I do?"

"Stop talking to me and split," the announcer answered.

"Thanks," said Shiro, shouldered his flight bag, and took off.

But others besides himself had been watching their TVs, and a huge crush had developed in the corridor before him, vast numbers of farmers and farm animals all rushing from the various gates.

Pausing, he looked the other way. He was very nearly at the end of the terminal, and as the tornado drew near, he raced to a doorway marked AUTHORIZED PERSONNEL ONLY. A stairway took him down onto the tarmac.

Trying to put as much distance between himself and Gate 22 as he could, he sprinted along the runway. But looking over his shoulder, he discovered to his horror that the twister was shifting course, as though it had been after perfectly-innocent little him after all.

For some reason, the builders of the airfield had left a small wooden farmhouse beside the runway. Thinking it might have a storm cellar, Shiro rushed around to the back, only to discover a "No Cats Allowed" sign tacked to the cellar door. Ignoring the sign, he immediately flung the hatch open----and found himself contemplating a half-dozen double-barrelled shotguns manned by surly looking hayseeds in checkered shirts, sprigs of alfalfa cocked at agressive angles in their mouths.

"Can't read, can you sonny?" one demanded.

"I'm not a cat," Shiro protested, waving his phony credentials. "I'm the Speaker of the House."

"And I'm the Chief Justice of the United States," the other answered.

"Prove it," Shiro demanded.

The farmer rushed up the steps, flashed his Chief Justice card, grabbed the cellar door, and went down again, pulling it shut above him.

The house was between Shiro and the tornado, but he heard the twister roaring close...pelting up the back steps and into the kitchen, he saw a little abandoned black dog writing out its last will and testament. Wearing a wool poochie sweater on which the name Tototo was blazoned, the bowser spotted Shiro, left off writing, and rushed over to him, leaping into his arms, smelling right doggily.

The roar of the tornado grew deafening, and the house began to shudder. Still clutching the dog, Shiro slipped underneath the dinner-table. Things were crashing all around, dust and debris rained down, and with a terrific lurch, the house heeled upwards, the floor pitching at a steep angle. Shiro and Tototo would certainly have slid out from under the table if the table hadn't been merrily sliding along with them. With a *bam*! so loud that Shiro clearly saw the letters hanging in the air before him, his head struck something. His vision darkened, and Tototo's powerful bouquet began to fade. Shiro was dimly aware of a sickening spinning motion----was *he* going round and round, or was the house? Pondering this question, he faded into a dream that consisted primarily of Tototo scrubbing his face with his raspy fido tongue.

At least, Shiro *thought* it was a dream until he felt a tremendous impact that came up through the floor, and he opened his eyes open to see the dog lapping away furiously. That close, the tongue looked like a sopping-wet throw-rug being snapped in his face.

Shiro fended the dog off. The kitchen table was halfway across the room. Much of the ceiling had caved in.

The kitten stood, brushing plaster dust from his kimono. Setting a fallen stool upright, he climbed up on it and looked out through the window over the sink.

More barren than the Kansas landscape but resolutely, even fiercely, in color---technicolor to be exact---a bright red desert stretched to the horizon, baking under a hot blue sky. The tornado had plainly transported the house some distance.

Trailed by Tototo, Shiro went to the back door. It was unopenable, the doorframe partially crushed.

He went into the living room. The front door had fallen from its hinges, and he stepped out onto the porch, from which a large cluster of fairy-tale dwarfy dwellings were visible, looking most out of place in their arid surroundings.

He descended from the porch...As yet he could see no sign of life among the little houses, but just in case, he took out his Micro-Uzis, loaded them up, and primed them.

There came the sound of a motorcycle being kick-started. The engine sputtered, began to rev; a bunch more soon joined in. Out from behind the houses thundered a troop of very salty-looking marauders sporting mohawk haircuts and football shoulder pads. Armed with makeshift crossbows, they drew up in a semi-circle before the farmhouse, eyeing Shiro malignantly. One in particular drew the kitten's attention, a tall dude with a highly egg-shaped head, very dark eyeliner, and a feather boa.

"Yer Ladyship?" the fellow cried over his shoulder in I-gargle-with-acid tones.

The bikers behind him parted, and up rode one very wicked witch on a great big hog. Her tall black hat was pointy as pointy hats come, which is to say, most pointy, and her railroad-spike nose was even sharper than the chapeau. Her skirt was hiked up a bit, revealing red-and-blue striped stockings; sparkly red slippers shod her feet.

"Do you *really* think those slippers go with the rest of your outfit?" Shiro called, straining to be heard over the idling bikes.

The witch signalled.

The engines cut off in unison.

The witch dismounted from her bike, looked down at her shoes, then back at Shiro.

"Yeah," she said, and squirted a long stream of tobacco juice through a gap in her front teeth.

Shiro stepped aside.

Tototo yelped.

"Is that your house?" the witch asked.

"No," Shiro replied.

"You didn't try to drop it on me and my men?"

"No," Shiro said. "It was picked up by a tornado in Topeka, and--- just where *are* we, exactly?"

"Oz," growled the guy in the feather boa.

"Oz?" Shiro asked.

"You know. Australyer."

37

"Australia?" Shiro asked, puzzled. "You mean it's a real place?"

"Of course it's real," snarled the witch.

"I thought it was like Canada."

"Canada's real too," said the witch.

"That's what *I* thought till I went there," Shiro replied.

"What shall we do with him, My Lady?" Feather Boa asked the witch.

"Can't say I care for his attitude, Wugh," she answered.

Wugh cocked his crossbow. "Just say the word."

Shiro trained his Uzis on the witch.

"You don't frighten us," said Wugh. "No one's had ammunition for years!"

"How depressing," said Shiro, most heartfeltedly.

"Waste him," the witch commanded.

Marvelling at her lack of judgement, Shiro stitched her good with both Uzis, pummelling her back over the handlebars of her hog head over heels. She landed upright in the seat with a thud, her witchy dress mostly matching the ruby slippers now. A thunderstruck look frozen on her face, she listed slowly to the right, tilting the bike, tipping six marauders beside her like dominos.

On the left, Wugh gaped dazedly at her corpse for a few more moments, then shook his head and turned towards Shiro once more, loading a quarrel into his crossbow.

"Why didn't you tell us you had ammo?" he demanded.

Shiro shrugged. "Bullets speak louder than words."

Wugh shrieked and loosed the bolt, but Shiro, twisting from its path, blasted him off his bike with a burst to one shoulder, then retreated into the farmhouse before a storm of missiles launched by the other bikers.

Brandishing a cleaver, one of the marauders came riding up the front steps and through the door. Shiro blew him out of the saddle, back out onto the porch, while the riderless bike careened into the kitchen.

Shiro rushed to a window. Outside, bikers were scrambling onto their choppers, or respanning their crossbows. He peppered several, clips running out just as Wugh got back onto his hog.

"You!" Wugh cried, pointing at the kitten.

"Me?"

"You can run, but you can't hide!"

"It's very hard to hide when you're running," Shiro acknowledged.

Growling, Wugh turned his bike round and fled, followed by his surviving comrades. Shiro watched them disappear in the distance beyond the dwarfy dwellings, then went back out onto the porch. Tototo was lying on his side, whining, still trying to paw the witch's tobacco-juice out of his eyes.

As Shiro went down the steps towards the witch's corpse, he saw the ruby slippers vanish from her feet...hardly had they disappeared when he began having difficulty walking, and looked down to see the slippers on *him*. Pausing, he tried to kick them off, but in spite of the fact that they were way too big for him, they remained resolutely on his feet.

Tototo appeared at his side, blinking. The dog started to bark, and Shiro noticed a very large iridescent bubble drifting out of the sky. Settling on the ground, it popped, revealing a woman in pink with a tall silver crown.

"Are you a good witch, or a bad witch?" she asked, soap dripping from her chin and limbs.

"Aren't witches bad by definition?" Shiro asked, provoking a lot of tinkly laughter from unseen inhabitants of the midget mansions.

"Certainly not," said the bubble lady. "I'm a good witch."

"Exactly what a plain old *bad* witch would say," Shiro answered.

"Well yes, but... I'm all dressed in pink, see?"

"And you're all covered in soap. So what?"

"The idea that witches are *necessarily* bad is a medieval misconception," the bubble lady said. "The word witch is from the Anglo-Saxon *wicca*, meaning a wise person."

Shiro was skeptical. "Do you have a dictionary?"

"No, but the Twonchkins do," she replied.

"Twonchkins?"

The little people who live in this land." Cupping her hands beside her mouth, she bellowed: "Get a dictionary out here, pronto!"

Carrying a big blue book, a diminutive man came out of one of the houses He was wearing a green hat with a yellow flower nodding on the peak, and stripey shoes with curled up toes. The buttons on his bright yellow vest seemed to be jingle bells. Shiro found the overall look more than a tad on the eccentric side.

"Look up the derivation of the word *witch*," Shiro told the Twonchkin.

41

The Twonchkin cracked the dictionary open and flipped some pages. "It's from the Anglo-Saxon *wicca*, a witch, a practitioner of sorcery."

"Look up sorcery," Shiro said.

The Twonchkin did so. "Synonymous with black magic," he announced.

"But I'm a nice person, really," said the bubble lady.

"Then you're not a witch," Shiro said.

"Thank goodness," she replied. "But what am I then?"

"Do you have supernatural powers?"

"I'm not sure," she answered. "My wand does. Oh, I really don't know about any of this. I wish my husband Cosmo was here. He's had a lot of experience with the supernatural, you know..."

"What's your name, by the way?" Shiro asked.

"Bubbles, of course. I float around doing good deeds. I thought you might need some advice."

"Err, excuse me," said the Twonchkin. "But the wicked witch *is* dead, isn't she?"

Bubbles struck the corpse with a sprightly little kick.

"Deader than Rock Hudson," she declared.

"All clear!" the Twonchkin called.

Within moments a huge crowd of goofily dressed midgets assembled and performed a very long musical number, raising a vast cloud of choking red dust. For some reason, Shiro found the scene curiously devoid of charm. But just when he decided the sawed-off extravaganza would never end, it ended.

"We owe you a great debt," said the Twonchkin with the dictionary. "The witch and her flying punkies raided our village every month."

"For what?" Shiro asked.

"Topsoil. To understand, you have to go back to another time, when there was topsoil everywhere, things growing in it, lovely shiny plastic plants...gone now...swept away...For reasons long forgotten, two mighty warrior tribes went to war, and touched off a blaze that engulfed them all...engulfed *who* all?... I don't know....Badly put, I suppose...Anyway, without soil they were nothing... They'd built a house of straw, and now the Big Bad Wolf was at their door, huffing and puffing...Two pigs bought it...Third one killed the wolf, but it was too late for the rest of us...Dirt embargo...dirt crisis...Had to settle for scraping it from under our fingernails...Yucchh...The world crumbled...Cities exploded...DVD players stopped working...Chinese restaurants would only serve Cantonese...On the roads it was a white-line nightmare...The wicked witches and flying punkies took over the highways, mooning Paul Hogan, ready to wage war for a wheelbarrow of humus...Get the picture?"

"Yes, thank you," Shiro said. "How does one get out of this country?"

"Same way you got here," the Twonchkin answered. "Qantas."

"I think I'd rather not. "

"I'd magic you out with my wand," said Bubbles, "but it can't transport you outside the Barrier Reef."

"What about the Ruby Slippers?" the Twonchkin suggested.

"Good heavens, of course," said Bubbles, and told Shiro: "Just click them together three times and keep repeating `There's no place like home.'"

"Give me a break," said Shiro.

"No, seriously---"

"Got any other ideas?"

"He could go see the Wizard," the Twonchkin said.

"The Wizard?" Shiro asked.

"Of Australia," said Bubbles.

"Where can I find him?"

"Australia."

"Yes, but---"

"Follow the Yellow Brick Road," interrupted the Twonchkin.

Another Twonchkin ran up, seconding: "Follow the Yellow brick Road."

A third ran up, thirding: "Follow the Yellow Brick Road."

They indicated a highway leading out of town.

"That's concrete," said Shiro.

"Just pretend," said the First Twonchkin.

"Actually," said the second, "There *is* a short brick stretch, right before you get to Zirconsville, the Wizard's city. Just enough to convince the Wizard that it's all like that."

"Ah," said Shiro. "A *Potemkin* Yellow Brick Road."

Bubbles directed his attention to some of the fallen motorcycles. "You could take one of those."

"Why don't you magic me to Zirconsville with your wand?" Shiro asked. "It isn't outside the Barrier Reef, is it?"

"No. But I never claimed I could get you anywhere *inside* the reef, either."

"You implied it."

"Oh well, la-di-da."

"You've been very helpful," said Shiro. "Farewell."

Righting one of the hogs, he climbed aboard; Tototo jumped onto his lap. The Twonchkins all came near and began a merry ditty that reminded Shiro to FollowtheFollowtheFollowthe, but he swiftly started the Harley up, blotting the song out as he roared from town.

Once the racket of the cycle faded, the dictionary Twonchkin told Bubbles: "You didn't warn him about the Wicked Witch's sister."

"What a lapse," Bubbles said, and giggled; the Twonchkins giggled too, then warbled a Twonchkinland favorite about the inevitability of death, Bubbles handling the refrain, which involved her singing out a midget from the crowd and laughing:

44

"It tolls for *theeee*!"

Shiro went a considerable distance through the waste; growing hungry as the sun neared its zenith, he stopped the bike by the side of the road, guessing the Harley's original owner must've stashed some grub in the storage containers in back. But the compartments held only dry red soil...he scooped up a pawful disgustedly.

"Dirt," he said, letting it drift through his fingers. "What *are* we going to do for food?"

Tototo nodded back in the direction of Twonchkinland.

"Eat the Twonchkins?" Shiro asked.

Tototo's tongue lolled out in enthusiasm.

"Nah," Shiro said, although not from any moral scruples. "I suppose we could go and ask for some provisions, though." He shaded his brow with his paw. "Long way back."

"Eat the dirt," a voice said.

Shiro turned.

There was nothing in sight but a ragged-looking scarecrow, lying flat on its back.

Shiro looked back at Tototo. "Who said that?" he asked.

Tototo shrugged.

"*I'd* eat the dirt," came the voice again.

Shiro whirled.

"Who said that?" he demanded.

"Me?" the scarecrow asked.

Shiro went nearer. "You can talk?"

"Can I?"

"Yes."

"Is that good?" the scarecrow asked, looking up at the kitten.

"Not so far," Shiro replied.

"Would you mind getting me down from here?"

"Down from where?" Shiro inquired.

"This post."

"You're lying flat on your back."

"Get me down anyway."

Shiro remained where he was, but just to test the straw man, said: "There."

"Thank you," the scarecrow answered.

"It was nothing."

"You're very kind," the straw man said. "I suppose you've already told me who you are, but would you be willing to do it again?"

"My name's Miaowara Shiro."

"What's the dog called?"

"Tototo."

"I see," said the straw man. "I suppose you've already told me who you are, but would you be willing to do it again?"

"Your brain doesn't work very well, does it?" Shiro asked.

"I don't have a brain. All I have is straw." To prove his point, the scarecrow dug into the side of his head and pulled out a piece of kapok. "Where are you going, by the way?"

"We're off to see the Wizard."

"What's a Wizard?" the straw man asked.

"Someone who can help me get out of this country," Shiro said.

"Would he help me?"

"With what?" Shiro asked.

"I'd really like it if my head wasn't full of straw."

"You want a brain?"

"No," the straw man said. "I was thinking of kapok."

"You're head's already full of kapok."

"*That* must be why I think it's full of straw," the scarecrow answered. "Can I come with you?"

"Well," Shiro said, "I'm not generally known for lending a helping paw, but... you really are a case. Let's go."

The kitten returned to the bike; the scarecrow remained on the ground.

"Can you walk?" Shiro asked.

"I thought I *was* walking."

"Do I have to carry you over here?"

The scarecrow promptly mosied over, got on behind Shiro, and said:

"Maybe you'd better at that."

Something occurred to Shiro. "You wouldn't be that straw man that people always talk about, would you? A lousy argument put forward as someone else's position?"

"I don't think so," said the scarecrow.

Shiro took this as a yes.

Tototo bounded back into the kitten's lap.

Shiro started the bike once more and sped away.

"*Dead*?" screamed the Wicked Witch of the Southeast, the double-headed koala beside her throne starting violently. "My sister's *dead*?"

Grovelling before her, Wugh lifted his face slightly. "There was this little Jap kitten, My Lady, and he had two machine guns..."

"Loaded?"

"Yes, Yer Ladyship."

"With *bullets*?"

"Yes."

"Did you kill him?"

"We were no match for those guns, My Lady. I was wounded..."

"What was he doing in Twonchkinland?"

"He fell out of the sky in a farmhouse."

"Ah," said the witch. "Qantas."

The koala nodded both its heads, muttering: "I hate Qantas."

She pulled out a huge Gasser Montenegrin revolver. "Seeing as how that joke was your whole *raison d'etre...*"

Two eleven milimeter bullets turned the koala from a warm fuzzy to a red wetty.

"Yer orders, My Lady?" Wugh asked.

"Stay here," she replied. "I'll go scope that kitty son of a bitch out myself."

"Can I have the koala, yer ladyship?"

The witch signalled him to take it. "You must have quite a collection by now."

Wugh cuddled the small corpse against his breast. "I think I'll call him...Headless."

"Isn't that what you call the rest of them?"

"Makes it easy to remember their names," Wugh replied.

"Must at that," said the witch.

The scarecrow kept up a steady stream of talk as Shiro rode along, and while the kitten tried to be polite, he'd never heard such unimaginable twaddle in all his life. The topics, just to name a few, included the pros of making a sequel to *Newsies*, holding a Worldcon in Yugoslavia, and terraforming the planet earth.

What a way to spend an afternoon, Shiro thought. Tototo had both paws pressed against his ears; Shiro would certainly have followed his example if he hadn't had to steer.

As the day wore on, the road entered a stretch of dead forest, thousands of fallen dessicated trees. Shiro theorized that the topsoil must have been plundered out from under them.

He was still very hungry. Sighting a pastel cottage beside the road, he decided to investigate, and dismounting from the chopper, was about to enter the dwelling when he heard someone wail:

"My baby! Please don't kill my baby!"

"Really," someone else answered, in bloodless tones. "It's for the best."

Out back, Shiro found a tin woodsman about to hack a baby wallaby lying bound and gagged across a chopping block, the youngster's mother and siblings looking on in horror.

"What can I do for you?" the woodsman asked Shiro, pausing in mid-stroke, the baby wallaby's eyes bulging in the shadow of the axe.

"You wouldn't have any food, would you?" Shiro responded.

"In a second," said the woodsman. "That's if you like wallaby."

"Save my baby!" cried the mother to Shiro. "*Please!*"

"Why are you going to chop that tyke?" Shiro asked the woodsman.

"It's the pragmatic thing to do," the woodsman replied. "His mother can't feed *all* her joeys, so I figured I'd kill two wallabies with one blow--- decrease the number of mouths she has to fill, and get her some grub in the bargain."

"Wallabies engage in cannibalism?"

"I don't believe so, but it's time they started."

"Very pragmatic, all right," Shiro said. "What a cold fellow you are."

"I have no heart at all," the woodsman explained. "Does that lessen me, in your opinion?"

"Not really," Shiro answered. "I'm not too big in the heart department myself, although I try to maintain a bare minimum of empathy...makes certain movies more involving."

The woodsman laid his axe down. "Which ones?"

"*The Devils, The Untold Story, Sympathy for Mr. Vengeance...*"

"I'd like them more if I had a heart?"

"The gross-outs get more of a rise out of you, believe me.

"I'd actually feel something?"

51

"Yep. You get a much better idea of the pain being inflicted."

"I'm not interested in inflicting pain."

"Well, just think of how much more pragmatic you could be if you enjoyed your work."

"You know," said the Tin Woodsman, "I've been feeling like something was missing from my life...But it's not as if I can do anything about it."

"I'm going to see this Wizard," Shiro said. "I've been told he might be able to help me."

The scarecrow had wandered up at some point. "Maybe he could give the woodsman a brain," he said.

"*You're* the one who needs a brain," Shiro answered.

"Maybe he could give him a brain, then."

"You think he might grant me a heart?" the woodsman asked Shiro.

"I don't know," Shiro answered. "It's worth a try, though."

"Pardon me," said Mrs. Wallaby. "Can I have my son back?"

"That reminds me..." said the woodsman, raising his axe once more.

"Don't," said Shiro.

"Why not?" the woodsman asked.

"It would piss the readers off too much."

"Now *that's* pragmatism," said the woodsman.

Mrs. Wallaby snatched junior off the block and went bounding away over the dead trees, her other young bringing up the rear.

"You have a raincheck," the woodsman promised.

As it turned out, the tin man had some non-wallaby provisions; Shiro cleaned the dirt out of the storage compartments on his bike and filled them with food and bottled water before he, Tototo, the scarecrow, and the woodsman all crowded onto the Harley and hit the road.

Slowly the sun sank in the West---as if it ever sank swiftly somewhere else. In the thickening dusk Shiro discovered that the bike's headlight didn't work; there was no choice but to stop and make camp. The tin man made a fire, and Shiro broke out the wienies and marshmallows.

"Do any dangerous animals live around here?" the kitten asked the woodsman.

"You mean, lions or tigers or bears?"

"Yes."

"No."

"What about other dangerous animals?" asked the scarecrow.

"Well, we have dingos, echidnas and ticks."

"Oh my," said the scarecrow, quivering.

"Echidnas are dangerous?" Shiro asked.

"If you eat them," the woodsman answered.

"I ate one, once, I think," said the scarecrow. "But I'm not sure how it came out."

Shiro watched, fascinated, as the straw man incinerated one marshmallow after another.

A twig snapped, somewhere in the darkness.

"Ah, come on!" Shiro cried. "That device gets used far too much."

"Which device?" a voice cried quite witchily.

"The snapping twig. Haven't you ever read *Fenimore Cooper's Literary Offenses*? Alert us to your presence some other way, *please*."

There came a series of crashing sounds, like an entire stack of wedgewood saucers falling one plate at a time.

"Okay," said Shiro. "Who goes there?"

"Do you have a place at your fire for an old woman?"

Shiro trained his Uzis in the direction of her voice.   "Show yourself."

Out of the blackness emerged an ancient crone who bore more than a passing resemblence to the wicked witch he'd zorched back in Twonchkinland.

"Don't have a sister, do you?" he asked.

"Why, no," she answered.

"You're not a wicked witch, by any chance?"

"Do I look like one?"

"As a matter of fact..."

"Nice," she said, leaning on her broomstick.

"She *is* a wicked witch," said the Tin Man. "She's the Wicked Witch of the Southeast. And she *does* have a sister."

The witch chortled. "You recognize me, eh Tin Man?"

He nodded. "From back before you lost all that weight. Called yourself Mama Cass, as I recall. Always *thought* you faked your own death."

The witch just smirked, humming a few bars of *Monday Monday*.

"You're here for revenge, I take it?" Shiro asked.

"You're assuming I know that you killed my sister."

"I am."

"Well, when you assume, you make an ass of *u* and *me*."

"That gag doesn't work if you don't have a blackboard."

"What gag?" the witch asked.

"So," said Shiro, "If you're not here for revenge..."

"I'm collecting ammunition."

"For who?"

"The poor."

"Let 'em get their own ammunition," the tin man answered.

"Perhaps there should be a government program," said the scarecrow.

54

"Frankly," said Shiro, "I incline towards the Tin Man's position. I paid for my ammo, and I should get to waste whoever gets wasted by it."

"Suppose I was willing to buy it from you?" the witch asked.

"What's you offer?"

"Five tons of grade-A topsoil."

"Dirt's not exactly hard currency where I come from," said Shiro. "You know what I think?"

"No, what?"

"I think you're trying to part me from my ammo so you can kill us all."

The witch laughed. "Ahh...could be."

"Can't you do anything with that broom of yours?" Shiro sneered.

"Like this?" she answered, and stamped the butt against the ground.

A huge crack opened in the earth.

Crying "You just had to ask, didn't you?" the tin man dropped in, saving himself only at the last second, hooking the blade of his axe over a stony rim.

Shiro, meanwhile, had hurdled the fissure, Uzis spraying slugs. But the bullets all splattered before they struck the witch, as if they'd encountered an invisible wall.

Uglier than she looks, Shiro thought. Chortling, she made as if to stamp her broom-butt again...he was completely at a loss. Luckily, Tototo rushed to his rescue, clamping his jaws on the witch's leg.

Seeing his chance, Shiro charged, catching her with a flying kick, driving a nasty hobnailed ruby-slipper heel straight into her forehead. She collapsed, dropping the broomstick. Seizing it, Shiro tried to throw it into the fissure, but the scarecrow grabbed it out of sheer stupidity.

"Don't throw it in the chasm!" the kitten cried.

"Oh, I get it," said the Scarecrow. "You want me to do the opposite of what you told me."

He proceeded to stand there and examine the broom most minutely.

Hoisting himself out of the crack, the woodsman snatched the broom away and chucked it into the abyss.

The witch rose, tore Tototo from her shin, punted him a fair distance, then put her pointy hat back on, said, "Never in all my life...." and marched off, the very picture of offended dignity.

"Think that's the last we'll see of her?" Shiro asked the Tin Man.

"How many pages are we into the story?"

Shiro checked. "About 51. That's manuscript, of course."

"She'll be back," the woodman opined.

"Sounds like this robot I know," Shiro said.

"Are you preparing the readers for some future appearance of this robot?" the tin man asked.

"No. But the author is."

"Don't you do just what the author wants you to do?"

"Nope," Shiro replied. "Never made him any money, at least."

They knew better than to let the scarecrow go on watch, so they took turns during the night; long about sunrise, Shiro heard another twig---or perhaps the same twig, broken in another place--- break again.

Assuming the witch had returned, he cried: "Didn't I already tell you about that?" Jumping to his feet, he kicked the tin man awake. The woodman clattered up, hefting his axe.

Into the firelight swaggered a lion in a U.S. Cavalry bluejacket with the epaulets ripped from the shoulders. He held a Winchester 73 with an enlarged circular lever in his left paw, and a shortened saber in his right; the blade, which had obviously been a full-length "wristbreaker," appeared to have been snapped over some superior officer's knee. Overall, the beast rather resembled a leonine Chuck Connors.

"What do you do when you're branded, and you know you're a man?" the lion growled.

The Scarecrow sat up, rubbing his eyes. "Beats me," he said.

"Who are you?" Shiro asked the lion.

"I used to be known as the Riflelion," the other replied. "Now I'm the Branded-A-Cowardly-Lion. Want to make something of it?"

"Do you have any ammo for that gun?"

"Want to find out?" the lion demanded.

"I thought you said there aren't any lions in Australia," Shiro told the Tin Man.

"Maybe he's only passing through," the woodsman said.

"I came to escape my past," the lion answered.

"But?"

"It followed me. People keep learning about my reputation."

"How?" Shiro asked.

"I tell them."

"Why don't you stop?"

"You think I'm *afraid* to tell them?" the lion roared. "Want to tie one on with me right now? I'm not scared of you."

At that, the Scarecrow broke in senselessly: "What if he was a muse named Thalia?"

"I'd show *him* who was King of Australia," the lion answered. "Come on, kitty, let's party."

"You're serious, aren't you?" said Shiro.

"Damn straight," said the lion.

"Even though I'd blow you to bits with these machine-guns?"

"I laugh at death."

"Ho-ho-ho or ha-ha?"

"I sort of snort through my nose."

"Look," Shiro said. "I really don't want to fight you. I rather like your attitude, as a matter of fact. But you present me with a real problem."

"Oh?" the lion asked.

"Well, we're going to see the wizard," Shiro answered. "I want to get out of this country. The Scarecrow there needs a brain desperately, and the Tin Man could really use a heart. But what could the wizard do for you? You're not a coward. He can't give you courage---you've already got that."

"Wait a second," said the tin man. "In the movie, the scarecrow was actually smart, and I was actually sentimental. But the cowardly lion was *actually* a coward."

"What's your point?" Shiro asked.

"Well, in this version, the scarecrow's stupid, and I'm heartless. But the lion's actually brave."

"So?"

"It's just puzzling, that's all."

The scarecrow said: "Maybe the Wizard could make the Lion a *real* coward."

The lion ignored this. "I *would* like my epaulets back."

"Were they very nice?" Shiro asked.

"The *best*," said the lion.

"I guess you'd better join us, then," said Shiro.

"Will that motorcyle hold us all?"

"Maybe not."

"You could drag me," the scarecrow offered.

"You wouldn't mind?" Shiro asked.

"Not as long as it's on my face," the scarecrow answered.

The tin man produced a rope. "We can manage that," he said.

The day after Shiro's visit, the Twonchkins heard a tremendous crash and came running out of their homes to see that another farmhouse had been deposited atop the first. Bubbles was still in town, and went to confront the large Germanic type that thrust his way out of the wreckage, a triple-barrelled recoilless rifle slung across his back.

"

Are you a bad witch or a bad witch?" Bubbles asked, remembering Shiro's lecture on etymology.

"Haff you seen a kitten named Miaovara Shiro?" the Terminationer demanded.

"You didn't answer my question," Bubbles replied.

The robot drew his longslide with all the lightning speed of someone really fast.

"Well, just to set a good example," said Bubbles, "I'll answer yours. We haven't seen any kittens lately."

The Terminationer looked about with slitted eyes, spotting a spent cartridge. The precision lenses concealed within his organic eye-casings zoomed the image.

"Nine milimeter," he said. "The kitten bought two nine milimeter submachine guns at Baltimore-Vashington Airport."

He pushed his pistol into Bubbles's face.

"It's from my wand," she replied.

"A nine-milimeter *vand*?"

"Let me show you," said Bubbles.

The robot lowered the .45.

Drawing the wand from its scabbard, she pointed it directly at his face.

"Dot's forty-four magnum," he said, looking straight down the bore.

"Isn't it though?" she asked, and pulled the trigger.

The bullet tore half his upper lip away, and that was a very dramatic sight, but she also heard a ricochet, and realized the slug must've bounced from his glittering metal teeth even as it laid them bare---she hadn't blown a gap through them, and he wasn't even swaying, not the least tiny bit.

"Silly old me," she said. Like most wands, hers was only single shot.

He lifted the longslide once more.

"Forty-five ACP," she observed.

"Dot's right," he replied, and gave her one in the shoulder. Gown flouncing up, arms whipping, she whirled back, right through the Twonchkins, sending little bodies flying as she opened a lane.

Grinning with fright, the midgets still on their feet all pointed to the Yellow Brick Road, saying, in perfect unison:

"Kitten went that way."

The robot holstered the pistol, straddled an orphaned Harley, and roared out into the waste.

The Twonchkins gathered around Bubbles. Rubbing her shoulder, she sat up groggily.

"Thank goodness I was wearing my kevlar gown," she said.

Reaching the Potemkin section---that is to say, the yellow brick section---of the Yellow Brick Road, Shiro and company came within sight of Zirconsville. True to its name, the city resembled a gigantic mass of varicolored sub-valuable gemstones; this was plainly intended as a magical fantasy conceit, but it fell well short of that, by at least fifty percent. More than anything else, it reminded Shiro of cheesy American theme parks fallen on hard times because the main highway had been moved.

He rode right up to the huge front doors, got off the bike, and banged a knocker...a whimsical circular hatch opened, and out looked a grown man with a big green spitcurl and lots and lots of latex character makeup all over his face.

"What the Hell do you want?" he snarled.

"We're here to see the Wizard," Shiro said.

"No one gets to see the Great Australia, no way, no how!"

Shiro twisted one of the doorknobs, pushing the lefthand valve inward.

"Hey!" said the gatewarden, swinging the door on its hinges. "These things open!"

"Still can't let anyone in," said another guard, beckoning to a horde of pikemen up the hall.

"If I blot the sun from the sky," Shiro said, "Would you let us pass then?"

"The Wizard would want to see you, I expect," replied the first guard.

"Come on out," said Shiro, "And behold!"

To the amazement of the guards---not to mention Shiro's companions--- a black shadow crept across the disc of the sun.

"All right," said the guards. "Go on through."

The tin man untied the scarecrow from the back of the motorcycle, then followed Shiro, the Lion and Tototo.

"See to my bike!" Shiro told the guards.

"How did you know there was going to be an eclipse?" the lion whispered in Shiro's ear.

"Sometimes you just have to trust to luck," Shiro replied.

A guard guided them to a huge palace done up in art-deco kangaroo motifs. Quivering with dread, the man clicked on an intercom in the vestibule, notifying the Wizard that visitors were coming.

"I'm not in!" the Wizard thundered through the speaker. "And I don't want to see anybody, either!"

"But one of them made the sun disappear!" the guard answered.

"And I won't bring it back unless we're granted an audience!" Shiro cried.

"According to my charts," the Wizard said, "There was *supposed* to be a solar eclipse today."

"Who do you think scheduled it?" Shiro replied.

"Eclipses aren't *scheduled*," the Wizard answered.

"No? What about earthquakes?" Shiro asked, just before a fierce tremor went through the floor.

"All right, all right," said the Wizard.

The vestibule's inner doors opened.

"Come ahead," the Wizard said.

Shiro and the others entered a dark cavernous hallway.

"Regarding that earthquake," said the lion to Shiro, "Were you just trusting to luck again?"

Shiro showed him a nifty little Sony pocket seismograph.

"Seismographs *measure* earthquakes," the lion said. "They don't predict them."

"You got me," Shiro answered. "It *was* another coincidence."

"I knew it," said the lion, very much relieved.

"Here," said Shiro to the scarecrow, handing him the seismograph.

They came at last to a vast chapel-like room notable for eerie lighting and extreme shinyness of floor. On the far side, twin geysers of oily flame erupted at regular intervals from the polished blue-black linoleum. Between the flames a huge hovering disembodied head covered by a KKK hood slowly materialized.

"Nobody told me he was a *Grand* Wizard," said Shiro to the tin man.

"I am Australia, the great and powerful," said the head. "Who are you?"

"I am Miaowara Shiro, the small and psychopathic," the kitten answered.

The lion said: "I am Chuck, branded a coward but actually your worst nightmare."

"My worst nightmares involve me being naked in public," said the Wizard.

"Mine too," answered the lion. "Boy, you've got an ugly bod."

After a pause, the wizard demanded: "And who are *you*, tin man?"

"I'm the tin man," said the tin man.

The scarecrow said: "Damned if I know who *I* am."

Tototo just barked.

"Why have you come?" the Wizard asked.

"Bubbles said you might be willing to help me," said Shiro. "I thought you might also be able to do something for my friends."

"Why do you need my help?" the Wizard asked. "You can blot the sun from the sky."

"Yes, but not all situations call for that," said Shiro. "Suppose I was missing an article of clothing, a sock perhaps. Blotting the sun from the sky might even *hinder* my efforts."

"Very true," said the Wizard.

"Suppose I were an astronomer, looking for sunspots," Shiro continued. "Or what if I was trying to prove that solar power was actually practical...?"

"You've made your point," said the Wizard.

"In any case," Shiro resumed, "I want to get out of Australia. The Scarecrow needs a brain---desperately. The tin man wants a heart. And the lion wants his epaulets back."

"I can give you what you desire," said the Wizard. "But first you must prove yourselves worthy."

"How?" asked the lion.

"By going on a quest," the Wizard answered.

"To achieve what?" Shiro inquired.

"The destruction of the One Ring."

"To Rule Them All?"

"The very same."

"It's been done," said Shiro.

"Are you *sure*?"

"Yes," said Shiro.

"But I have the One Ring in a safe upstairs."

"Does it have an inscription on the inner surface?" Shiro asked.

"Yes," the Wizard answered.

"What's it say?"

"'This Is The Inscription The One Ring Has On Its Inner Surface..'"

"That's not the One Ring," Shiro assured him. "Give us another quest."

"Very well then. Since you're wearing the ruby slippers, I assume you must've killed the Wicked Witch of the Southwest. But you may not know that she has a sister..."

"We had a run-in with Sis on the way here," said Shiro. "She was out for revenge."

"Her prize possession is a tanker-truck full of first-class topsoil," the Wizard went on. "If you capture it, and bring it to me, I'll do whatever I can for you."

"This doesn't feel right," said the lion to Shiro. "How much faith can we put in a floating Ku Klux Klan head?"

"*Are* you a member of the Klan?" Shiro asked.

"I was when I was younger and more insensitive," said the Wizard. "Now I'm a Republican. Of course, when I actually *belonged* to the Klan, I was still a Democrat..."

"Where can we find this truck?"

"In the Wicked Witch's castle. You go back out on the Yellow Brick Road, take a right at the second light, and follow Route 88 straight through the Foothills of Anxiety to the Mountains of Terror. The Castle will be on your left. It's balanced precariously atop a needle-sharp pinnacle, and overshadowed by a gigantic swirling cloud of bats and vultures. You can't miss it."

"If we bring the truck back here, you'll do whatever you can for us?"

"Didn't I already say that?" the Wizard asked.

"Yes, basically," said Shiro. "But there's a young fellow by the name of Kyle Stiff, from Hardinsburg Kentucky, who skimmed over that earlier line."

"You know that for a fact?"

"Nope. But I expect he'll enjoy seeing his name in print, all the same."

"A nice personal touch," the Wizard admitted. "Now beat it, the bunch of you."

The straw man tugged Shiro's sleeve. "Bunch of us?" he whispered. "I'm alone."

"No, you're with me," Shiro said.

"So...*you're* alone?"

Shiro smiled uncomfortably, then bowed to the wizard. "Thank you for seeing us," he said.

He and his companions headed back the way they had come. The tin man said gloomily:

"We're being sent off to certain death."

"I laugh at death," the lion reminded him.

"What is it about death that makes you laugh?" asked the woodsman.

"The funny part," the lion replied.

Returning to their bike, Shiro and company did about what you'd expect them to do: they travelled some distance having wacky adventures and uttering lots of loony dialogue. Some of the things they did and said were so fantastically funny---by far the funniest stuff that happened during Shiro's trip to Australia---that I was overcome with laughter and couldn't set any of them down.

Sorry.

Anyway, they raised the Foothills of Anxiety long about sundown. At the base of the first swell was a gas station with a sign that read: *Last Chance Petrol and Valium.*

"Any of you guys need a pit-stop?" Shiro cried.

Tototo barked, and the Tin Man admitted that halting might be the pragmatic thing to do. Shiro pulled up beside a gas-pump.

As the engine cut off, the kitten thought he heard the scarecrow mumbling something; the straw man was burbling in the grit, puffs of orange dust rising beside his head. Going back and taking him by the scruff of the neck, Shiro pulled his face up. Needless to say, after being dragged for much of the afternoon behind the Harley, the scarecrow was looking right threadbare in the features department.

"Kind of hard to understand you when you have a mouthful of sand," Shiro said.

"Oh, I wasn't trying to say anything," said the scarecrow. "I just like burbling in the dust."

Shiro lowered the straw man's head and went into the station. Tototo, the woodsman, and the lion were already inside, arguing with the attendant.

"But we don't *want* any valium," said the woodsman, shifting his weight anxiously from foot to foot.

"That's what you think now," said the attendant. "Why do you think they call 'em the Foothills of Anxiety?"

The lion cocked his Winchester. "Think I'll get frightened, do you?"

"No, but you don't get to use the loo if you don't buy anything," the attendant insisted.

"Fill my bike up," said Shiro. "I need a headlight, too."

The man tossed Shiro the bathroom key, got a headlamp, and walked out muttering. Shiro handed the key to the tinman, who made a beeline for a door marked 'gents.' Going back outside, the kitten joined the attendant at the pump.

"Just what sort of horribleness can we expect up ahead?" he asked.

"Nothing explicit," said the attendant. "Lot of moody stuff with shadows and suggestion, but no steak with your sizzle. It's sort of a Val Lewton haunted forest."

"Are there actual ghosts?"

"Yes, but they're lazy."

"What about when we reach the Mountains of Terror?"

"The gnarly trees disappear, but louder sound effects and greater heights more than compensate."

By this time, the attendant had long finished pumping the gas and was replacing the burned-out headlamp. Rising at last, he looked past the cycle at the Scarecrow, who was still lying on his face, although he seemed to be actually speaking now. For a few moments the pump jockey seemed to listen closely to the stuff issuing from the straw man.

"You're wondering why we're dragging him," said Shiro.

"Why you're *bothering* to drag him," said the attendant. "Did I just hear him say something about a lifetime achievement Oscar for Lou Ferrigno?"

"I bet you did, yes."

"Pay me and take that idiot far away, please," said the attendant.

"You take Visa, I presume," Shiro answered.

Once the Harley disappeared into the gathering dusk, the attendant rang up the witch.

"You have something to report?" she snarled.

"A kitten, a tin man, a scarecrow, and a lion who, if you ask me, fears he's actually a coward, all headed your way, Your Ladyship."

"What are they after?"

"Well, they came from the direction of Zirconsville---"

"The Wizard's sent another bunch of suckers to steal the Tanker-Truck," said the witch. "It's either that, or my button collection. Did you give them the standard bullshit about the Haunted Forest?"

"Yes, your PointedHattyness. 'Steak but no Sizzle,' that's what I told them. They're expecting Val Lewton."

"When they're going to get Lucio Fulci," said the witch. "May not be scarier, but the bad taste alone should kill them."

"Personally, My Lady," said the attendant, "I find the understated approach more frightening."

"Scary *is* subjective," replied the witch, waxing philosophical. "Frankly, I've never recovered from seeing *The Crawling Eye* when I was a kid. I know it's stupid, but that one really got to me."

"I know just what you mean, My Lady," said the attendant.

"Something about that crack opening up in Janet Munro's room at the observatory....Brr. I was also scared by a birthday cake once, don't ask me why. In any case, I'm going to go hide the buttons."

The witch rang off.

The attendant stood awhile in silence. He too had been deeply frightened by *The Crawling Eye*---he'd seen it under the title *Trollenburg Terror*---but he'd found Forrest Tucker more disturbing than any of the monsters.

That night he dreamed of Forrest Tucker, and Larry Storch, his unconscious mind writhing as it tried to fathom what exactly the joke was with the Hekowi tribe. Screaming at the top of his lungs, he awoke drenched in sweat.

But that's another story.

And rather a scarier one.

At first, as the night deepened, it seemed to Shiro that the attendant had gotten it exactly right: what haints there were in the uplands were far more bent on evoking mood than doing any real damage. There was a lot of creeping ground fog, churned by occasional gusts of wind full of dead leaves, and all the trees were gnarly and expired and hung with great big nets of silvery spiderweb. The lighting was very dramatic, with the most innocent objects, like empty Dinky-Di dogfood cans, cast-off vegemite sandwiches, and roadkill Olivia Newton-Johns casting gigantic threatening shadows.

But as Shiro drove deeper and deeper into the foothills, he began to notice some very un-Val Lewtonish things: blood dripping from overarching branches, fresh human skeletons that appeared to have been munched quite free of meat, Olivia Newton-Johns trying to get to their feet even though they gave every sign of having been squished beneath semis, intestines *a la Fulci* cascading from their mouths. Soon the headlight began to reveal all manner of undead Aussie-fauna shambling through the trees, Jolly swag-men, Bush-veldt carabineers (each squad led by their very own Breaker Morant), poor wasted youths slaughtered in their prime at Gallipoli, Rolf Harrises, self-righteous bald rock stars maintaining ferociously that it should all be given back, expatriate film-directors just returned from Hollywood; unemployed members of Men-at-Work lunged at the bike from right and left, only to be taken down by the lion's Winchester or one of Shiro's Uzis. Digger hats cocked at rakish angles on their rotting noggins, a whole brigade of decomposed Kylie Minogues formed a cordon across the road, brandishing boomerangs; Shiro hit the brakes just as they loosed their missiles. The kitten's timing was absolutely perfect; the bike slewed sideways, halting just outside Boomerang-range; barely missing the noses of Shiro and his companions, the boomerangs promptly boomeranged, braining the Minogues in a collective splash of down-under putrescence.

"The scarecrow!" the tin man cried.

Shiro looked round.

Three Mel Gibsons were staggering towards the straw man, explaining none-too-convincingly how the South Africans had managed to establish air superiority over downtown L.A. in *Lethal Weapon II*. For his part, the scarecrow was sitting with his back towards the oncoming corpses, looking at the rope tied to his ankles.

"Hey guys!" he called to his companions, lifting the rope. "If I follow this, will I get back to the bike?"

Shiro bagged one of the Gibsons, the Lion another, but the third hauled the straw man to his feet and started chewing on the back of his head.

Chambering a fresh shell, the lion put one right through the scarecrow's cheek, sending Mel number three rocking back with a great big wad of kapok clenched---again, rather Fulcily---between his teeth, and a hole where his nose had been. But the scarecrow didn't even seem to notice that a slug had just gone through his head, let alone the fact that a bunch of his non-brains had been torn out; looking down down at the rope, he asked:

"So this *won't* get me back to the bike?"

A gang of moldy opal-miners---moldy miners, not miners of moldy opals--- surged out of the woods behind him. Shiro wrenched the front wheel round and hit the throttle, yanking the straw man from their clutches, blitzing forward over the still-twitching Minogues.

Ahead, the zombies and trees thinned out, then disappeared. The ground grew arid and rocky as the road wound its way in and out of deep valleys and up the sides of steep cliffs.

"I guess these must be the Mountains of Terror," said Shiro over his shoulder.

"I wonder why they're called that?" asked the Tin Man. "No zombies."

"No guard rails, either," said Shiro. "Maybe the Witch takes it for granted we'll speed."

He eased back on the throttle, cruising along at twenty-five, nice and easy, congratulating himself on his restraint.

No crash-and-burn for this little bastard! he thought.

Rather prematurely, though: a swarm of headlights appeared in his sideviews, swinging out of a ravine he'd passed some distance back. Quarrels streaked by.

He sped up, but the lights gained steadily. Negotiating one hairpin after another, he zig-zagged his way up the mountainside. Glancing at a mirror, he saw two of his pursuers blow the last turn and go shooting out of sight; he wondered how long it would be before he followed their example.

The lion was banging away with his Winchester. Trailing long shlorps of blood from his back, a Mohawked marauder passed Shiro on the right. Sitting rigidly astride his chopper, he seemed to be unaware that he'd been shot, or of anything else, for that matter, gradually veering towards the void on the left, finally rocketting over the side of the precipice.

Shiro reached the top of the mountain, plunged into the trough. The road narrowed; the turns grew tighter. The engine maxed out, the speedometer- needle striking the side of the gauge with an audible clang; but the bike kept accelerating on the decline. The punkies hard behind, Shiro couldn't afford to brake. He took each turn faster, the wind sharpening in his face. Blasted flat against his cheeks, his whiskers dug into his flesh like wires, and after a depressingly short while he could feel his eyesockets knocking against the back of his skull---Buddha only knew where his brain had been squeezed. He had no doubt that the gale would've knocked him from the saddle if the tin man and the lion hadn't been behind them---he couldn't imagine what was holding *them* in place.

The distance between turns grew shorter and shorter, a hundred yards, then eighty, then forty, then ten, then three, then one, then whatever ridiculously short interval you're silly enough to buy. Knowing now why the mountains bore the name they did, he negotiated the last seventy miles of the descent in a daze of terror; only the sheer magnetic stickiness of his fear kept his cycle clinging to the road...falling punkies rained past him, yodelling with regret at having been insufficiently frightened.

At last, though, he reached the bottom--- where, without warning, a score of headlights blazed before him.

He lifted an Uzi, released a short burst---then felt a dozen quarrels nick him, though not in the same place. There was a pop, and the bike wobbled and flew out of control. Soaring through the air, he guessed that the front tire had been hit.

The headlights careened close. Something snagged him, and he found himself astride another hog, in front of someone very big, a knife at his throat. He didn't remember dropping the Uzi, but it was gone all right, and he couldn't reach the other, which was pinned between him and the punky.

"Got yer," growled Wugh's voice in his ear.

When the tire blew, the lion sailed into a roadside gully, cold-cocking himself on a rock; one of Wugh's minions snatched Tototo as the tin man disintegrated against the macadam in a glittering sliding explosion of metallic junk. That left the straw man standing alone, surrounded by a circling, snarling ring of bikers. Handing Shiro to a flunky, Wugh dismounted and strode up to the scarecrow with the kitten's Uzi.

"I know what you're thinking," said Wugh.

"I'm glad someone does," said the scarecrow.

"You're wondering how you got yourself into such a situation."

"I suppose I'll have to take your word on that. What situation am I in, by the way?

"You're in grave danger," Wugh chortled.

"Would it help if I close my eyes?"

74

"Absolutely," Wugh answered, allowed the straw man to shut them, then sprayed six bullets into his stomach. Ripping through the scarecrow in a blizzard of straw, the slugs shipped one of the circling mohawks off to punk perdition, much to the amusement of his colleagues..

The scarecrow opened his eyes. Blissfully short of internal organs, he looked down at the ineffectual holes that had been drilled in his shirt.

"It worked," he said.

Growling, "Die, damn you!" Wugh gave him three in the hat.

"If you insist," said the scarecrow, and laid down.

"Back to the castle!" Wugh cried, returning to his chopper. The punkies *vamanose muchachado'd* like Aussie versions of the heavies in the next story.

Rubbing a bleeding wound in his head, the lion staggered up from the gully and over to the scarecrow.

"Straw man?" he asked. "Hey? Anybody home?"

"Perhaps you'd better not talk to me," said the scarecrow.

"Why?"

"I won't answer."

"Why not?"

"Just between you and me, I'm dead."

"You were never alive to begin with."

"How does that help?"

"You're *not* dead," said the lion, untying the rope from the scarecrow's ankles and pulling him to his feet before asking, "What did they do to you?"

"Well, first they tore my legs off, and they threw them over *there*. Then they pulled my arms off and they threw them over *there*..."

"What, and they put them back on again?"

The scarecrow inspected his limbs. "They must've," he answered. "*I* didn't do it. I think."

"They shot him, but it didn't take," said the tin man's head, which lay nearby.

The lion surveyed the scattered wreckage that had been the woodsman and said, "I could make some bucks recycling you."

"Put me back together please."

"Is it possible?"

"Sure," said the tin man. "I'm a three hundred series. Breakaway model, designed to come apart if I'm hit hard enough."

"What was the point of that feature?" asked the lion, screwing an upper arm into a shoulder.

"Chief of the design team had a brain tumor," said the woodsman's head. "Sales were kind of slow at first, but then the model was discovered by rich five year-old boys. Shattered all sales records. I spent three straight months having my head smashed off with a baseball bat. Then the kid who owned me bought himself a small South American country, was overthrown and killed, and I was put out to pasture."

Soon the woodsman was sufficiently reassembled to begin aiding the lion. Once he was good as new, he went to pick his axe up.

"At least we've still got wheels," he said, indicating the bike that had belonged to the punkie Wugh had shot.

"Shh," said the lion, craning his head back, scanning the cliffs

above. "I think I hear something."

After blasting his way through the zombies in the foothills, the Terminationer had rolled on into the Mountains of Terror, whistling Austrian folktunes, reminiscing about edelweiss and lederhosen and Christopher Plummer's glorious voice. Having heard about the kitten's companions back in Zirconsville, he wasn't entirely surprised to find them blocking the road in front of him, the lion drawing a bead with a Winchester. The robot slowed to a stop.

"Give us your bike," said the tin man.

"Youff already got vun," said the Terminationer.

"Yeah, but we're tired of all this piggyback business," the lion answered.

"Vun of you vill *shtill* haff to ride piggy-back," the robot pointed out. "Unless you intend to drag somevun."

"Just get off the bike," said the lion.

The robot didn't stir. "Vhere is ze kitten, by ze vay?"

"He was captured by the witch's men," said the woodsman. "Who are you?"

The robot didn't answer at first, giving serious thought to kneecapping all three. Then it occurred to him that they might come in handy at the witch's castle.

"His lawyer," the robot said.

"They allowed him a phone call?"

Studying the woodsman's reaction, the robot decided that Shiro hadn't told them that he was being pursued---or if he had, that he'd neglected to describe his pursuer.

"No," said the robot, "But zere are some tort matters I need to discuss viss him."

"Perhaps we should join forces," said the lion.

"*Ja*," the robot replied.

As soon as Wugh's band arrived at the castle, Shiro and Tototo were imprisoned in the northwest tower. The witch came to the cell post-haste.

"Would you like to know why you're still alive?" she asked the kitten.

"No," he said.

"Sure you do."

"Nope," he replied. "I figure your reasons must be pretty stupid, so I really don't care."

"Just for that," she cried, "I'll tell you anyway!"

He stamped. "Don't, dammit!"

"I will!" she answered.

Clapping his paws over his ears, he proceeded to walk up and back, making loud gargling noises.

"Wugh!" the witch shouted.

Wugh seized the kitten, uncovering one of his ears and slipping a palm over Shiro's yap.

"I wanted the ruby slippers, so there!" the witch crowed. "You can let him go, Wugh."

He released the kitten.

"But what did you need me for?" Shiro asked. "Why didn't you just tell your flunkies to kill me and take the damn things?"

"They have little experience at removing other people's shoes," said the witch. "They have a hard enough time with their own."

Ever since Twonchkinville, Shiro had been trying to work his feet free of the slippers; now, at last, they seemed to have loosened.

"You want 'em?" he asked. "Here!" Eyes blazing, he kicked them off at the witch.

"Put 'em back on!" she commanded.

"Why?"

"These things must be done *carefully*."

"No way."

"Wugh!" she cried.

Taking the slippers, the Punky tried to restick them on Shiro, but evidently Punkies were as bad at resticking other people's shoes as they were at removing them. At last the witch howled in rage and upended a conveniently-placed hourglass.

"If you haven't put those slippers back on by the time these sands run out," she told the kitten, "I'll kill that little dog of yours!"

With that, she stormed out with Wugh. The door boomed shut.

Shiro looked at Tototo, who looked back at him just as cutely and sadly as only a small black dog named Tototo could.

"Sorry, pal," Shiro said. "But I really hate those shoes."

The Terminationer and Shiro's pals clapped eyes on the castle long about sunup. The view was very spectacular, with the fortress atop its crag, and the cloud of bats and vultures swirling above the fortress, and not surprisingly, there was a broad stretch of widened shoulder on the precipice side of the road marked "scenic overlook," where one could pause and take in the vista at one's leisure---or hash over one's plans to invade the castle.

But the overlook was a trap. The witch knew well that it was a perfect spot for plan-hashing, and always kept three men there, concealed among the rocks. Hardly had the robot and Shiro's chums halted their hogs when the punkies cried "Aha!" and came leaping out of hiding, crossbows at the ready.

"Take off your clothes," said the Terminationer to the Mohawks.

The Punkies blushed, one answering: "We hardly know you."

The robot dismounted and lumbered towards them, and as they stood there dithering, distracted by his intimidating approach, the lion smoked all three with his Winchester.

"Put on zere duds," said the robot to his allies.

"Why?" asked the tin man.

"Vhen ve get to ze castle, you can pretend you took me prisoner."

"What about the bloodstains?" asked the lion, divesting a punky of his shoulderpads.

"I vounded you," said the robot.

"I thought you liked him," said the scarecrow, appalled.

"You only hurt ze vuns you luff," said the robot. "Now dress up!"

After hiding the corpses, they rode to the castle gate, the tinman sitting behind the Terminationer, holding a crossbow to the robot's head. A group of punkies with halberds stood beneath the raised fangs of the portcullis.

"Caught this one at the scenic overlook," said the woodsman as he and the robot got off the bike. "Says he's the kitten's lawyer."

"Scenic overlook, eh?" a punky answered. "What's that blood on your clothes?"

"He wounded us," the said the lion.

"You know," the punky continued, "I don't recognize you guys at all."

"Gosh," said the lion. "He must've wounded us worse than I thought."

"Where'd that Winchester come from?" the punky asked.

"Took it from the prisoner."

"Why'd you leave him with that pistol and the recoilless rifle?"

"He said he'd shoot us."

"Very well," said the punky. "Go on through."

"Where's the kitten?" asked the tin man.

"Northwest tower."

As the four entered the courtyard, the woodsman indicated a huge tanker-truck to the lion. A wicked-looking steel dozerblade-cum-plow-cum-cowcatcher had been attached to the front end; the words *My Dirt* were blazoned in tall red letters on the trailer.

The quartet made their way to the tower and up the spiral steps, following green arrows accompanied by the international symbol for *cell,* which, for those of you who are hopelessly insular, like from Delaware or some such hole like that, is three vertical lines with a little guy looking out glumly. At the top was a single doorway with two guards sitting on either side of it, twiddling their thumbs.

"New prisoner," said the tin man.

The guards took up the crossbows and stood.

"We've heard nothing from Her Ladyship," one said.

The tin man stepped out from behind the Terminationer, and without giving the guards the slightest warning, swept his axe left and right.

"Closer!" whispered the lion.

The tin man stepped forward, this time connecting.

"Whew!" said the lion. "That was cold!"

"I only vould'ff vounded zem," the robot admitted.

"Wuss," said the tin man, and picked up the keys.

Shiro was explaining various theories about the afterlife to Tototo as the door swung open. In rushed the tin man, the lion, and the scarecrow.

"Brought your lawyer," the scarecrow said.

Sweeping them all to one side with a stroke of his arm, the Terminationer strode in, reaching for the Colt longslide at his belt.

"He's not my lawyer!" Shiro cried.

"Why'd you fire him?" asked the scarecrow from the floor.

Staring into the red glare of the .45's laser sight, Shiro thought fast. Stepping aside, he held up a little makeup mirror which he'd never known why he carried until now...the laser-beam bounced from the glass, depositing a neat red spot right between the Terminationer's eyes just as the robot pulled the trigger. Shiro stood congratulating himself on his cleverness---until he realized that the bullet had simply shattered the mirror, cutting his paw.

Fighting to his knees, the tin man hacked at the Terminationer's leg, the axe bouncing off. The robot turned, swinging his gun round.

Shiro cupped both paws beside his mouth.

"Fat science-fiction fans!" he cried.

The Terminationer cringed and dropped his pistol, looked up at the ceiling, and bellowed, "Vhere, vhere?", giving Shiro, Tototo, the lion, and the woodsman time to scramble out the door.

"Eight hundred knee-bends!" cried Shiro over his shoulder.

"Very Vell," Terminationer answered dispiritedly.

Shiro was halfway down the circular staircase when the lion asked:

"Where's the scarecrow?"

"Wait here," Shiro told the others, then pelted back up to the cell. The straw man was raptly watching the Terminationer doing his callies.

"I wouldn't have fired this guy," he told Shiro. "My lawyer can't do half this many knee-bends."

"Take him viss you, please," the Terminationer begged the kitten.

Shiro went to grab the scarecrow's sleeve---and accidentally stepped back into the ruby slippers, which glommed right on to his feet. Cursing, he led the straw man down the stairs.

The others were waiting at the bottom. Looking out into the courtyard, Shiro could see a large delegation of punkies led by Wugh hastening towards the doorway.

"Company," the kitten said.

"How many?" asked the lion.

"Too many. And Wugh's got my gun..." Shiro paused, hearing heavy footbeats on the stairs...he turned.

Recoilless rifle on his shoulder, the Terminationer was charging down towards them.

"Whoa!" said Shiro, backpedalling through the doorway.

The robot loosed his first shell, which struck the ground just outside the threshold. Still standing within, Shiro's buddies took no damage; neither did the kitten, as he was one hell of a backpedaller. Nonetheless, the concussion chucked him twenty feet across the courtyard, straight into Wugh, bowling him over. Shiro had his gun and ammo back in an instant, and leaped to his feet. The punkies seemed stunned, gaping at the doorway.

Shiro heard the lion's Winchester, then three shots from the robot's longslide. Out came the Terminationer, holstering his pistol, readying his three-barrelled weapon once more.

Most of the punkies paid Shiro no attention, but he dusted two who did, scooted behind the rest and kept running, making for the truck.

Just to get a clear shot at the kitten, the Terminationer put a recoilless round into a punky's shoulder...even though the shell wasn't meant to kill, the robot didn't mind a bit when it turned the guy into a bone-laced human slurpee, killing five of the surrounding marauders with punky shrapnel.

Shiro was in plain sight now. Ignoring crossbow-bolts from the surviving mohawks, the robot took aim once more, and was just about to make a *feline* slurpee out of the kitten when something struck him from behind, knocking him forward. His last shell went wild, taking out another bunch of punkies and sending the rest running for cover. Tossing the rifle aside, he whirled, reaching for his Colt.

A neat round hole in one shoulder (opened by the same .45 back inside the door), the tin man swung his axe once more, knocking the gun from the robot's grip. Bleeding from a wound in the leg, also inflicted by that pesky Colt, the lion stepped up beside the woodsman, cranking out three shots from the Winchester. The robot went over on his back, temporarily stunned. The tin man, the lion, and Tototo rushed past, the scarecrow bringing up the rear.

Shiro, meanwhile, had shot out a window and clambered into the truck. Swinging the seat forward to the kitten position, he hotwired the ignition with all the effortless speed of an action-adventure protagonist and pulled up to his friends, opening the passenger's side door. The tin man and scarecrow piled in with Tototo; hanging onto the bar-handle attached to the cab, the lion remained on the running-board.

Behind, the Terminationer turned over onto his stomach, snatched up his pistol.

Shiro floored the fuel-pedal. The truck lunged forward, a real jack-rabbit for a semi, let alone one hauling such a heavy load.

The robot got off two shots. A pair of frosty-white bullet-holes opened in the windshield, spraying the inside of the cab with powdered glass. Then the front end planted a big dozerblade kiss on the Terminationer's face, sending him flying like a four-bagger hit by the Babe himself, although, in truth, Mr. Ruth never smacked any robot assassins from the future out of the park---unless you want to count that time in the '32 world Series where the robot veered over the foul line just before clearing the wall.

Shiro braked, popped the tranny into reverse, and swung the truck round. Off to the right, he could see the witch emerging from a doorway looking wondrously rabid; some of the punkies were beginning to venture forth again. A few quarrels struck the cab, one shattering the passenger's side window...Shiro snorted with contempt, pointing the semi's nose at the gateway.

The portcullis was dropping; the lion took cover behind the cab. A line of punkies had formed in front of the threshold, but they all scattered as the truck drew near, with the exception of one really foolish fellow who stood his ground and put a quarrel through the windshield (and the scarecrow too, for that matter); the dozerblade mashed the punky through the portcullis in nice neat squares like scarlet Playdough before shattering the gate itself. Bursting out onto the road in the biggest blast of toothpicks since Tunguska, the truck roared downhill, Shiro smacking his paw again and again into the center of the steering-wheel, the horn bellowing like the last trump on the *Dies Irae*.

"Zirconsville here we come!" Shiro cried.

"Isn't this stealing?" asked the scarecrow.

Pit-bull murdering pissed, the witch went over to Wugh, who still lay senseless; plucking a long stiff straw out of her broom, she jammed it up his left nostril---his right, not your right---with roughly the force of a tornado driving a sprig into a telephone pole, and he woke with a howl. Seizing a handful of mohawk, she twisted him round, pointing.

"What's that?" she screamed in her shrillest out-Heroding Herod voice.

"I don't see anything, Your Warty-Chinnedness," he answered.

She ripped out a fistful of mane. "That's the empty space my tanker-truck used to occupy!"

"I believe you're right, Your Ladyship."

"The kitten stole my dirt!" she shrieked.

Wugh rose. "We'll get it back, My Lady."

"You're damn right we will," she said, plucking the straw from his nose and waving its bloody tip before his eyes. "Because there's a lot more where this came from!"

Wugh sniffled.

"Call out *all* the men!" she cried. "Put every vehicle we've got on the road---especially the stuff the readers haven't heard about yet!"

"Even the Yugos?"

She screeched in rage, popping every vein in her bulging eyeballs. "Even the pogo-sticks and the surfboards! Now see to it!"

"Seeing to it," said Wugh, rushing away, gathering up the men nearby. The whole troop vanished into the garage.

As the witch stood fuming, the Terminationer came up, asking, "Ze kitten escaped, I take it?"

"Who are you?" she demanded.

"A robot assassin from ze future."

Her Ladyship laughed. "And I'm the Wicked Witch of the Southwest!"

"Ja, you are," the Terminationer replied.

She had no answer for this.

He marched out the gate, straddled his chopper, and took off.

Careening down the switchbacked road from the castle, Shiro glanced into one of the sideview mirrors to see the robot approaching swiftly, one arm outstretched. The kitten couldn't hear any shots above the roar of the truck's engine, but saw pistol flashes, and the black splintery explosion of one of the rearmost tires, retread flying everywhere; the robot casually drove his bike over a lengthy piece of rubber, then popped a new clip into his gun.

Shiro snapped his eyes back to the road just into time to snake the tractor-trailer round the next bend. The robot made the curve too and started back up with his .45. Another tire blew, and the trailer's rear end began to judder, but this time the robot caught a four-foot strap of rubber across the chops. His bike swerved toward the edge of the cliff, catching between two boulders on the brink; the Terminationer soared out of the saddle, way out into space. Dropping two hundred feet, he landed on a section of road below, was stunned for an appropriate interval, then got up and dusted himself off---just in time for the semi to smack him over like a snowplow making love to a mailbox.

Shiro looked in the sideview, hoping to see the robot go shooting out from under the back of the trailer; but the Terminationer didn't reappear. Was he clinging to the bottom of the tank?

Whatever had happened to him, the question was swiftly driven from Shiro's mind as a huge fleet of very funky marauder-vehicles came steaming around the last turn: stripped-down buggies with rollbars, pickup trucks with quadruple-barrelled spear guns mounted on the beds, New York Checker cabs, top-of-the line if extremely filthy-looking RV's made in Elkhart, Indiana, Honda Civics huffing and puffing to keep up, bumper cars, airline catering vans, bookmobiles, welcome wagons, golf carts, 40-inch cut riding mowers, Toddlin Trains, outrigger canoes, and Bactrian camels, the Wicked Witch riding herd from above on her broomstick, black cape streaming behind her in the wind.

The tin man had been keeping track of the situation in *his* sideview. "We're going to be boarded," he told Shiro, pushing the scarecrow off his lap. "Me and the lion will climb up on the trailer, see what we can do."

Opening the door, he went out on the running-board. The lion looked round the corner of the cab at him.

"Let's head on back," said the woodsman.

They went up to the cleated chase-sequence walk on the top of the tank, and, half-crouching, footed their way carefully to the back of the trailer, deciding there was really no point in going any further.

Looking like something out of a Lea and Perrins commercial, a mail-draped pantomime cow came galloping up, a punky astride its awfully-sagging back, squinting along the top of his crossbow at the lion.

The lion nailed him first, then roared: "Eat this, bossy!" and drilled the cow in the head. Going all the way through the lead man in the costume, the slug put a second hole in the rider before slanting at last into the guy in the costume's rear end, fetching a perfect E above high C from the poor fresh-cut soprano. Legs buckling, the cow crumpled and rolled, exploding in flames as its gas-tank went.

For a moment the road was obscured by a wall of fire. Then a double-decker London tour-bus and a Manilla Jeepney burst through the blazing remains of the cow, both trailing burning petrol. The lion swiftly picked off the drivers; swerving in front of the bus, the jeepney burst like a nuked junkyard, the bus careening into the cliff-wall and coming apart in turn.

Two VW convertibles bounced and butted their way through the jetsam, bracketting the tank-trailer as the lion reloaded his rifle. Taking the next turn, the semi squished one bug against the mountainside, but several punkies managed to leap from the other before Shiro nudged the Volkswagen over the brink...within moments the mohawks clambered onto the trailer-top from the hose-container shelf, drawing meat cleavers from their belts.

The tin man stepped to meet them, hooking one's ankle with his axe and flipping him onto his back. A second man charged forward, grinning hideously.

"You really should see a dentist," said the woodsman, parrying a cleaver-blow with his axe.

"I would, but who has the time?" the mohawk answered, laying on a second stroke.

Guessing the fellow had no intention of going, the woodsman dealt out some emergency dentistry of his own. Showing not the least bit of gratitude, the punky took a header from the starboard side, snatching teeth from midair.

"Keep 'em on ice!" the woodsman advised.

A third punky strode over the first, who was still on his back, wind apparently knocked out.

"How are *your* teeth?" the tin man asked.

The third mohawk flashed him a fierce and quite perfect smile, but the woodsman, noticing that one of the man's arms was longer than the other, shortened it thoughtfully by a hand. The punky toppled to port, howling.

The first marauder got up, pressing the small of his back.

"Do you have any Tylenol?" he groaned, grimacing.

The tin man tossed him a bottle.

"This is aspirin!" the punky said.

"Better for your heart," said the woodsman, burying his axe in the punky's forehead.

"I've heard that," said the punky, eyes crossed as if to better observe the blade. The tin man wrenched him to one side, axe pulling loose in the process.

The lion's gun was cracking again. The tin man spun to see the witch not far astern of the trailer, jinking and dodging in the air, lighting a molotov cocktail as she avoided the bullets. But as she cocked her arm back to chuck the bomb, one of the lion's slugs shattered the bottle, dousing her cloak with fiery fuel. Screaming, she set her broom down in the back of a Ram pickup, the punkies there rushing to slap out the blaze.

The Dodge slowed. Bristling with hostiles, an Edsel convertible passed it by, a marauder in the front seat rising, whirling a grapling-hook. The lion greased him, but the hook was already sailing, and caught the lion by his purloined shoulder-pads. The dead punky's comrades immediately lunged to grab the rope, pulling the lion from the trailer.

Rushing to the tank's end, the tin man saw the lion spreadeagled--- or spreadlioned---on the hood of the Edsel, the punkies struggling to reel him up over the windshield.

Suddenly the lion reared up and leaped the barrier, swinging the Winchester, evidently out of ammo once more. A terrific melee erupted inside the Edsel, with torn-off shoulder-pads, crossbows, and hanks of Mohawk and upholstery flying into the air. The Ford swerved right and left, falling back; the last the tin man saw of the lion, the beast had just torn off the passenger's side door and was busily bashing away at someone in the back seat.

The Edsel vanished behind a huge prairie schooner sporting a huge red W on its billowing sail. Whirling his very own grapnel, Wugh stood in the bows. The tin man raised his axe to bat the hook away.

Shadow covered him; pivotting, he saw that the truck's cab had just entered a tunnel. *Clearance 14' 3"* warned a sign above the arch. The tin man read the message with no difficulty whatsoever, as his face was headed right for it. His first thought was that he was all right, as he was barely five eleven. Then he realized that he'd made an intellectual error worthy of the scarecrow himself; also that it was too late to duck, as the impact had already smashed him into far more pieces than he cared to count.

Oops, thought Shiro, turning the headlights on. *Forgot about the tunnel.*

The truck barrelled on through, emerging in half a minute or so.

I wonder if the lion and the woodsman are okay?

His first indication that something had gone very wrong was when he noticed the scarecrow waving to someone on the passenger's side running-board. A dude in warpaint was glaring in.

"He doesn't look very happy," the scarecrow told Shiro. "Maybe you should wave too."

The punky thrust a gauntletted fist through the window, grabbing the scarecrow by the throat. With a yelp, Tototo leaped at the marauder's face. Loosing the scarecrow, the punky ripped Tototo from his nose and flung him to the floor.

"Duck!" Shiro cried to the scarecrow.

Apparently expecting to see one flapping about in the cab, the scarecrow tilted his head back just enough for Shiro to pepper the punky's brow with the Uzi. The mohawk dropped from sight.

The scarecrow turned to Shiro, looking somewhat concerned. "You know, I think someone just fired a gun in here."

Detecting motion on his right--- this is an aussie truck, mind you---Shiro immediately swung the Uzi round, blasting a punky off the running board on his side.

Footsteps clanged on the roof of the cab; a long gleaming projectile burst through the ceiling, driving into the seat between Shiro's legs.

Shiro fired a blast straight upwards.

"Missed me!" a man cried, then stamped on the roof. "Over here! Yeah, right here!"

Shiro obliged him, firing at the sound.

The Punky yelped: "No, I meant...over *there*..."

Shiro saw the body drop between the cab and the tank.

More footbeats banged onto the roof, and a crudely-fabricated morningstar-head crashed through the windshield. Shiro fired another burst through the roof, but whoever was up there swung the mace again, this time through the hole in the glass, just missing the kitten's face.

Shiro jammed on the brakes.

Wugh ended-over-ended from the roof, bellowing, "I'm doing this on purpose, really!"

He dipped from view beyond the front end.

Coming to the bottom of the slope, Shiro accelerated, crossed the valley, and started up the next mountain. Losing speed on the grade, he glanced at the sideviews; another group of punkies had clambered onto the trailer, and were advancing along the hose-container shelf on the right side.

"I'm going outside!" Shiro cried to the scarecrow. "You'll have to drive!"

"Sure," said the scarecrow.

With that Rototo began to bark furiously, shaking his head and raising his paw.

"Okay," said Shiro. "*You* drive."

Still holding the wheel, Shiro opened the door and stood out on the running-board. Rototo swung the seat forward to the little black dog position and took the wheel, grinning maniacally, honking the horn.

Shiro felt a projectile tug at his topknot. Unbound, his locks whipped back in the breeze.

"Ruin my topknot, will you?" he screamed, whirling, spraying his Uzi into a punky on the container-shelf, who was even then in the process of trying to re-span his crossbow. The mohawk dropped from the shelf, revealing the next guy in line, who looked very much out of place, timorously proffering a cardboard container.

"Jerry's Kids?" he asked.

Shiro flipped him a quarter. Catching it in the slot, the man cried: "Thanks!" and climbed up over the top of the trailer.

The third man in line was trying the charity-routine too, dressed as old St. Nick.

"Better not cry," he said.

"I was thinking of pouting," said Shiro.

"Don't do that either!" answered the other, but just then the wind blew his Kris Kringle hat off, revealing a haircut like the crest on a Roman helmet. Dropping his tin cup, the fellow whipped out a cleaver.

Shiro ventilated the man's Santy-suit but good.

Three more marauders remained on the shelf; Shiro's clip was empty, but the punkies didn't know that...a Rose-Bowl float proclaiming "One Hundred Years of Internal Combustion" had snuck up alongside the tanker-trailer, and the Mohawks dived right in among all the petals, mightily discomfitting the Queen of Internal Combustion and all her Internal Combustion handmaidens, who, if the knives between their teeth were any indications, had clearly been intending to board the trailer.

Shiro slid a new clip into the Uzi and blew out one of the float's front tires. The vehicle slowed, slipping back.

Shiro blew out the other front tire. The float boat-tailed and flipped, disintegrating in a vast blizzard of red, white and pink perianths, which isn't exactly another word for *petal*, although it says it is in my thesaurus.

Is there a synonym for thesaurus? Shiro wondered.

The road levelled off for a stretch.

Scenic overlook's just ahead, the kitten thought. He opened the cab-door.

"I'll drive," he told Tototo.

The dog snivelled but surrendered the wheel. Shiro slid the seat back to the kitten position, and when the truck reached the overlook, eyed the sideview to ascertain that none of his pursuers had cleared the incline yet, then wrestled the wheel all the way over to the left, swinging the truck round.

Suddenly a hand appeared over the front end, gripping the wombat-ornament on the radiator cap; an instant later, Wugh lunged up onto the hood, scrambling towards the windshield, smashing it out with his face, hurling himself onto the scarecrow as the truck started back down the slope. Stuffing the straw man down into the space between seats, he knocked the Uzi from Shiro's paw.

"Don't you like car-crashes?" the kitten demanded.

"That's why I got into this line of work!" the punky chief replied.

"Then watch this!"

Wugh turned to see the remaining two-thirds of the witch's fleet steaming up the grade, heading right for the semi's dozer-blade.

He could only grin.

Shiro floored the pedal.

Three bikers rode up the blade like skiers at the tip of an Olympic ramp, one clipping the top of the cab, the other two missing it clean. Two dune buggies struck the front end and went off like grenades; Mr. Toad's motorcar caught it next, the amphibian himself sailing into Wugh's lap mumbling "poop-poop" as he succumbed to brain-damage.

The next several vehicles swerved out of the truck's way, pitching over the edge of the cliff; but the succeeding drivers had more gumption...looking very much like Stephen Boyd, a charioteer in black drove his team directly into the blade, whereupon a wave of fresh-ground dogfood came cresting over the hood, half-flooding the cab.

Shiro swore, brushing guck from his face. The charioteer's head was hanging over the dashboard.

"Look for them in the valley of the lepers," the fellow gasped, and died.

Wugh nudged Shiro. "So far so good," he said, and tossed Mr. Toad and the charioteer out his window.

"Ain't it?" said Shiro, Jeepneys and Hyundais and Fords (oh my!) shattering against his front end. Wugh's landschooner came apart with such a flourish of fragments that Wugh himself roared out a laugh of the sheerest delight; vehicle after vehicle bit the big blade and was blown to flinders. It was a carnival of havoc, a Roman orgy of devastation, a Mongolian cook-out of chaos; Shiro was so filled with joy that he could barely control his little Bushido bladder. So much twisted garbage piled up on the hood that he couldn't even see the road anymore, but still he refused to let up on the pedal, relishing each jolt of impact, reaching out with his feelings, somehow keeping the truck on the serpentine road, whether from Zen inspiration or a perfect lust for destruction, he didn't know.

After several more minutes of such wonderfulness, the crashes came less frequently, then stopped altogether. Shiro sighed, then looked over at Wugh.

"Was that something, or what?" the kitten asked.

Wugh gave him a big thumb's up. "Very spectacular, I must admit," he said. "I'm afraid I'm going to have to switch sides, just to show my gratit---"

With a tremendous squeal of metal on metal, all the wreckage on the hood was wiped to one side.

Wugh howled in surprise and terror.

The Terminationer, having hauled himself along the underside of the truck, was crouching on the hood; rising, he kicked the roof off the cab, and looming over Shiro, pointed his Colt at the kitten.

Scooping up a big mess of horsemeat, Wugh hurled it into the robot's eyes.

Looking out between the Terminationer's legs, Shiro saw a turn approaching; even as he steered round the bend, a blurred object came hurtling into view, travelling so fast he didn't even recognize it as the witch, airborne once more, until she was a scant few yards from the robot. The kitten had a brief impression of her eyes bugging out so far that they must've struck the Terminationer a good half-second before the rest of her did. Then the robot's whole body was outlined by a titanic crimson splash as she ruptured like a paintball against, well, a *very* sturdy automaton.

"Gonna have to clean this cab before long," Wugh told Shiro earnestly, blinking.

Feeling rather like the floor of a movie theater, Shiro found some merit in this proposition.

Having kept his feet, the Terminationer reached up to wipe the horsemeat from his face.

Wugh snatched Shiro's fallen Uzi, blasted the .45 from the robot's hand, then gave him the rest of the magazine in the face and body, the pelting slugs tossing the Terminationer off the hood and down the cliff.

That left only one bit of unfinished business. A last pickup, the one in which Her Pointyhattedness had lit after catching fire, was careening towards the rig. But the dozer blade made short work of it.

"Where we going now?" Wugh asked.

"Zirconsville," Shiro said. "But I lost the lion and the tin man somewhere, and I'm going to look for them."

"Could you let me out here?" Wugh inquired. "I think I'd like to go back and bask amid the wreckage."

"Sure thing," Shiro said, stopping.

Wugh gave him back his gun and got out. "Once again," he said, "Primo destruction. Be seeing yer."

Shiro started down the slope once more.

The scarecrow hauled himself up out of the dogfood on the floor and slumped back in his seat.

"I never got to perform any heroics," he said mournfully.

"We're still alive, too," Shiro said.

As they were crossing the valley floor, Shiro saw a sorry-looking vehicle approaching, the remains of an Edsel, little more than the frame and motor and the grille. The kitten started to accelerate before noticing that the Ford's driver was none other than the lion.

Shiro halted, looking down into the Ford. Busily reassembling himself, the tin man was sitting beside the lion.

"Sorry we're late," the lion said. "But I thought I'd better gather up our friend here."

"What happened to the witch and her men?" the tin man asked.

"Whacked 'em all," Shiro answered. "With the exception of Wugh. He recognized some of my sterling qualities, so I let him off the hook."

"And the robot?"

"Went over the cliff. I passed him on the way down here. Still seemed to be stunned. I think we'd better find an alternate route back to Zirconsville. Are you back together yet?"

"Just about," said the tin man, snapping something into place below the knee. He and the lion got out of the car and climbed up to the cab. Opening the door, the lion eyed the horsemeat.

"You *have* been busy, haven't you?" he asked Shiro. "Oh well, at least I'll be able to snack."

The tin man stayed outside on the running-board; refusing to let the scarecrow sit on his lap, the lion made him get down between the seats again. Shiro started forward once more. Snacking *very* heavily, the lion had the cab clean in short order, with a little help from Tototo.

There was a road-map in the glove-compartment, and it showed Route 88 looping back towards Zirconsville on the far side of the mountains. The truck arrived in the city after a twenty-three hour haul. Accompanied by a large troop of guards, Shiro and his companions were ushered into the Wizard's presence.

"This had better be good," growled the hooded head. "Woke me up, dammit!"

"We brought the truck," said Shiro.

"*What?*" the Wizard demanded.

"It's true, sir," said one of the guards. "It's at loading dock A."

"You're sure it's *the* truck?"

"Yes sir."

"We fulfilled our part of the bargain," Shiro said.

"So?" the Wizard asked.

"Fulfill yours."

"Nope," the Wizard replied.

"You promised me epaulets," said the lion.

"You promised me a heart," said the tin man.

"You promised you'd send me back home," said Shiro.

"You promised me *something*," said the scarecrow. "Didn't you?"

"Sorry," answered the Wizard. "Can't hold up my end, I'm afraid."

"Why not?" Shiro cried.

"It's beyond my abilities."

"You scumbag," said Shiro. "You're a very bad man."

"No," the Wizard answered. "I'm a very *good* man. I'm just a bad wizard, that's all."

"You're a liar and cheat, and you sent us off to be killed."

"Well, maybe I'm *not* a good man. Guards!"

Shiro and his friends felt spearpoints at their backs.

"Drop your weapons," said the Wizard.

Uzi, axe, and Winchester all clattered to the floor.

"What are you going to do with us?" the lion asked.

"Frankly, I'm rather partial to lynchings," answered the Wizard.

Five nooses, one doggy-sized, dropped out of the ceiling.

"You *are* still a member of the Klan!" the tin man cried.

"A regular Aristotle, aren't we?" the Wizard laughed. "String 'em up, boys!"

The guards fastened the nooses and yanked the prisoners up off the floor. Legs kicking as they dangled, Shiro and his companions died slowly in horrible agony...

Just fooling.

This is what *actually* happened.

An instant before the guards could fasten those neckties, a loud commotion started up behind a drape off to the left.

"Pay no attention to that little Klan fellow behind the curtain!" the Wizard's voice boomed. "He's not the one you want---!"

The floating head vanished; a roundish object wrapped in a blood-spotted white hood rolled from under the curtain. One of the guards ran over and dumped it from its covering...the severed noggin that dropped out was blond and Aryan and showed every sign of having had a recent nosejob.

Eyeing the thing with horror, the other guards asked, "Who's that?"

To Shiro's astonishment, Tomokato stepped out through a break in the curtains, and, sword dripping, told the men-at-arms, "Your glorious leader."

"The Wizard?" they cried.

The cat nodded.

"Uncle-*San*!" Shiro shouted. "How did you know I needed rescuing?"

"I didn't," said Tomokato. "That swine was simply on my list." He regarded the Wizard's troops. "Are you going to try and avenge your Master?"

They huddled, whispering.

"Hell no," a spokesman answered at last. "Bastard owed us six months back pay. We're off to loot the treasury."

They clattered out of the audience-chamber.

Shiro and his friends flipped the nooses from around their necks.

"This certainly turned out to be a pointless trip," said the lion.

"We got nothing from it whatsoever," said the Tin Man.

"*I* learned something," the scarecrow said.

"What?" Shiro asked.

"Don't go see the Wizard," the straw man replied.

The tin man asked, "Can it be you've actually gotten smarter after all?"

"I suppose it would if I meant it," the scarecrow answered. "But I don't."

Tomokato said: "You haven't introduced me to your friends, nephew."

Shiro obliged him, then added: "You'd better get used to their company, too. I don't think we can leave this country---unless we happen to be sucked up by a tornado." He thought a moment. "That *is* how you got here, isn't it?"

"No," said Tomokato. "I needed magic ruby slippers, which I lost upon arrival. But I notice you have a pair."

"Huh?" Shiro asked.

"Just click them together three times and say, 'There's no place like home.'"

"Really?"

"Really," Tomokato answered. "I'll hold on to you, and off we'll go."

Shiro turned to his companions. "Guess this is good-bye."

He shook paws with the lion.

"You make me proud to be a feline," the lion told him.

Shiro shook the tin man's hand, and said: "Sorry you didn't get your heart."

"Oh well," said the woodsman. "I suppose I appreciate *The Untold Story* enough as it is."

Shiro picked up Tototo and let the dog slobber on his face for a bit; then the kitten went on to the scarecrow, saying, "I'm going to miss you least of all."

"I miss me already," said the straw man.

"Let's be off, nephew," said Tomokato, wiping his sword, sheathing it, then kneeling and wrapping his arms around the kitten.

Shiro clicked the slippers three times, closed his eyes, and said, "There's no place like home."

A mighty wind swept him. He felt a cool tingly sensation. When it subsided, the scent of marinara sauce filled his nostrils. Somewhere a chorus was chanting in Latin. He opened his eyes to find himself in the Vatican. The Pope was just concluding an audience with Dick Van Patten.

Shiro looked down at the slippers in disgust, whispering: "I said *home*, dammit!"

Van Patten dragged away from the dais, a dejected expression on his pudgy mug.

"Now remember!" the Pontiff called after the chubby actor, "Stop trying to be funny!" He beckoned Shiro and Tomokato, holding out his ring to be kissed.

"I don't want to kiss it," Shiro said.

"I don't want you to, Shiro," said the Pope.

"How did you know my name?" Shiro asked.

"I didn't. Sometimes you just have to trust to luck."

"Do *I* have to kiss it?" Tomokato asked.

"Not if you don't want to," said the Pontiff. "Seeing as how you're probably a Buddhist or somesuch, I'll kiss it for you."

He smacked it but good.

"How can I repay you?" Tomokato asked.

The Pope replied: "Perhaps I could pick what gets parodied next."

"That's not unreasonable," Tomokato answered.

The Pope considered his options. "*The Seven Samurai*, I think."

"Good choice," said Tomokato, a split instant before this story ended.

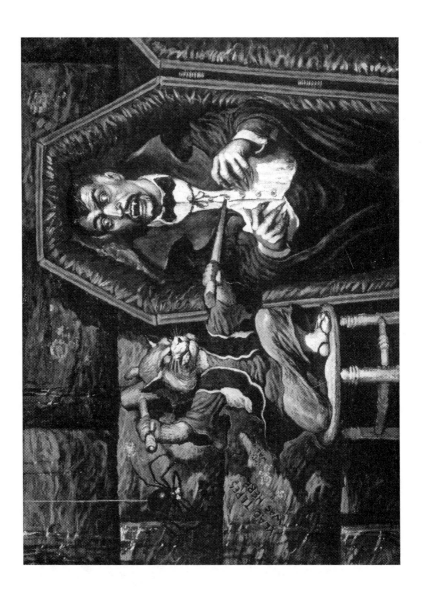

THE MAGNIFICENT SEVEN SAMURAI CATS

Tomokato and Shiro lingered at the Vatican for several days, during which Tomokato gave some pointers to the Swiss guards, and Shiro, posing as Cardinal Ratzinger, tried to sell the Pieta. The deal fell through when the real Ratzinger showed up, declaring Shiro to be glaringly deficient in the matter of faith and morals. Agreeing with him and apologizing most profusely, Tomokato accompanied Shiro to the airport, deciding at the last moment to join him on his visit home....

From: *Cat Out of Hell*

Huki, Duki, Luki, and Agamemnon were very worked up.

"Don't get so excited," said Shimura. "Dinner's not the time for such carrying-on."

"But papa-*san*," cried Huki. "The whole scene is a total rip-off from *The Kremlin Litter!*"

Tomokato laughed, sipping his sake. "Let me see if I understand. You say there's a ghost---"

Huki broke in: "And he's trying to make Whoopi Goldberg do what he wants."

Agamemnon took up the thread: "He's annoying her on purpose, singing *I'm Enery the Eighth I Am*, over and over again."

"Just like when like when you were torturing that torturer in the Lubyanka," said Luki to Shiro.

"Hmm," said Shiro.

"Enery the Eighth, eh?" Tomokato mused. "It could be a coincidence, I suppose."

"That's what *I* think," said Hanako.

"With all due respect, no way, mama-*san*," said Duki. "Those Hollywood guys are always on the lookout for material to rip off. And the movie was directed by a man who worked on all those Leslie Neilsen comedies. It's exactly the same type of humor as in these books."

"What do you suggest we do about it?" Tomokato asked.

"Hunt down the guilty and kill 'em like dogs," Huki said.

"My schedule is full enough," Tomokato said.

"But Uncle-*san*..." Agamemnon whined.

"I'm *too busy*," Tomokato insisted.

"You had time for this visit," Agammenon sulked.

"Which means I have even *less* time for killing Hollywood types. I've already killed enough as it is. I mustn't lose sight of my paramount goal: vengeance for My Lord."

Hanako observed wistfully: "How relatively uneventful your life was before Nobunaga's death."

Tomokato sighed: "My victims barely numbered in the hundreds of thousands."

"Ah," Shimura said. "I can remember when you hadn't proved yourself at all. To me, at any rate."

"That far back?" Tomokato chuckled.

"Doesn't seem that long ago to me," Shimura answered. "My little green brother, tagging after me, making a nuisance of himself..."

"I never made a nuisance of myself," said Tomokato. "You refused to give me a chance."

"Have I heard this story, uncle-*san*?" asked Shiro.

"If not, it *would* be rather surprising," Tomokato replied. "After all, you've spent so much time in my company. But seeing as how this story's going to be trotted out no matter what, I suppose you haven't."

"Better get to it then, brother," said Shimura.

Tomokato took another sip of sake, and began:

"There's a village in Shinano Province, typical in every respect. Indeed, it's *so* typical that it's the only village in all Japan called Anytown..."

"I've always thought it ironic that there's only one Anytown," Shimura said.

"So have I," answered Tomokato, and resumed: "Twenty years ago, things were very bad in Anytown. Shinano Province was overrun with brigands, and worst of them all was El Pacino, who ravaged the land with his four hundred Bandoleros---"

"*Mexican* bandits, uncle *san*?" asked Shiro.

"Yes," said Tomokato. "There was an exchange program, since discontinued..."

"*Our* bandits were in Mexico?"

"Yes."

"I see," said Shiro.

Tomokato went on: "El Pacino swept down on Anytown every year. He was after the *bonsai* trees, of course. The peasants would spend ten years training a sapling, binding it with wires, stunting its growth, and then El Pacino and his brigands would swoop in, snatch the trees, and ride off to Edo or Kyoto and trade them for baseball cards, which were the hot item then.

"It was a terrible situation, to say the least. And it grew particularly ugly that spring..."

"Which Spring?" asked Shiro.

"The spring in question," said Tomokato. "One fine afternoon in prime bandit-swooping weather, the brigands appeared atop the hills south of Anytown, silhouetted most strikingly against the sky. After giving the peasants a good long time to be awed by the tableau, the *banditos* came thundering down the slope, hooting and howling and firing their pistols into the air.

"Panicked, the peasants fled indoors. Most of the bandits halted outside the village, but thirty or so led by El Pacino himself rode into the common.

"'Watanabe!' the bandit chief cried. 'Watanabe! Come out and cho us some hospitality!'

"Kazuo Watanabe, the wealthiest peasant in the village, came from his house with three other men, the lot bowing and scraping.

"'As ju have probably noticed by now,' said El Pacino, 'We have returned.'

"'It's so nice to see you again,' answered Watanabe.

"'Bah,' said El Pacino. 'Ju know what we've come for.'

"'You need some of those little fringie-balls for your sombreros?'

"'Would *we* come *here* for those? Come now, Watanabe! When a man wants little fringie-balls, he goes to Osaka or Edo, doesn't he?' El Pacino climbed from his mount, stretching his back. 'No, my old prend. We've come for what we've always come for--- those precious stunted trees of jurs. Although I noticed, on the way in, that jur nursery was miserably lacking in trees suitable for plunder.'

"'It was plundered last week,' said Watanabe.

"'And who committed this crime?'

"'Canadian bandits.'

"'Please,' said El Pacino. 'Have ju ever seen a Canadian bandit in action? They lie on the ground and bleat until they die of starvation. No, Watanabe. I think ju are hiding jur trees.'

"'I swear to you---'

"El Pacino drew his Walker Colt and drilled a hole, big but bloodless, in the forehead of one of Watanabe's companions; there was a whole lotta splash out the back, though.

"'Cut the chit, Watanabe,' said the bandit chief.

"'We mislaid them,' answered Watanabe.

"'Jur trees?'

"'It's easier than you might think. They are, after all, very small.'

"'But where did ju lose them?'

"'We don't know.'

"'I'll tell ju what I'll do. I'll give ju six weeks. If ju haven't found the trees by then, I'll raze this town to the ground.'

"What a guy,' Watanabe said.

"'I know,' said El Pacino. 'But in the meantime---'

"He plugged another of Watanabe's companions.

"'Why did you do that?' Watanabe demanded.

"'Story needed a bit more gratuitous violence,' the bandit chieftain answered.

"'If the story needed it, it wasn't gratuitous.'

"'But that would mean I chouldn't have killed him even *if* the story needed it.'

"'Precisely.'

"El Pacino wrinkled his brow in deep thought. 'Screw it,' he said at last, and shot a third spear carrier. 'Six weeks, Watanabe.' Getting back on his horse, he lifted his arm. '*Vamanos, muchachos*!'

"'What did ju say?' his men asked.

"'Time to say bye-bye!' El Pacino answered.

"'Bye-bye!" they bellowed fiercely, and galloped from the square behind their leader.

"'How very tiresome,' said Watanabe.

"The other villagers came out.

"'So,' said Watanabe, 'We have six weeks until he returns."

"'Then what?' asked the village agronomist, Hanbei Izaka.

"'We're all dead meat,' replied Watanabe. 'Unless we let him have the trees.'

"'Actually, why don't we?"' asked Brzezinksi Tatsuya, Watanabe's security advisor. 'What good are the damn things?'

"'They're much smaller than regular trees,' Hanbei answered.

"'That loses its charm after a while,' Tatsuya said. 'Especially when you need lumber.'

"'We can trade them for baseball cards,' said Hanbei.

"'What good are baseball cards?'

"'They give us a reason to grow bonsai trees,' Watanabe said. 'In any case, I think we'd better go talk to the old man. Maybe he can tell us what to do.'

At that, Shiro interrupted: "How come they never asked this old guy for advice before, uncle-*san*?"

"Same reason you never heard this story," Tomokato replied. "Now where were we?"

"Wait, wait," said Shiro. "Unless I'm badly mistaken, Unc, you weren't present during any of this, right? At least, you've made no mention of yourself..."

"'That's true."

"Well, if you weren't there, how come you have a such detailed knowledge of what happened?"

Tomokato looked as though he were at something of a loss for an explanation, but Hanako leaped to his aid:

"Perhaps he interviewed everyone concerned, some time after the events described."

"Yes," he said. "Perhaps I did."

Shiro opened his mouth to make some objection, but Tomokato continued:

"Do you want to hear this story or not?"

"On balance..." the kitten said.

"So then," said Tomokato. "Off they went to the old man's place, and laid the problem out before him in full.

"'Strange you never came to me with this before,' he said.

"'Shiro said much the same thing,' said Watanabe.

"'Who's Shiro?' asked the old man.

"'Damned if I know,' said Watanabe. 'Anyway, what would you advise us to do?'

"'To *do*?" asked the old man. 'I'm afraid I have a much clearer sense of what you *shouldn't* do.'

"'Very well then,' said Hanbei. 'What *shouldn't* we do?'

"'Thrusting one's tongue against hot metal is generally pointless,' said the old man.

"'And how exactly does that advice help us?' asked Tatsuya.

"'How would you cope with the bandits if you had glowing ingots depending from your mouths?' the old man asked. 'You'd have to run hunched over, your tongues swinging down below your knees, smoking and stinking horridly. And what exactly would you gain by having your taste-buds welded to the metal? The satisfaction would be temporary---at best.'

"'He speaks the truth, Tatsuya,' Watanabe was forced to acknowledge.

"What else shouldn't we do?' Hanbei asked the old man.

"'Don't go see the Wizard,' the elder replied.

"'The Wizard?'

"'And now that I think of it, don't come see *me*, either,' the old man said. 'If you'll excuse me, I have a cake rising---'

"He stumped off into the kitchen. Watanabe, Hanbei and Tatsuya went back outside.

"'Oh Hell,' said Watanabe. 'Why don't we just go hire some samurai?'

"Hanbei and Tatsuya immediately saw that this was the only solution; together with Watanabe, they persuaded the rest of the villagers. It was decided that sufficient funds were available to offer seven samurai a reasonable *per diem*, in addition to all the bonsai trees they could carry. Watanabe, Hanbei and Tatsuya departed the next day for Samurai City.

"This was a very good place to look for samurai, although, strangely enough, the name was mere coincidence; the burg had been founded by one Milton Samurai, an eccentric Kyoto millionaire who'd made his fortune manufacturing weird feet for *anime* characters.

115

"In any case, Watanabe and his companions took a room at the Holiday Inn and began looking for suitable warriors, but after an exhaustive search, failed to find any in their room.

"After that, they looked outside. Prospects were better there, although the peasants still had a difficult task. This may be hard to understand, but not all samurai are humble moral paragons like myself; indeed, most have personal deficiencies, and some are very arrogant, if not downright snotty.

"Such was the first man the fellows from Anytown approached, a scarred swordsman with ostentatious sideburns strutting down the street.

"'Excuse me, sir,' said Watanabe, bowing, 'I couldn't help but notice your sideburns strutting down the street, and---'

"The samurai gave him the back of his hand and kept walking.

"A second warrior approached, longsword resting over his shoulder.

"'A thousand pardons,' said Watanabe.

"'Yes?' the samurai asked.

"'We were wondering if you might be willing to spare a moment, kind sir...'

"'What is it?'

"'Are you currently employed as a samurai?'

"'My Lord is dead,' the warrior replied. 'I'm ashamed to say that I've been forced to seek employment in the service economy. I'm starting tomorrow at that Domino's Pizza in the middle of town. As a slicer, of course.'

"'Would you be interested in protecting a village from Mexican bandits?' Hanbei asked.

"'You know,' said the warrior, 'Seven Samurai is a classic of Japanese cinema, one of my all-time favorites, and it sounds like you want to involve me in some sort of half-assed parody of it, perpetrated, no doubt, by some gaijin.'

"'I'm afraid so, sir,' said Tatsuya. 'But we're willing to pay you all the bonsai trees you can carry.'

"'All the *bonsai* I can carry," said the samurai. He opened his kimono; the garment was stuffed with little trees. 'My aesthetic compunctions aside, I am *so sick* of protecting you peasants...I really should kill all three of you.' He paused. 'Did you bow to me, by the way?'

"'No!' they cried, hurling themselves to the dirt. 'But we're prostrating ourselves now, most abjectly!'

"'Stay like that for the next seventy-two hours, or I'll come back here and cut you a bunch of new bodily orifices.'

"He stalked off. Trembling, teeth chattering, the poor peasants remained there in the middle of the road, where they were subjected to considerable punishment from wagon-wheels, hooves, rain-storms, and the Mysterians, who just happened to be invading Japan that week.

"Once the three days were up, the peasants got disgustedly to their feet.

"'The Hell with this,' Hanbei declared.

"'We're never going to find anyone,' said Tatsuya.'I vote we go home.'

"'We only tried two men,' Watanabe answered. 'Let's speak to a few more, at least---'

"'I'm leaving,' said Hanbei.

"'Me too,' said Tatsuya.

"Watanabe waited a few moments, then trudged after them.

"On their way back to the hotel, they encountered a large crowd.

"'What's happening?' Tatsuya asked a man, who pointed, saying:

"'See that barn? There's a thief inside. He was discovered stealing gravel from a gravel garden, and he took a little boy hostage as he fled. He says he'll kill the child if anyone comes too close."

"'Is there anything to be done?' Watanabe asked.

"'Perhaps," said the man. 'At least that cat over there says he has an idea.'

"He indicated a large orange tabby in a blue kimono---"

Shiro broke in: "Was it you, uncle-*san*?"

"No," Tomokato said. "Your *father*. And he had a very good idea indeed. He simply started towards the barn, going as close as he might before the thief cried:

"'Not a step further!'

"'As you wish,' Shimura said, halting. 'But really, you have nothing to fear from me. I've merely come to serenade you.'

"With that, he commenced to yowl as hideously as he could.

"'Stop it!' cried the thief.

"But Shimura only continued to caterwaul.

"'Stop it, or I'll kill the kid!' the thief yelled.

"'Kill your hostage?' Shimura asked. 'That would be very foolish.'

"He resumed his horrible song.The thief repeated his threat, but Shimura was unimpressed.

"'Scat!' the man bellowed, hurling a large and malodorous western-style boot. Shimura dodged it with ease. The thief threw the boot's equally stinky mate; Shimura dodged that as well. In the next fifteen minutes, the thief threw every object in the barn at him, pitchforks, horsecollars, cultivators, combines, hayseed Kansans from the last story, and several black-and-white cows of the sort that used to appear in Disney cartoons from the early 1930's. Shimura sidestepped every missile with ease, yowling all the while.

"At last, in desperation, the thief was reduced to hurling his hostage. Shimura snatched the child from the air, set him gently on the ground, then drew two model 1911 Colt autos from his kimono and rushed into the barn.

118

"Shots rang out, and bullets hurled tufts of thatch from the roof. Then the thief staggered from the doorway in slow motion, riddled and bloody, a shortsword in his hand. He paused, swaying in the midst of a sluggish cloud of dust.

"Shimura came up at his side, saying:

"'Serves you right. Stealing people's gravel.'

"It's society's fault,' said the thief. 'I had no gravel at all when I was a kid.'

"'Neither did I,' Shimura answered scornfully. 'Of course, I didn't want any.'

"'Moralist!' groaned the thief, and tried to stick him, still in slo-mo.

"Shimura finished him off with one last bullet. The thief crumpled.

"The crowd surged forward. The child's parents thanked Shimura profusely, offering him a reward, which he politely declined. The *bonsai* farmers waited until the throng had broken up before approaching him.

"'You're tremendous!' they all said, bowing.

"'Actually,' said Shimura, 'For a housecat, I am rather on the large side.'

"'You're a cat, sir?' Hanbei asked.

"'That explains the fur,' said Tatsuya to Watanabe.

"'I was hoping there was an explanation,' said Watanabe.

"'Well," said Shimura. 'My work here appears to be done, so I think I'll be on my way---"

"'You have work elsewhere, sir?' asked Watanabe.

"Shimura smiled again, this time ruefully. 'I am, as we say in the samurai business, between jobs.'

"Hanbei said, 'We might be able to help you sir, if you're interested.'

"'What's your proposition?' Shimura asked.

"Watanabe laid it out for him.

"'El Pacino,' said Shimura.

"'You know of him?' asked Hanbei.

"'I fought against him, once,' Shimura answered. 'It was when my former lord, Kiyoshi Kagamura, met Santa Ana at Vicksburg. There I was at the Bloody Angle, and up rode El Pacino with Nathan Bedford Forrest, Bloody Bill Anderson and Cyrus Vance.

"'In any event, when it was over, I alone of all my company was still alive. I wouldn't mind meeting El Pacino again.'

"'Even though you did so badly the last time?' asked Watanabe.

"'I'm presuming I'd do better,' said Shimura.

"'You'll help us then?' asked Tatsuya.

"'Certainly,' Shimura answered. 'Provided we can recruit some other samurai. But that shouldn't be too difficult. If the film we're parodying is any indication, samurai are perfectly happy to help farmers for no reason whatsoever.'

"'Now sir, to be honest,' said Hanbei, 'In that movie the samurai were offered three bowls of rice a day.'

"'Not to mention their paychecks from the studio,' said Shimura. 'But enough of this. Where are you staying?'

"He spent that night with them at the Holiday Inn, and began making inquiries the next day. Learning of a samurai employed by the hotel, Shimura went out back where the warrior was cutting firewood. As should come as no surprise to anyone who's read the title of this story, the woodcutter turned out to be a cat too, chubby and dirty-white except for black ear-tips and topknot. Sitting on his chopping-block, he was taking a mid-morning break, a half-eaten *fugu* hoagie in one paw.

"'Down on your luck, eh?' asked Shimura.

"'Nope,' said the other. 'I'm simply waiting for a chance to defend some *bonsai* farmers from Mexican bandits.'

"'I have just such an opening for you---'

"'Excellent,' said the other cat.

"'---Provided you give me a suitable demonstration of your skills.'

"'I can manage that,' said the woodcutter. 'Who are you, by the way?'

"'Miaowara Shimura, Colt Auto School.'

"'I'm Toru Takemitsu, Chainsaw School.'

"Finishing his sandwich, he took up an enormous top-of-the-line Shindaiwa treekiller, rose, and yanked the priming cord. The motor came to life with a murderous ripping sound.

"'Wood can't fight back,' cried Shimura dubiously.

"'I know,' Toru answered, and emitted a piercing whistle.

"Ten ninjas burst from various ninja hiding-places, brandishing exceptionally fanciful ninja weapons. Shimura stepped out of the way. Toru dodged and leaped, sweeping his Shindaiwa as the ninjas closed in.

"Blood spewed from sawed flesh. An arm dropped here, a head rolled there; a JAL 747 called in for an emergency landing after thirty feet of intestine fouled its left starboard engine. Before long, only a very prejudiced observer---perhaps an East German Olympic judge--- would've denied that Toru had wrought some very serious carnage. Once the last ninja collapsed, firehosing the surrounding landscape with gore as only a sliced native of Nippon can, Toru turned off his engine of slaughter.

"'Thank you for helping me achieve my career objectives,' he said to any ninja who might still be able to hear.

"'Glad to do it,' said the last living assassin, just before going down for the third time in a lake of his own juice.

"'Do I get the job?' Toru asked Shimura.

"'You're in,' Shimura assured him. 'You wouldn't know of any other out-of-work samurai cats in the general vicinity, would you?'

"'As a matter of fact...'

"They went into the hotel. Toru informed the manager that he'd found other employment.

"'Where will I locate another such chainsaw artist?' the manager asked.

"'Same place you found me,' said Toru. 'The Kotani temp agency. Farewell.'

"'Farewell,' said the manager.

"As Toru and Shimura were passing through the lobby, Watanabe, Hanbei and Tatsuya joined them. Shimura introduced Toru, and all five went off to find the cat of which Toru had spoken.

"'Saito Suguyama is his name,' said Toru on the way.

"'I've heard of him,' said Shimura. 'He's said to be a consummate master with a blade.'

"'He practices all the time,' said Toru.

"'Even in his sleep?' asked Hanbei.

"'Even then.'

"'Doesn't sound very restful,' Hanbei said.

"Toru replied: 'He makes up for it by sleeping during practice. Look---there he is, practicing right now.'

"Apparently quite conked out, Saito, a very long lean black cat, lay with his head propped up against a fence-post on the edge of a field.

"Three men were marching towards him. The leader, a truculent-looking chunky brute, kicked Saito on the foot.

"'Wake up, cat!' the man cried.

"Saito cracked open a yellow eye.

"Chunky-*san* indicated one of his companions. 'Tetsugoro here told me what you said.'

"Saito closed his eye.

"Chunky kicked him again.

"'*I* say *you're* nothing.'

"'Say what you please,' answered Saito.

"'Let's do it,' said Chunky.

"'If I oblige you, will you stop bothering me?'

"'I'll leave you alone,' Chunky promised. 'Now get up.'

"'I don't have to,' Saito answered.

"'What?' Chunky cried.

"'Not to deal with *you*.'

"'Hah!' said Chunky, taking a wooden training-sword from one of his companions. 'We'll see about that. Where's your *bokken*?'

"'It's around somewhere,' Saito said.

"'You might at least want to open your eyes.'

"'No.'

"'You're ready?' Chunky asked.

"'I am,' Saito answered.

"Chunky grunted, stood a few moments with his *bokken* raised, then rushed up alongside Saito and rapped him smartly on the chest.

"'You didn't even try!' he cried.

"'You lost,' said Saito.

"'You were lying there the whole time!' said Chunky.

"'You lost,' Saito answered. 'Now leave me alone.'

"'The Hell I will!' Chunky shouted. 'Let's do it for real!'

"Saito folded his paws on his chest.

"Chunky kicked him yet again, then tossed his *bokken* aside and stepped back, reaching for the hilt of his *katana*.

"'Fight me, or I'll kill you where you lie!' he cried.

"'As you wish,' said Saito.

"'What a waste,' said Toru to Shimura.

"'It was so obvious,' Shimura said.

"Watanabe could only agree; the much-vaunted Saito had been completely humiliated through his own overconfidence, and now he was about to die---for nothing.

"'I'm waiting,' said Saito.

"Chunky began to draw---

"Then let go of his hilt, swaying. His blade whispered slowly back into its sheath, *tsuba* clicking against the mouth of the scabbard.

"Watanabe glanced at Saito. Saito was still on the ground, paws on chest.

"Watanabe looked back at Chunky, who had a very puzzled look on his face. Chunky turned, carefully like a drunken man, taking a step towards his friends.

"'Are you all right?' cried Tetsugoro.

"'Never better,' said Chunky.

"He took another step, then parted from crown to crotch in a crimson gush, the halves of his body scissoring past each other to the grass.

"His friends rushed towards the remains.

"'Are you *sure*?' Tetsugoro asked.

"Toru led Shimura and the peasants over to Saito.

"'Toru,' said Saito, eyes still shut.

"'Saito,' said Toru. 'I have someone I'd like you to meet.'

"Saito stood up. Toru introduced him to the others.

"'Very impressive performance just now,' Shimura told the lean black cat.

"'Substandard, in my opinion,' said Saito. 'Once, on my very best day, I halved a man with such speed that my sword cauterized every bloodvessel it sliced. Even he congratulated me on my skill.'

"Shimura didn't doubt it. 'Would you be interested in working for these peasants here?'

"Saito gave them a cursory glance.

"'*These* louts?' he asked.

"'Yes.'

"'Perhaps if they were oafs...'

"'We can be right oafish, sir,' said the peasants.

"Saito laughed, acknowledging:

"'Only oafs would claim such a thing.'

"'Okay,' said Toru. 'We've established that Saito will join us. There's no more reason to continue this scene.'

"Shimura nodded. 'What we need is a lateral wipe across the screen, so we can just go to the scene where my brother is introduced.'

"'That would be very Kurosawa-like,' Toru said. 'But wipes are a cinematic device. You can't do wipes in a book.'

"'Sure you can,' Shimura answered. 'When I say three, everyone shout *wipe*!'

"He counted.

"'Wipe!' they all cried---

"And found themselves in the farmers' room at the Holiday Inn. There came a knock at the door; a silhouette was visible through the paper partition.

"'Who's there?' Watanabe called.

"'My brother,' said Shimura. 'Who did you think?'

"'I've heard you're looking for samurai,' I said. 'Let me in.'

126

"Shimura slid the panel back, and I entered---a callow, rather less muscular me, just out of my teens.

"'Brother-*san*!' I said. "'Haven't seen you in---what is it---five years?'

"'Hasn't been long enough,' Shimura replied.

"'Father asked me to find out if you were still alive,' I said. 'Took me some time to track you down. I understand you're a *ronin* now.'

"'I've been *ronin* all over the place,' Shimura said.

At that, Shiro said: "My own father cracked such a joke?"

"I've cracked worse," Shimura replied. "And if you don't stop interrupting uncle Tomokato, I'll crack them again."

Tomokato resumed:

"I told Shimura that I'd heard about the Anytown job.

"'That doesn't concern you,' Shimura answered. 'You've seen that I'm well. Go home.'

"'I'd rather join you.'

"Shimura shook his head.

"'The last thing I need is to be worrying about my little brother. Do you have the slightest idea of how to use that sword?'

"'I've been training,' I replied. 'Will you at least allow me to prove myself?'

"'What can it hurt?' Saito asked Shimura.

"'It's a waste of time,' Shimura answered. 'He's a clumsy fool, utterly devoid of talent. You've heard of idiots who can't chew gum and walk at the same time? When I left home, Tomokato here couldn't chew gum. `Gum don't work,' he used to say.'

"'It *didn't* work,' I replied, quite truthfully. The gum he used to give me was horrible stuff.

"'See?' Shimura said. 'He hasn't changed. Good-bye, Tomokato.'

"'You're making a mistake,' I replied.

127

"'Go home, baby brother,' Shimura answered. 'Practice chewing.'

"Frankly, I was taken rather aback, and let him herd me out into the hall. The panel shut in my face.

"I told myself that I should leave. Shimura had nothing but contempt for me. Having located him, I was under no obligation to help him fight the bandits.

"I had a room at the hotel; after getting my things, I went down to the lobby and decided to send a telegram ahead of me, notifying my parents that I had found Shimura.

"While I was filling out the paperwork, I saw Shimura and his party going outside. Immediately I changed my mind. After hurriedly altering the message--saying I'd be delayed---I followed at a distance, far enough back to remain undetected, yet close enough to hear everything that was being said, or thought, for that matter.

"A great believer in air superiority, Shimura had been told by Saito of a Zero pilot employed as a crop-duster, one Curtis Kondo. Yet another cat, Curtis had, through no fault of his own, survived four suicide missions in the service of Mori Monotari, and ultimately he'd concluded that the gods had some special purpose in keeping him alive, although he proudly retained the nickname `Kamikaze Curtis.' He was in the process of dealing with an infestation of American Beetles when Shimura and company arrived at the farm.

"Back and forth Curtis roared over the fields, scarlet rising sun blazing on the fuselage of his Zero. The beetles were well equipped with triple-A, and the air was full of tracers and exploding flak; fearlessly Curtis made pass after pass, picking off some bunkers with cannon-fire, destroying others with bombs, always careful to avoid damaging the crop. It was an astounding display of skill----hardly a stalk of barley was severed. I for one was overcome with delight--- few things excite my admiration more than a true Zen bomb-run.

"At last, his work completed, Curtis set down, Shimura's group approaching him as he climbed from his plane. Wearing a long white scarf and a leather flyer's helmet, Curtis was a rather Siamese-looking cat with bright blue eyes.

"'Hello, Saito!' he said.

"'Curtis-*san*,' Saito replied.

"'Who are your friends?'

"For the next-to-last time in this story, there was a long round of introductions, after which Shimura explained the peasant's plight.

"'Is there plane fuel at Anytown?' Curtis asked.

"'We have a splendid tank-farm, sir,' said Hanbei. 'Plus everything you'd need for repairs.'

"'What are *bonsai* farmers doing with such facilities?' Curtis asked.

"'Up till now, not much, sir,' Tatsuya replied.

"'I'll also need bombs and ammunition,' said Curtis.

"No problem either, sir,' said Watanabe.

"'Who's that cat watching us from a distance, by the way?'

"'That would be my brother, I expect,' Shimura said, turning and squinting. 'Where is he?'

"'Well, he's too far back to be detected,' said Curtis. 'But he's close enough to hear what we're saying.'

"Cupping both paws to his mouth, Shimura shouted:

"'Get lost, baby brother!'

"To which I answered: 'Just on the off-chance that you're speaking to some other baby brother, I will *not* reply!'

"I was somewhat sillier then.

"'Let's just ignore him from now on,' said Shimura.

"My brother agreed upon a rendez-vous with Curtis; then he and his company returned to the hotel. I elected not to go up to my room, taking a walk in the twilight instead.

"Not far from the Holiday Inn, I saw a powerfully-built cat in sunglasses push what appeared to be a large baby-cart into an intersection ahead. Abruptly he paused, right in the middle of the junction.

"Three men appeared across from him, in huge straw hats that made them resemble nothing so much as mushrooms from the Nutcracker Suite sequence in *Fantasia*. One was armed with a sword, one with a spiked mace, and the third with rakes attached to the backs of his hands.

"'We are the three Masters of Sadistic Behavior,' announced the fellow with the rakes.

"'I am Origami Ito,' replied the cart-pusher, 'Known otherwise as Lone-Wolf-Except-For-The-Fact-That-I'm-Accompanied-By-My-Midget- Buddy-Sue.'

"A small cat, not much bigger than a kitten, popped up in the cart.

"'A tomcat named Sue?' laughed Mister Mace Master.

"How do you do!' answered the midget belligerently.

"'Might make a good country and Western song,' opined the sword-master.

"Origami Ito shook his head.

"'It could never hope to compare with *Little Bitty*. Why have you blocked my path?'

"'Well,' said the rake guy, 'As our collective name clearly implies, we do vicious things purely out of cruelty. It's simply your bad luck to have run into us.'

"'We haven't butchered anyone in at least four minutes,' said the Mace Master.

"Origami Ito removed a square of white paper from his kimono.

"'Any requests?' he asked.

"'Make something that'll get you out of this situation,' said the Sword Master.

"Lone Wolf began creasing furiously, so proficient that the paper got *bigger*, even as he folded it; in a startlingly short time, he was standing atop a forty-foot tall battlement, setting an arrow to string.

"The swordsman ran up next to the baby-cart, aiming his point at Sue's chin.

"'Loose, and your dwarf's dead!'

"'He's not a dwarf!' answered Origami Ito. 'He's a midget!'

"'What's the difference?' the swordsman demanded.

"'Midgets are better armed!' Sue answered, priming a potato-masher grenade. Stuffing it into the swordsman's mouth, he clapped the canopy down on the baby-cart. Gagging, the swordsman tottered back several paces, grabbing at the grenade's handle. He managed to pull the bomb out only to have it explode in his face, wiping his head clean out from under his mushroom-hat, which fluttered up a few feet, then settled lazily on his shoulders. He staggered off like a chicken with its head cut off, or at the very least, a Master of Sadistic Behavior with such an injury.

"Origami Ito put an arrow into the rake-master, who immediately toppled. The mace-master brandished his weapon up at the figure on the wall.

"'Come down and fight like a man!' he cried.

"'And waste this perfectly good defensive position?' replied Origami Ito, and shot him in the base of the throat.

"'But the mace-master kept his feet. Going to the baby-cart, he flipped the top back, whereupon Sue jabbed him with a pair of twelve-gauge bangsticks. The last Master of Sadistic Behavior went to the street looking like he'd been splashed down with two buckets of Sloppy Joe."

Tomokato paused to wet his whistle with a bit of sake, but before he could begin again, Hanako said:

"Excuse me, Tomokato. Something is puzzling me."

"Yes?" Tomokato asked.

"While telling this story, you seem to have adopted the author's prose style. `Two buckets of Sloppy Joe?'"

"How do you know that he didn't filch *my* style?" Tomokato

asked.

"Because it's the style of a Twentieth Century barbarian, beyond a shadow of a doubt," Hanako answered. "Can you even tell me what Sloppy Joe is, by the way?"

"Please wife," said Shimura. "Let him continue."

"Very well," Hanako replied.

133

Tomokato said: "'Origami Ito climbed down from his fortress, folding it back into a small square of paper as he went. When he reached the bottom, he very conscientiously deposited the used sheet in a trashbin, and went over by the baby-cart, electing to take notice of me at last; Sue had been glaring my way for some time.

"'He's another Master of Sadistic Behavior,' the midget said.

"'He has no mushroom-hat,' Origami Ito pointed out.

"'I might've taken it off,' I said, going closer.

"'Why would an MSB point out such a possibility?' asked Lone Wolf. 'No, my friend. Only a *non*-MSB who had *not* taken his hat off---probably because of a lack of hat--- would say such a thing. Besides. MSBs cannot take off their mushroom hats, as they are born with them, much to the discomfort of their mothers.' He paused. 'You know, my friend, you bear a certain resemblence to a comrade of mine. You could almost be brothers...'"

"'Is his name Miaowara Shimura?' I asked.

"'No,' said Origami Ito. 'Although that's who we're searching for. The word's out that he's hiring Samurai...'

"'That's true,' I said. 'He's staying at the Holiday Inn, room 502. I expect he'd be delighted to talk to you.'

"'*Are* you his brother?' asked Sue.

"'Yes.'

"'Would you be willing to introduce us?'

"'It would do you no good,' I said. 'Shimura and I are on bad terms. Who's that comrade you mentioned, by the way?'

"'Kaki Kakizaki,' said Sue.

"'The Pee-Wee Herman of Japan?' I protested. 'He's not even a cat! I don't look anything like him!'

"'My pal here thinks *everyone* looks like Kaki Kakizaki,' said Sue, pulling the sunglasses from Origami Ito's face.

"On each lens were excellent likenesses of Pee-Wee Herman doing the Tequila dance. After examining the pictures, I handed the shades back to Origami Ito, saying:

134

"'Isn't that rather a handicap in a fight?' I said.

"'Seeing properly *is* difficult,' Lone Wolf allowed, donning his specs. 'But that just makes my victories more glorious.'

"I agreed wholeheartedly, having won my first hundred swordfights operating under just such a theory, with my lower lip safety-pinned to my ears. Only the eventual rusting-through of the pins had induced me to revert to sighted combat. I'd considered getting another pair, but my sentimental attachment to that first set had simply been too great...

"Origami Ito and Sue took their leave of me. When I spotted my brother's party departing the hotel the next day, Lone Wolf was trundling his midget accomplice along at the forefront of the troop.

"The bunch of them headed out of Samurai City, in the direction of Anytown. Kamikaze Curtis's Zero soon appeared overhead, accompanying them at a slow walk, drifting through the sky like a big Zero-shaped Macy's Thanksgiving parade balloon. Used to planes that had to maintain a minimum speed to keep from crashing, I found the effect somewhat surreal. Unreasonably so, perhaps; after all, seeing is believing.

"I trailed the group at some remove, but made no attempt to conceal myself. They paid me no attention. After several hours, I decided to try and force the issue, rushing ahead of them through the woods and sitting down directly in their path. They went right by. During the afternoon I paid a local advertising firm to paint my portrait and the message 'Give your little brother a shot, Shimura,' on billboards along the way. The ads were huge and striking, but they failed to melt my sibling's heart.

"I spent the night by myself, huddled by my little fire, smarting at the humiliation that Shimura was inflicting on me. It was some time before I could sleep.

"But as I lay dreaming, a stratagem occurred to me, and I woke in the morning with a triumphant `ha!' or some Japanese laugh-word to that effect.

"The others were already back on the road, trying to put as much distance between themselves and me as they could.

"'No sign of your brother yet,' said Saito, looking over his shoulder.

"'I'd wager he's still asleep,' said Shimura. 'After all, babies need their rest.'

"'Don't you think you're being a bit hard on him?' said Toru.

"'Not as hard as those bandits would be,' said Shimura. 'I'm doing him a kindness, believe me---'

"'Look there!' cried Lone Wolf, pointing.

"Before them a lone Master of Sadistic Behavior had appeared, sporting an especially large mushroom hat that obscured not only his face but a considerable portion of the surrounding landscape as well. With surpassing speed and grace he drew his sword, which flashed in the morning sun.

"'A magnificent glint,' Shimura acknowledged.

"The MSB bowed.

"'Nonetheless,' Shimura continued, 'It would behoove you to get out of our way. We *are* samurai, and *will* give you what for."

"'Pish,' answered the Master of Sadistic Behavior.

"'Would you repeat that, please?' Shimura asked. 'I thought I recognized your voice.'

"But the MSB wouldn't pish again.

"Toru slipped his chainsaw from its scabbard.

"'I'll deal with him,' he said, and strode forward.

"The MSB waited motionless.

"'Toru Takemitsu, Chainsaw School,' Toru said.

"'Incognito, Big Hat Disguise School,' answered the MSB, in a voice quite different from the one he'd pished in.

"'I'll give you one last chance to surrender,' said Toru.

"'That's big of you,' Incognito replied. 'But surrender is too similar to capitulation, in my opinion. As the Buddha said: capitulators never triumph, and triumphers never capitulate.'

"'The Buddha never said that,' answered Toru.

"'Who did?'

"'It was either Vince Lombardi or Mohammed,' said Toru.

"'Well, whoever it was,' replied Incognito, 'We owe him our thanks, for expressing such a valuable thought so nicely."

"'Agreed,' said Toru, and pulled the primer-cord on his chainsaw.

"'Am I a tree, that you would saw me?' said the MSB, dodging Toru's first stroke.

"'Huh?' asked Toru.

"Incognito said it again, lowering his voice.

"'What?' Toru asked, striking again.

"Incognito parried the stroke, repeating the question in a whisper.

"'I'm sorry,' said Toru, shutting off his saw. 'What was that again?'

"'Forget it,' said the MSB, stepping in close before Toru could pull the cord again, bashing him between the eyes with the pommel of his sword. Toru keeled backwards, knocked senseless.

"'My turn," said Saito, advancing within lying-down range of the MSB. Stretching himself out, he announced: 'I will not tell you my name, as you plainly will not tell me yours. Nonetheless, I *will* inform you that I am of the Apparently Motionless School, and that you may attack any time you like.'

"'That is very generous of you,' said Incognito. 'But I have *already* attacked you."

"'Forgive my scepticism, but---'

"'As you were approaching, I ran several rings around you, touching various pressure-points. You didn't lie down of your own free will.'

"'That's not my recollection,' said Saito.

"'I am *most* adroit,' answered the MSB.

"Saito attempted to rise, but his body wouldn't respond.

"'You plainly know a thing or two,' he admitted.

"'Or three, even,' answered the MSB.

"'Would you be willing to give me lessons when all this is over?'

"'I'll consider it,' said Incognito. 'In the meanwhile, who's next?'

"'We are!' cried Origami Ito, wheeling Sue towards the MSB.

"'You cut a most eccentric figure pushing that baby-cart,' said Incognito.

"'Taunt us all you please,' said Sue.

"'Is it true that you're named Sue?' the MSB inquired.

"What if it is?' Sue demanded.

"'That would be very sad,' said Incognito. 'It would be pathetic beyond belief, as a matter of fact. A tomcat named Sue. What a hopeless little eunuch you must be, to have gone through life with such a name and not have killed yourself, even once.'

"Sue vanished briefly inside the cart, reappearing with a flame-thrower strapped to his shoulders.

"'That's all I'm going to take from you!' he cried, trying to ignite the pilot-jet with a sparker.

"'You said I should taunt you all I liked,' replied the MSB.

"'You did,' Origami Ito reminded Sue. 'Honor demands that we put up with as much verbal crap as he's willing to dish out.'

"'Thank you,' said the MSB, going very close to the baby-cart. 'Just look at you, Sue! Not only do you have that ridiculous name, you're also a preposterous teeny-tiny runt! A flea-sized cat! A feline paramecium! A molecule, an atom, a pi meson! There you are, as grown up as you'll ever be, and you're still being wheeled around in a baby-cart as though you were still in diapers!'

"'Yeah, well, it's made me very tough,' answered Sue.

"'Oh yes, you must be very tough,' said Incognito. 'Eating all this abuse from me and not striking back. Most people would say that you're just the kind of little midget simp your name would imply. How does Lone Wolf put you in that cart? With a pair of tweezers? Does he find you with a magnifying glass, or does he need an electron microscope? Has he ever lost you in his kimono? Inhaled you accidentally? Let you swim in his favorite bottle-cap---?'

"'Yah!" cried Sue, totally losing it, desperately resuming his efforts to light the pilot-jet. But Origami Ito snapped the lid down on the baby-cart and padlocked it.

"'I apologize for my companion,' said Lone Wolf. 'When it comes to his sense of honor, he's a little short.'

"'Apology accepted,' said the MSB.

"'Are you going to insult *me*?" asked Origami Ito.

"'Who'll lock *you* in a baby-cart?"

"Origami Ito smiled, saying: 'Will you, perhaps, fight me the way you fought Saito?'

"'That would be repetitious,' the MSB replied.

"'An answer worthy of a warrior of your stature,' answered Lone Wolf. 'Boring *is* the worst. Let's tango.'

"Juggling his *katana, wakizashi* and a sheet of paper, Lone Wolf held the MSB at bay, simultaneously creating a gigantic and completely functional origami dragon that breathed out vast clouds of orange paper flames.

"Unimpressed at first by the billowing pseudo-fire, Incognito quickly discovered to his regret that it was every bit as hot as the real thing. Hat singed, he retreated swiftly, the dragon crawling in pursuit.

"But the MSB wasn't without his own paper-creasing credentials. Sheathing his sword, he withdrew a sheet of Teutonic Grey number 5 from his kimono, and, scissoring and folding, rapidly produced a half-dozen sturdy Sigurds, who just as rapidly dug a line of pits across the dragon's path and leaped inside. Concentrating entirely on the MSB, and quite ignorant of the Volsunga Saga (as most oriental dragons are) the beast crawled blithely over the pits---and was stabbed through the belly. Roaring, spewing flame, the monster dragged itself from the highway only to be swept up by a sanitation truck that was even then passing by.

"The Sigurds climbed up from the pits, and Incognito pointed to Lone Wolf, who, folding frenziedly and evidently less concerned than Incognito about repreating himself, recreated the fortress from which he'd battled the three MSB's back in Samurai City.

"But Incognito wasn't about to give up, and responded with a crackerjack siege tower, fifty feet tall. The Sigurds immediately climbed aboard, one manning the powerful caterpillar tractor concealed in the tower's base, the others clambering to the top.

"Lone Wolf cut out a lengthy chain of samurai paper-dolls to man the battlements with him; Incognito replied with a score more Sigurds. Samurai and ancient Teutons locked in battle, and paper bodies drifted from the walls, curled in death.

"While Lone Wolf was preoccupied with the siege, the MSB quietly made a troop of very hungry goats, who promptly began to devour every bit of paper in sight, seige tower, wall, warriors...before long, Origami Ito was back on the ground, trying to shoo the goats away. Instead of fleeing, however, they started to eat each other, the last soon vanishing into its own mouth with a loud `baaa!'

"With that, Lone Wolf met Incognito sword to sword, but he was far less adept with steel than paper; the MSB disarmed him with ease, sending his longsword and *wakizashi* flying.

"'I fear I have blown it,' said Lone Wolf.

"'Justifiably,' said Incognito, and stunned him with a kick to the jaw.

"Kamikaze Curtis had been circling all this while, and when he saw Lone Wolf go down, he sent his plane screaming towards the MSB, jettisoning an emptied fuel-tank at the last instant. Incognito stepped directly towards the container, bisecting it cleanly, point to tail, with a single stroke, the pieces passing on either side of him.

"Curtis swept round at him once more, tilting his Zero up on its side, wing-tip all-but scraping the ground. Incognito refused to budge, holding his sword above his head in a *Jodan* position; as Curtis's wing whistled near, the MSB sliced it vertically from guns to tip before bounding out of the way. The pieces of the wing began to flap most horridly, approximating the rudest of Bronx cheers. A cat of impeccable civility, deeply committed to the ideal of understated good taste, Curtis couldn't bear to have his very own plane emit such a sound; he landed on the road, fully prepared to apologize to anyone who might've heard.

140

"But the instant he slid the canopy back, there was Incognito leaping up on the wing, clambering towards him. Curtis pulled his Nambu 14th Year automatic, and squeezed off three rounds. Yet so huge was Incognito's hat that it was extremely difficult to tell what part he was under, and the next Curtis knew, the MSB had him by the flight-helmet. After yanking Curtis's head forward, Incognito slammed the canopy against it---twice.

"'Was it necessary to give me that second slam?' Curtis groaned. 'The first one knocked me unconscious!'

"'Why are you still talking?' Incognito asked.

"Why does Desdemona keep talking after Othello's strangled her?'

Incognito just slid the canopy forward again. This time Curtis piped down.

"The MSB leaped from the wing. Shimura was walking unhurriedly towards him.

"'You're a brilliant fighter, beyond a doubt,' Shimura said. 'Too bad I have to kill you.'

"'Don't fret,' Incognito replied. 'That's not in the cards.'

"Shimura examined his cards.

"'Nuts!' he said at last, unable to find anything. 'Pinochle deck!'

"He hurled them to the earth.

"'If my fate were truly sealed,' said Incognito, 'even such a deck would be sufficient."

"'Pinochle is the silliest-named game in the world!' Shimura shot back.

"'No,' answered the MSB, a sudden gust of wind tossing his kimono. 'Parchesi!'

Refusing to concede this, Shimura whipped out two .45's.

"Incognito improvised a shield out of bullet-proof paper and marched briskly towards the blazing automatics. Shimura advanced as well, leaping high into the air, landing behind Incognito.

"But his magazines were dry, and as he reached for two more pistols, the MSB whirled upon him, tossed away his sword and the shield, and closed with him paw-to-paw, wresting the guns from Shimura's grip. For the next three hours the pair chucked each other all over the island of Honshu in an epic ju-jitsu battle that wreaked so much havoc that it lowered *Dai Nippon's* GNP forty percent over the next five years.

"At last, as their struggles brought them back where they'd started, Incognito's mushroom-hat flew off, and Shimura found himself looking straight into the face of...

"*Me.*

"'Tomokato!' he cried in amazement.

"'Shimura,' I answered, grinning.

"The peasants and the other samurai came up.

"'I suppose you'll have to let him come after all,' said Saito to Shimura.

"'If *he's* not worthy to share our company,' said Toru, 'We're hardly worthy ourselves.'

"'Toru's right, Shimura," said Sue from his carriage. 'I, for one, am proud to have been humbled by your brother.'

"'I too,' said Kamikaze Curtis, picking bone-splinters from under his flight-helmet. 'He slams a mean canopy!'

"'We need all the help we can get, sir,' said Hanbei to Shimura.

"'Aww, grumble grumble,' Shimura grumbled.

"Origami Ito patted me on the back.

"'Don't worry about your brother,' he said. 'You just come and join us.'

"'Absolutely!' cried everyone else except Shimura.

"Shimura smiled grudgingly at me.

"'It seems I'm out-voted,' he said. 'Welcome, brother-*san.*'

"I bowed.

"'Your efforts to keep yourself from looking smug are not entirely successful,' Shimura observed.

"'I'm sorry,' I answered, although I wasn't convinced for one moment of his assertion. I'm never smug, even when a situation positively demands it.

"We arrived in Anytown the next morning to find the hamlet apparently deserted.

"'Come out!' shouted Watanabe. 'Where is everyone?'

"But there was no response.

"'They're all afraid,' said Tatsuya.

"'Of us?' asked Toru.

"'Probably,' said Hanbei.

"'This is extremely rude!' cried Watanabe. 'These cats have come to help us!'

"'How do we know you're actually Watanabe?' asked someone from the darkness of a doorway.

"'What?' Watanabe answered.

"'How do we know that you, Hanbei and Tatsuya weren't actually replaced by dead ringers, and that those cats aren't from the C.I.A., and that this whole thing isn't part of the plot to assassinate John F. Kennedy?'

"'Please excuse them,' said Tatsuya to Shimura. 'We peasants are a fearful lot.'

"Right then, Toru ran and climbed a watch-tower and started banging on the drum suspended at the top. For some reason, this brought the peasants rushing from their houses.

"'Why did they all come out?' I asked Hanbei.

"'I presume, sir,' said the farmer, 'That they were all pointed towards the doors when they started to move.'

"Toru descended from the tower and swaggered among the peasants.

"'You dolts!' he shouted. 'Did you really believe all that crap about the Kennedy assassination?'

"'Do *you* think Oswald acted alone, sir?' one asked timidly.

"'Hell no,' answered Toru. 'I find the single bullet theory profoundly unpersuasive. But it sure wasn't *me* on the grassy knoll.'

"The farmer jerked a thumb towards Saito, asking:

"'What about him?'

"'He was with me,' Toru answered. 'We were over by the Book Depository. But enough of this. Why wouldn't you come out, really?'

"The peasants toed the earth.

"'We thought you'd yell at us,' they answered. 'And make fun of our conspiracy theories.' Tears welled up in their eyes. 'And you did! You *did*!'

"'Sorry,' said Toru.

"'Oh, it's all right,' they answered. 'Let's hug.'

"'No thank you,' said Toru.

"'Bitch,' they said.

"'What was that?' he demanded.

"'Bitch-*san*,' they replied.

"'Well, now that we've broken the ice,' said Shimura, 'Let's start planning the defense of the village.'

"Watanabe took us on a tour of the hamlet, after which Shimura drew a map of the town and the surrounding terrain.

"'That's quite a nice map,' said Saito. 'I particularly admire your use of color, and the deft way you rendered the buildings. The forms are simple yet full, and your suggestion of detail is superb.'

"'Thank you,' said Shimura, and pointed his blue marker at the map. 'The way I see it, there are four approaches to the village--- East, West, North and South. I suppose we could add an additional four approaches, namely Southeast, Southwest, Northwest and Northeast, but then we'd have eight approaches--- in short, twice as many. Also, there's the whole matter of the slippery slope--having to add North-Northeast, and suchlike. I say we settle for the four.'

"'But what if the bandits *approach* from the North-Northeast?' asked Origami Ito.

"'We'll have to make them pay---and pay dearly---for getting so specific.' Shimura indicated a blue line on the map. 'This represents that much bigger blue line off to the east. Boy, I'd like to see the marker that made that.' He indicated another blue line. 'This, on the other hand, represents the millrace, which I intend to dam. The resulting lake should cut off the eastern approach--- especially after we fill it with alligators.'

"'Where are we going to get alligators?' ask Hanbei.

"'Do you have a sewer system?' Shimura asked.

"'No, but we could build one,' said Tatsuya.

"'That's the kind of can-do attitude I like!' Shimura said. 'Now then. I noticed a volcano off to the west. Is it extinct, or merely dormant?'

"'Dormant,' said Watanabe.

"'Excellent,' said Shimura. 'We'll start an eruption and divert a stream of lava into a channel on the village's west side, thus blocking that approach.'

"'Start an eruption?' Hanbei asked. 'Divert lava? How will we do that?'

"'We'll have to use our heads.'

"'Won't that hurt?'

"'I never said it would be painless.'

"'What about the southern approach?' asked Toru.

"'No problem,' said Shimura. 'All we need to do is move some cliffs closer to the village.'

"'There are no cliffs around here,' Hanbei protested.

"Shimura smiled, quoting one of his favorite proverbs, 'The warrior is not dismayed by a lack of precipices.'

"Hanbei nodded, replying, 'I am comforted.'

"'As for the northern approach,' said Shimura, 'We leave that open, so that we can lure El Pacino's men in piecemeal and trap them.'

"'But even with all your defensive measures,' Watanabe said, 'Will the seven of you be enough to cope with four hundred bandits?'

"'Oh, it won't just be the seven of us,' said Shimura. 'You peasants will fight alongside us.'

"'That was never part of our arrangement!' Tatsuya cried.

"'It's not as though you have any choice,' said Shimura.

"'Would you force us at swordpoint?' asked Hanbei meekly.

"'No,' Shimura said. 'I'd have Curtis bomb the village. That way I'd get to watch the explosions.'

"'I don't believe it,' said Watanabe. 'You're just trying to scare us.'

"Shimura's eyes bored into his; whistling, he simulated the sound of a falling bomb, then made a loud blast-cum-rumble.

"'And doing a damn fine job,' Watanabe added.

"'Obey us,' said Shimura.

"'Sure,' said Watanabe.

"Afterwards, once he, Hanbei and Tatusya had gone off to speak with their fellow villagers, I asked Shimura:

"'Would you really have told Curtis to bomb the village?'

"'Don't *you* like explosions?'

"'As much as the next cat. But---'

"'If these peasants want to live, they'll have to comply with our orders. No egalitarian bullshit here. This is Sixteenth-Century Japan, and it would be totally anachronistic for us samurai to be anything other than authoritarian.'

"'But these stories are full of anachronisms,' I answered.

"'Yes, but the line has to be drawn somewhere,' Shimura replied. 'And since we're the authoritarians around here, *we're* going to draw it.'

"'That's to say, *you're* going to draw it.'

146

"'I'd be less authoritative otherwise.'

"'Should we organize a secret police?' Toru asked.

"'We're not going to be here that long," Shimura replied. 'By the time we had a reliable roster of informants, our work would be done...'

Tomokato broke off, noticing that Huki, Duki, Luki and Agamemnon were looking at their father in dismay.

"Papa-*san*!" Agamemnon said. "You weren't opposed *in principle* to forming a secret police?"

Shimura shook his head.

"Gross!" said Luki.

"Those were different times," said Shimura. "So much so that we referred to them by different dates. I've changed in many ways. I'm much less concerned about maintaining order now. So shut your little traps, or I'll shut them for you. Tomokato?"

Tomokato went on:

"And so we made our preparations. In a remarkably short span, the physical defenses were realized in accordance with Shimura's plans; then we began to train the villagers in the art of war, drilling them in the use of bamboo spears, running them all over the place, and making them do lots and lots of jumping-jacks.

"Early on Toru noticed that one of the farmers, a fellow named Takashi, wasn't carrying a bamboo pigsticker, but a real spear with a winged steel head, very finely crafted. Taking Takashi aside, Toru asked him where he'd come by such a weapon. Takashi was reluctant to answer, but finally spilled the beans--- much to the annoyance of his fellow peasants, who had to clean all those beans up.

"By killing samurai fleeing from the many battles that raged during that time, the villagers had amassed quite a trove of looted armor; led to the hoard by Takashi, Toru donned a choice outfit for himself, then had a group of peasants bring the rest to show Shimura.

147

"'Look what I found!' Toru cried, thumping himself on his armored chest. 'All the protection we could ask for!'

"'Correct me if I'm wrong,' said Origami Ito, 'But weren't those armors stripped from murdered samurai?'

"'What of it?' demanded Toru.

"'It would be disgraceful to wear them,' said Sue from his carriage. 'As shameful as going into battle in bunny-ears or a garter belt.'

"'What about going into battle in a baby-cart?' Toru shot back.

"'That's different.'

"'Sue's right,' I said. 'There's no comparison between bunny-ears and a baby-cart.'

"'They both begin with b,' said Toru.

"Before I could retort, Saito insisted:

"'We cannot wear the armor.'

"'Are you serious?' Toru demanded. 'We'll be putting our lives on the line, not playing a game!'

"'Your attitude isn't honorable,' said Saito.

"'Perhaps it's my upbringing,' Toru answered.

"'Are you of peasant origin, perhaps?' asked Shimura. 'Do you come from a village just like this one?'

"'Yes,' said Toru. 'Except that we had a much bigger stash of stolen armor. And this excellent municipal pool---'

"'What was the town's bond rating?' Shimura asked.

"'Triple-A,' Toru answered. 'We had all that armor to auction off--'

"'Disgusting!' Saito cried.

"'Don't judge us peasants so harshly!' Toru replied.

"'*Us* peasants?' Saito asked. 'Aren't *you* a samurai now?'

"'Not for the purposes of this speech,' said Toru. 'You think peasants are contemptible. Well, maybe we are. But who *made* us the way we are? Samurai! Who comes into our villages and forces us to bow and scrape? Samurai! Who compels us to say 'buck, buck, buck' and pretend to be chickens? Samurai! Who orders us to fart under our blankets and pull them up over our heads? Samurai!'

"Shimura shook his head, saying, 'I derive no pleasure from compelling peasants to inhale their own flatulence.'

"'But you've forced them to do it, haven't you?'

"Shimura averted his eyes.

"'But who made us *samurai* the way we are?' asked Kamikaze Curtis. 'Who made us force peasants to fumigate their own bedclothes? Who ordered us to go about with little bundles of hair sticking up from our heads like furry pee-pees? Who made us take all those ballet and elocution classes, and walk up and down stairs with dictionaries balanced on our melons?'

"'It wasn't us peasants,' said Toru.

"'I was just asking a rhetorical question,' Curtis replied.

"'It was the nobles,' said Origami Ito. 'They created us as surely as Aaron Spelling created *Charlie's Angels*.'

"'Does that truly count as being creative?' I asked.

"'I never cared for *Charlie's Angels*,' said Origami. 'Perhaps if it had been cats instead of those human females---'

"'It still would've stank,' said Sue.

"From there we passed into a lengthy discussion of why, which continued intermittently for the next four weeks, right up until three of El Pacino's scouts were sighted in the woods some distance outside the village.

"'Strange transition,' Saito observed.

"'Couldn't be helped,' Shimura replied. 'You and Tomokato go out and capture one of those scouts.'

"'Just one?' I asked. 'What about the other two?'

"'Under no circumstances allow them to return to El Pacino.'

"'What if they make an argument that even you would find compelling?' Saito inquired.

"'In my absence, it'll be impossible for you to determine that,' Shimura replied. 'But if you think they've indeed come up with such an argument, compliment them on their mastery of logic, then kill them. As an ancient monk once told me: 'The bandit who argues is merely a lawyer waiting to hatch out.'

"'Very well,' I said, and went off into the woods with Saito.

"We found the *bandoleros* about where we expected to, in a valley glade, its floor dotted with white flowers. Our approach went unnoticed by the scouts, who were busy making their lunch. By their uniforms, I determined that they were Eagle Scouts---renegades, obviously.

"'Wait here,' Saito told me, marched right up to them, and lay down. The bandits started, leaping away.

"'We only need one prisoner,' Saito declared. 'Which two of you would like to be killed?'

"They conferred briefly. Then all three put their hands up.

"'Which *two* of you?' Saito demanded.

"'Ju see, *senor*,' one of them said, 'we *all* put our hands up to confuse ju---and ju are confused.'

"'Do you really want to leave the decision up to me?' Saito asked.

"'Chure,' they said, and immediately drew their pistols, a Smith and Wesson Schofield, a LeMat, and a Pettingill.

"'Ju look like a real horse's ass, lying there like that,' said their spokesman. Then all three fired into Saito---

"An instant before their gun hands dropped from their wrists.

"'Aye, *caramba*!' cried the bandits, reaching for back-up pistols with their remaining hands.

"Breaking from cover, I dashed towards them, deflecting bullets with my *katana*. Two of the bandits tottered, struck by their own ricochets; one fell, but the other, apparently in the belief that he'd been shot by the third fellow, turned on his comrade and blew his brains out before expiring.

"I knelt beside Saito. His fur had paled nastily.

"'Who'd have thought it would take their hands so long to drop off?' he asked, chest squirting like a lawn-sprinkler..

"'This is quite a blow!' I said. 'I thought you'd make it to the end of the story, at least.'

"'I thought so too,' Saito coughed. 'But I'm clearly heading south--- unless all that stuff squirting from my chest is just red tempera paint, or something.'

"I opened the front of his kimono.

"'It *is* red tempera!' I cried. 'There's a Hefty trashbag full of it taped to your chest. That's the good news.'

"'I was *wondering* what was in that bag,' Saito said. 'What's the bad news?'

"'Bullets went through,' I said sadly.

"Saito closed his eyes.

"I felt for a pulse; there was none. Lugging him and the bandits' guns back to Anytown, I reported to Shimura.

"'At least the scouts didn't escape,' he said. 'Pity about Saito. Let's get him underground before he stinks up the place.'

"'Nothing worse than a dead cat,' Toru agreed.

"And so we planted him in the village cemetary, with Lone Wolf thrusting Saito's sword down into his grave. Rather to our surprise, we heard a loud *yow!* from out of the earth.

"'Oops!' said Origami Ito, putting paw to mouth.

"'Don't torment yourself,' Shimura told him. 'Good thing you finished him off. Being buried alive is worse than watching a Joel Schumacher film.'

"'Maybe we'd better dig him up and make sure he's dead,' I suggested.

"'No,' said Shimura. 'That was a definite death-yow.'

`"Perhaps it was at that," I replied.

"But that night we discovered that it had been nothing of the sort.

"Guessing El Pacino was about to show up soon, we were at Watanabe's house, formulating some last-minute plans, when in came Saito, risen from his unquiet grave!

"'Who stuck me?' he demanded.

"We all looked at Lone Wolf.

"'Thought you were dead,' said Origami Ito, shrugging.

"'Why *aren't* you, by the way?' Curtis asked Saito. 'And don't give me any stuff about cats having nine lives!'

"'Author's wife complained about me getting killed off too soon,' Saito answered.

"'So sucking up to her is the way to triumph over death?' Curtis asked.

"'For us,' Saito replied. 'Can't say if it'll work for the author, though.'

"'Let's see,' I said, and we all went over to the terminal-screen and looked out at the author. We were there for quite a long period, during which he was sweet to his wife three times and remained resolutely alive.

"'Isn't his room sloppy, though?' I asked.

"The following day, we received signals from various watchers that El Pacino was on the way. Our peasant trainees assumed their posts; Kamikaze Curtis got airborne. The rest of us samurai planted ourselves right in the middle of the common. With us were Watanabe, Hanbei, and Tatsuya, armed with the pistols I'd taken from the scouts.

"The bandits rode right up to the border of Anytown, pausing to consider the WELCOME BANDITS and DON'T WORRY ABOUT AMBUSH billboards we'd erected. Then fifty men advanced into the village, led rather imprudently by El Pacino hiself.

"'Watanabe!' the bandit leader cried. 'Ju seem to have made some changes around here!'

"'Civic improvements,' Watanabe answered.

"'Where did ju get those alligators and all that lava?'

"'Different places,' Watanabe replied.

"'And what's with these keetie-cats?'

"We came to protect this village,' Shimura answered.

"'Ju?' El Pacino asked. 'Why ju want to do such a thing? These peasants deserve everything they get. If God did not want them cheared, He would not have made them cheep.'

"'How do you go about chearing these cheep?' Shimura asked.

"'Smile, say *baa*. Not a bery demanding audience. Ju know. Cheep.'

"'How cheep are they?' I asked.

"'Did they offer to pay ju in rice and little trees?'

"'Yes.'

"'Thass how cheep.'

"'But aren't you here for the trees too?' Lone Wolf asked.

"'Jes,' said El Pacino. 'Just don't mention it again.'

"'Hit the road, El,' said Shimura.

"'Ju don't scare me,' said the bandit chief. He looked at Shimura narrowly. 'Say. Don't I know ju?'

"'We met at Vicksburg---briefly.'

"'I remember,' said El Pacino. 'Jur that Chimura pussy. I keeled all jur buddies. Me and Cy Vance.'

"'Go and don't come back,' said Shimura. 'This is your last warning.'

"'No, Chimura,' said El Pacino, hand drifting towards his pistol. 'That was *jur* last warning.'

"He unholstered the Walker and snapped off a shot. Shimura ducked.

"'Ju made me miss!' El Pacino cried.

"Shimura produced a Very-pistol and fired a flare, signalling Curtis to strafe the bandits who had been left outside the village.

"The men with El Pacino drew their pistols, but showers of spears, from peasants concealed in the houses surrounding the common, put them off their aim somewhat; so did the fusillade from the volley-gun concealed in the front of Sue's baby-carriage. Riders toppled from saddles; horses neighed and reared. Saito ran right up and lay down directly in the middle of the confusion, wreaking incredible havoc in his own inimitable style. Chainsaw coughing blue smoke, Toru leaped onto a riderless mount and slashed three *banditos* out from under their *sombreros* in bursts of blood and severed fringie-balls. I, on the other paw, preferred to bound from horse to horse or even rider to rider, chopping down into shoulders and heads. Somewhere Shimura's .45's were barking; as I paused to pose atop one horse's rump, perhaps to inspire a possible cover for this book, I saw a *bandito* with a Henry rifle suddenly erupt with bullet-impacts as he tried to draw a bead on me.

"'Thank you, brother-*san*!' I cried.

"'That was me!' answered Watanabe from off to the side, waving his six-shooters.

"Armed with scythes and flails and axes, the peasants began to pour out of the houses. Getting the message at last, the remaining bandits retreated from the village without even a *Vamanos muchachos*! from El Pacino, who fled with eight feet of bamboo spear through the crown of his hat. Rejoining the bandit main body--- or at least as much of it as had weathered Curtis's strafing---they galloped off into the hills.

"We counted up the corpses, both in and out of the village. Fully seventy-five bandits had been killed.

"'What a resounding triumph of good over evil!' Tatsuya exclaimed---

"And took a bullet in the back. He was face-down in the road before the sound of the shot reached us; two more peasants dropped in short order.

"'Snipers!' I cried, and we withdrew into the houses.

"Shimura said: 'They'll try to keep us pinned down, so they can advance on the village again.'

"'Curtis'll slaughter them,' said Origami Ito.

"'No,' said Curtis, coming through the door. 'I had to land for repairs.'

"'If we could make the snipers reveal their positions...' I said.

"'Do you have a plan?" Shimura asked.

"'One of us could walk back and forth on the road---'

"'Like a shooting-gallery duck?'

"'Yes.'

"'It would be most hazardous.'

"'I'll take the risk,' I said.

"'No,' said Toru. 'I have some experience in these matters. I was shot twenty-one times while duckwalking at the Third Battle of Kawanakajima.'

"'Were you under orders?' Shimura inquired.

"'No, medication,' said Toru.

"'For what?'

"'I was *convinced* I was Douglas MacArthur. Wrote a dynamite constitution for this country, by the way. Then the Chinese crossed the Yalu river, and---the rest is history.'

"'Who'll pick off the snipers?' Shimura asked.

"Sue pulled a Sharps-Creedmore rifle with a Vernier sight and a 34-inch barrel out of the depths of his baby-cart.

"'I will,' the midget replied.

"'With its gunports and inch-thick steel plates, the carriage was a perfect place for him to do *his* sniping from. For the next several hours, Origami Ito sprinted it from place to place before dashing back into cover---whereupon Toru would begin his marching-back-and-forth-duck behavior, clad in the heaviest armor from the peasants' trove. The bandit marksmen subjected him to the most accurate fire imaginable---until Sue, firing at the smoke-puffs in the hills, wasted every last one of them. As soon as the fire from the hills stopped, Toru limped over the baby-cart and wheeled it back indoors.

"'So," said Saito, 'How bullet-proof *was* that armor?'

"'Fairly,' said Toru, taking off his breastplate to reveal that his entire ribcage had been turned into something resembling red consomme.

"'*I'd* say you're a goner,' Saito opined.

"Toru sat down. 'Guess my last hope is the author's wife,' he said.

"'He's not telling her this time,' I said. 'He felt her intervention on Saito's behalf was an unwarranted infringement on his sovereignity.'

"'Understandable,' Toru answered.

`"Wait---' I said, eyeing the terminal-screen. 'She just sneaked into his room, she's looking over his shoulder, and---'

"'Yes?' Toru asked.

"'She's taking it up with him.'

"Toru sighed with relief.

"'Help me get this breastplate back on,' he said. 'Author's wife or no, quite enough of me has run out on the floor.'

"Playing slip-and-slide in his innards for the next few minutes, we were inclined to agree.

"That night the bandits tried several ways to overcome us; the first involved a large ice cream van. Blazoned with the name Mister Creemee, it was very authentic looking. Sue wanted to shoot the driver, but the rest of us decided against it on the off-chance that the guy was legit---much to our ultimate chagrin.

Loudspeaker playing an inane glockenspiel jingle, it came rolling slowly up the road, pausing just outside the village.

"Before they could be restrained, a horde of children rushed out of the houses and raced to the van, clamoring for vulgar western treats. It was a small matter for the bandits to jump out of the truck, scoop a bunch of kids up and chuck them into the vehicle; the van wheeled round and headed the way it had come. Undoubtedly, El Pacino's terms would be delivered in due time.

"But a Mister Creemee van can't do much more than thirty; Shimura and I sprinted after it. Noticing an *I Brake for Animals* sticker on the rear bumper, we rushed past the truck and placed ourselves directly in front of the it. The vehicle screeched to a halt.

"Two bandits came out, Remington revolvers drawn.

"'You wouldn't run us over, but you'd shoot us?' I asked.

"'We brake for animals so we *can* choot them,' the bandits replied.

"'And then you run over the bodies?' I surmised.

"'Ju bet."

"'Unattractive,' I said, flinging a *shuriken* into one man's throat; one of Shimura's throwing-knives appeared in the other man's forehead. A moment later, we were in the van.

"The hostages were all crying, their captors too busy trying to pacify them with lame magic tricks and fit-only-for-children-but-just-barely jokes to notice that we'd entered the vehicle. A half-dozen swordstrokes, and the bandits were dead.

"'I don't see any blood,' a child protested.

"'Sometimes you don't,' Shimura answered.

"'Yeah, but I don't have to like it,' the youngster replied.

"I got behind the wheel and drove back to the village, where the childrens' parents welcomed them with hugs and kisses--- then administered the most brutal spankings I've ever witnessed.

"Later that evening, El Pacino tried a different tack, entering into secret negotiations with the alligators guarding the east side. In exchange for allowing the bandits to swim the moat, the gators would be given an all-expenses-paid sex tour of various crocodilian hot spots throughout southeast Asia.

"But several of the alligators had second thoughts, and came crawling to Shimura. They had some trouble making themselves understood, but Shimura guessed what had happened just in time to prepare a welcome for the bandits, who were even then emerging from the moat. Seeing the *bandoleros* being axed and speared and sworded to death on the shore, the majority of the alligators decided to switch sides once more, and turned on the men still in the water, very few of whom managed to make it back to the farther bank.

"El Pacino wasn't about to give up, though, and set in motion his most ambitious plan yet. We'd set an insufficient guard on the cliff-moving devices we'd used to transport the precipices closer to the village's sourthern border; a group of *bandoleros* snuck in, killed our watchmen, and grabbed the equipment. It took them almost till dawn---they had to work *very* quietly, needless to say---but they gradually eased the cliffs back, and would've had an ideal avenue of attack if not for the fact that Toru and Saito discovered what was happening during a routine cliff-inspection.

"Attaching a silencer to his chainsaw, Toru went down amongst the bandits, hopping out on them from behind things large enough to conceal him, strewing the ground with *chile con carne* before jumping back into cover; Saito simply laid down in several locations, with the usual results. In a matter of minutes, the bandit cliff-moving team was annihilated, and Toru and Saito detailed a group of farmers to shift the cliffs back into their previous location.

"By then, of course, the sun had risen, and El Pacino launched a fierce attack on our work-gangs. But Curtis's plane had been repaired during the night, and he took off once more, pelting the bandits with bombs and bullets and cannon-shells, igniting the tree-line that they retreated into. The cliffs were securely back in place by noon.

"The remainder of the day was suspiciously quiet; flying back and forth over the forested hills, Curtis detected no trace of the bandits. Yet we didn't doubt that they were still in the area, and as the sun went down once more, I resolved to discover what El Pacino was up to.

"There were plenty of dead *bandoleros* about, and I had little difficulty finding a suitable Mexican trousseau. After donning a *sombrero* with particularly copious fringie-balls, guessing this would be sufficient to conceal the felinitude of my face, I sheathed my paws in leather gloves, then strapped on two pistols and went up into the hills.

"The smell of Spanish rice and the sound of Latin rap led me through the forest to the bandits. El Pacino's army had been reduced by perhaps half; the survivors were squatting by their campfires, listening to their leader, who was up on a rock. Finding a likely campfire to crouch by, I crouched. Two of the bandits looked round at me.

"'What an impenetrable curtain of fringie-balls ju have on that hat,' one said--- in Japanese, luckily for me.

"'This is my poker hat,' I answered.

"'Can it back there!' cried El Pacino. 'I'm outlining my plan!'

"We fell silent.

"'Okay then,' said El Pacino, 'In case some of ju just joined us, the plan is this. These samurai are plainly tough nuts to crack. So I've decided to hire some samurai of our own---already put in the order, as a matter of fact.'

"'Put in the order?' asked one of his lieutenants.

"'There's an 800 number,' El Pacino said. 'I dialed up Mehico City, and---'

"'Mehican samurai?' the other man asked.

"'It has the element of surprise,' answered El Pacino.

"'When will they get here?' I called.

"'Just about sunup---' Suddenly he squinted at me. 'One of my men would *never* wear so many fringie-balls on his hat.'

"'With all due respect,' I answered, 'I took this hat from one of your men.'

"'He squinted at me even more suspiciously; suddenly I realized what I'd said.

"How young and stupid you are! I thought.

161

"'What did ju say?' he asked. 'I took this hat from one of your men?'

"'That's what he said!' a chorus of bandits answered.

"El Pacino leaped down from his rock and strode over to me. 'Did ju not mean to say, "I took this hat from one of *jur* men?"'

"'*Si*.'

"'What's jur name?'

"'Sy.'

"'Do ju have a sister named Sue?'

"I almost said something about Lone Wolf's partner, but refrained.

"'No,' I answered.

"'Good,' said El Pacino, and turned away. 'Less get some chut-eye.'

"Once the bandits were asleep, I hastened back to Anytown.

"'*Mexican* samurai?' Shimura asked.

"'Do you have any experience of them?' Curtis asked him.

"'Does anyone?'

"'They'll be arriving at sunup,' I said.

"'How many?' asked Toru.

"'I don't know.'

"Sue said: 'We should go up and waste the bandits while they're asleep.'

"'And surprise the samurai when they reach the scene?' I asked.

"'Yes,' said Sue.

"We looked to Shimura, who signed off on the idea with a nod.

"'Should we bring some farmers with us?' I asked.

"'The best fighters,' Shimura said. 'And leave the rest to guard the village.'

"Once we assembled our force, I led the way, but this time there was no Spanish Rice to be heard or rap-music to be smelled...reaching the camp, we found it quite bandit-free.

"'What do you make of this, sir?' Watanabe asked Shimura.

"'I don't know,' Shimura replied.

"'Perhaps they've just called it quits,' said Hanbei hopefully.

"'No,' said Saito, picking up a flight-bag. 'Look.'

"He showed us the tag. It said Mexico City. There were hundreds of flight bags all over the camp.

"'El Pacino's samurai must've arrived early,' said Shimura.

"Saito nodded grimly, dropping the bag.

"Which means...' Toru began.

"'That he led his troops down to Anytown while we were sneaking up here,' I said.

"'Haven't heard any shots,' Watanabe said.

"'Fight hasn't started yet,' said Shimura. 'Come on!'

"Guessing the road would be watched, we approached the village from the alligator side, but hardly had we clambered from the moat when the houses disgorged a mob of bandits and Mexican samurai, many of them dragging hostages.

"'Boy I bet ju feel stupid!' cried El Pacino.

"'Yes, but you *look* stupid,' Shimura answered. 'And tomorrow, we may feel smarter.'

"Lay down jur arms!" El Pacino replied.

"'What about the rest of our bodies?' asked Watanabe.

"'Lay down jur *weapons*!' El Pacino roared. 'And no more of this pun chit!'

"We and our peasant auxiliaries did as we were told.

"'Now,' said El Pacino. 'I'll tell ju how it's going to be. My *compadres* and I have decided to settle down. We're not just going to take jur little trees. Ju are going to build us a fort up there in the hills, and ju are going to be *our* peasants. In chort, we're going to be the government around here. How do ju like that?'

"'Will you improve the roads?' Hanbei inquired.

"'Give us quality health-care?' asked Watanabe.

"'What about a space-program?' Hanbei went on.

"'Frankly,' said El Pacino, 'I wasn't going to do anything for ju at all.'

"'Haven't you ever heard of the social contract?' Watanabe asked.

"'Chure,' said El Pacino. 'Ju do what I say, right?'

`"That's not the social contract we were thinking of," replied

Hanbei.

"'It's the kind I'd sign,' said El Pacino, pulled his Walker, and blew him away. He trained the smoking barrel on Watanabe. 'Any more of this civics-class crap?'

"'Heck no,' said Watanabe.

"El Pacino turned to us cats.

"'And what am I going to do with ju?' he asked.

"'The cruellest thing would be to let us go,' Shimura said.

"'Ju know, that strikes me as counter-intuitive.'

"'We'd have to live with the humiliation of this defeat,' Shimura explained.

"'But why would ju suggest such a thing to me?'

"'Because we were defeated, and *deserve* to live with the humiliation.'

"'Can ju think of any reason why I chould let ju keep jur weapons as well?'

"'Not right at this moment,' Shimura answered. 'Perhaps if you gave me some time...'

"'Forget it,' said El Pacino, and detailed a group of his samurai to escort us from the village.

"These mexican warriors were a bizarre combination of foreign and familiar. Much of their armor was typical samurai style, but then there were the chaps and the sombreros. The hats in particular were very odd, made out of lacquered leather, and fitted with neckguards and horns and *fukigayeshi*, those little earlike things that western folks are generally unfamiliar with, but which we recognize as those little earlike things.

"'I didn't know there *were* Mexican samurai until a few hours ago,' I told one of our captors.

"'Most Mehicans don't even know,' the man replied. 'But the samurai tradition actually *started* in Mehico.'

"'Rather like the Cossack tradition?'

"'Jes, and about the same time too.'

"'Which would account for the more Cossack-like elements of the samurai tradition.'

"'Especially the onion domes.'

"'*I'm* very fond of them,' I said.

"'Now ju know why,' he replied.

"Our captors brought us several miles from the village, then headed back to Anytown just as the sun was coming up.

"'Did they take all your paper?' Shimura asked Origami Ito.

"'That I was carrying,' Lone Wolf replied. 'The rest was in Sue's buggy.'

"'I want my cart back,' Sue snarled. 'I'm way too stubby to spend the rest of my life walking.'

"'We have to re-take the village,' I said.

"'Let's go back to that ridge that overlooks it,' Shimura said. 'I'm sure I'll think of something. Maybe not a plan, but a tune or a funny story at least.'

"'That should lighten our spirits,' replied Saito.

"We made our way back toward Anytown, halting at last on the crest Shimura had spoken of. Almost immediately inspiration struck him.

"'What struck me?' he asked dizzily, picking himself up from the dust, rubbing the back of his head.

"'If I tell you,' Toru said, 'You will think me contemptible.'

"'Perhaps it's better you didn't,' Shimura answered. 'Anyway, *there's* the answer to our problem."

"He pointed at a terrace carved out of the slope below us. The earthen shelf was covered with immature *bonsai*, very elegantly potted. In a flash I realized what my brother was suggesting.

"'You're not serious,' I said.

"'It just might work,' said Toru.

"'The trees are too young,' Saito objected.

"'I think not,' answered Shimura.

"'What exactly is under discussion here?' asked several readers.

"Shimura snapped: 'If you can't figure it out, you're just going to have to wait.'

"'I can't wait!' one cried. 'It isn't fair!'

"Shimura seized him by the lapels and slapped him around a bit. The reader subsided, mumbling something about these books being too sadistic.

"'Hypocrite!' Sue answered. 'You didn't think so until *you* got hurt.'

"The reader said nothing else intelligible.

"'But what about the hostages?' I asked.

"'I looked back as we were leaving the village,' Saito said. 'The farmers and their families were being herded into that large maximum-security structure on the west side.'

"Shimura said:

"'Someone will have to go in ahead and deal with the guards.'

"'I'll do it,' I replied.

"'We strike tomorrow at dawn,' Shimura said.

"'Won't Dawn protest?' asked Origami Ito.

"'Let her," Shimura answered. 'She's getting off easy.'

"As sunup approached the following day, I worked my way down to the fringe of the lava-lake that warded the village's western side. A black crust had formed over the molten stone, but there was more than enough light for me to see by--- lava lamps, of course.

"*How to get across*? I thought.

"My kendo master had once assured me it was possible to walk on lava, but he hadn't mentioned whether it could be done successfully. Stone being more dense than the likes of me, there was no danger that I'd sink through the crust; on the other hand, there *was* the likelihood that I'd have my feet, then my legs, then my whole body burned off--- all of which I wished to avoid.

"Ultimately I decided that I had no choice but to cool a path for myself by blowing on the lava. That meant walking on my forepaws, so as to keep my mouth closer to the surface; but I was a practiced forepaw-walker, and for that matter, still am.

"The surface remained very hot, even though I cooled it sufficiently to keep my flesh from charring. The second-degree burns were no laughing matter, however.

"Three sentries, two samurai and a bandit, were stationed on the far side. They saw me in the glow of the lava-lamps, but so astonished were they by my prowess at lava-forepaw-walking that they allowed me to come up on the shore unmolested.

"'What a performance!' they cried.

"'That will be fifty thousand *yen*, please,' I answered.

"They totaled up their combined cash.

"'Sorry,' one said, 'we only have ten thousand.'

"'I'll take it---along with your sword and one of that fellow's pistols.'

"I nodded towards the bandit.

"'Not much to ask,' the samurai said, and handed me his *katana*. The bandit went so far as to cinch his gunbelt around my waist.

"'Have you fellows ever considered becoming good guys?' I asked.

"'Why would we?' the bandit answered.

"'Because you wouldn't be so eminently trickable.'

"They all looked at each other and laughed.

"'We live to be tricked,' they replied.

"'Then I don't even need to kill you now, do I?' I asked.

"'Nope, go on about your business,' they answered. 'We'll probably get killed later.'

"Going round to the front of the Maximum Security Structure, I confronted the guards at the door.

"'Can't let you in,' they said.

"'What if I trick you?' I replied.

"'Then we'll probably let you through,' they answered.

"Hardly were the words out of their mouths when I showed them that one where you fold your left thumb down, and put its knuckle up against the knuckle of your right thumb, and hold the first finger of your left paw over the joint, and then pretend to pull the end of your left thumb off...stunned, they admitted me forthwith.

"'Now go back to Mexico,' I said, over my shoulder.

"'Chure,' they replied.

"But there were six more *banditos* up the corridor, and when I asked *them* what they'd do if I tricked them, they all went for their guns; with my free paw, I slapped leather too, emptying my pistol into them, and they whirled to the floor in the best Sergio Leone style.

"Spotting some keys on one of them, I opened the gigantic cell where all the villagers were being held, then pointed to my latest victims, crying:

"'Take the guns from those bodies!'

"Watanabe and five others swiftly armed themselves, and we rushed back out to the doorway.

"Having heard the shots, El Pacino and a dozen samurai emerged from a house across the way; we opened up from the doorway. Returning fire, El Pacino's men backed towards the house they'd come out of. Six of El's men fell, but not before two of mine were shot as well.

"'At least you're dying as a free man,' said Watanabe to one of his stricken friends.

"'What a feeling,' the fellow exclaimed, blood foaming from his mouth. 'I'm looking forward to rotting as a free man too...'

"'Listen!' I cried.

"By the sound of it, a pitched battle had broken out on the village's south side.

"'Shimura,' I said.

"By the light of the moon, Shimura and my colleagues had selected the choicest *bonsai* from the south forty; catching the crackle of gunfire, they went out onto the road, trotted towards the village and, just before coming within rifle range of the sentries, raised their little trees on high.

"'*Bonsai!*' Shimura cried.

"'*Bonsai!*' the others echoed.

"They began to sprint, dashing along fearlessly in full view of El Pacino's men.

"It was a *bonsai* charge, of course.

"Apparently El Pacino's troops had never witnessed such an exhibition, and its effect on their morale was extreme. Few of them even got a shot off, and those that did didn't score. Shimura had counted on fetching such a reaction: the true value of the *bonsai* charge lies in the terror that it generates, which is immense out of all proportion to the fear it inspires.

170

"Shimura and the rest were among the opposition before you could say *Daruma-dera no Doitsujin*---not that you'd have any reason to. At close quarters, a warrior armed with a *bonsai* finally comes into his own, which is about what you'd expect, as the trees are truly small. The wounds they inflict are peculiar and extremely revolting in unmentionable ways; suffice it to say, the guardians of the southern approach took lots of them before they had the sense to lay down and die.

"Once the *bonsai* had served their purpose, Shimura's company cast them aside, looting weapons from the bodies.

"Small groups of Mexicans, samurai and *bandoleros*, began to rush them from the houses, but Shimura's party dealt with them in short order, then rushed deeper into the village.

"'Kamikaze Curtis split off from the main group, making for the airstrip. His Zero was well-guarded; eyeing the Mexicans from behind a row of fuel-drums, he considered shooting them, but was afraid of hitting his plane.

"'You know,' he cried, throwing his voice into the midst of the sentries' conversation, 'I've heard that guarding Zeros makes you impotent.'

"The Mexicans looked at each other, then withdrew a good distance from the plane. Curtis broke cover, making for the Zero.

"'Don't go near that!' the guards shouted.

"Curtis thanked them for their concern and fanned off ten shots---no mean trick for a cat a pistol in either paw. The guards bit the tarmac.

"'This tarmac tastes terrible,' groaned one.

"Another suggested: 'Perhaps if we added some guacomole...'

"Paying little heed to this discussion, Curtis climbed into the cockpit, revved up, and taxied down the runway. Within moments he was aloft, raining death on the enemy.

"Origami Ito and Sue, meanwhile, had also dashed off on their own, looking for the baby-cart. There was no particular place where they expected to find it, but fortunately, they were soon confronted by the two samurai who'd taken it from them; the smaller of the pair was hunched down inside the carriage while the larger puffed along behind. They seemed to be having trouble with the volley-gun.

"'Piece of junk,' said the one pushing the carriage.

"'Here,' said Sue. 'Let us show you.'

"The samurai in the cart surrendered it to the midget, and Origami Ito swung the carriage round.

"'You press the *red* button,' said Sue, firing all forty barrels, and as the Mexicans fell, Origami Ito thought he heard a calliope tooting out the beginning of *March of the Gladitors*; but it was only the wind rushing through multitudinous wounds.

"Lone Wolf reached into the cart, taking out a ream of rice paper.

"'Folding-time!' he said gleefully.

"Extremely pessimistic about his chances of finding his own chainsaw, Toru made a beeline for the first toolshed he spotted and kicked down the door. His eyes went immediately to a Poulan saw hanging from a pegboard, a custom job, modified to Japanese tastes. Toru took it down, shook it, felt a good supply of gas sloshing around in the tank, then started the saw with a single pull of the primer-cord.

"*All's right in the world*, he thought, marching back outside.

"A troop of mounted samurai were thundering towards him, nocking arrows. Grinning, he stood his ground, splitting every missile that screamed his way, head to tail. That alone should've told the riders something, but demonstrating exceptional obtuseness, they kept on coming, doing about as well against him as Danish ham does against a meat-slicer. Indeed, by the time he was done with them, horse and man alike, they wouldn't have looked out of place in the world's biggest submarine sandwich.

"Toru gazed admiringly at his weapon, savoring the fumes.

"*Better than my old one,* he thought. *What a creampuff!*

"Finding a good spot near the common, Saito stretched himself out. Bandits and samurai encircled him, one crying:

"'Jur going to take it lying down, hey?'

"'Are you embarrassed for me?' Saito asked.

"'Frankly, jes---'

"The bandit broke off, understandably, as his head slid from his neck.

"'Did ju do that?' a samurai asked Saito.

"'Impressed?' Saito inquired.

"'Bery.'

"'Then you're going to love this,' said Saito.

"'What?' the samurai asked---and parted at the waist, the upper half of his body spinning away from the lower.

"'Less all charge at once!' another samurai cried.

"Guns blazing, swords flashing, the Mexicans managed one step towards Saito, then flew apart in a fiesta of slashed flesh, human pinatas venting slippery scarlet treats that would've put a damper on most birthday parties.

"'Let's *not* all charge at once,' gasped one of the pinatas.

"Getting up, Saito graded his own performance.

"*B-,* he decided.

"At the same time, Shimura was making his way towards the Maximum Security Structure, striding unhurriedly through the village, taking no advantage of cover, relying entirely on his awesome prowess with a brace of pistols. Samurai backflipped from saddles; bandits plummeted from thatched roofs, weapons flying from their hands. Whenever his revolvers went dry, Shimura merely snatched two more from the air. Unopposable, unstoppable, he marched through the streets with an implacable expression, shooting in front of him, beside him, behind him, straight up in the air. His guns lunged everywhere, crossing over his chest, ducking under his armpits and behind his knees. Corpses flew backwards through doors, through walls, snapped off gingko trees of considerable thickness; others spun with such violence that they lifted off like helicopters, whirring as they bled. Brother-*san* was truly in top form that day.

"I was waiting for him in the Maximum Security Structure. We were still taking fire from El Pacino's men in the house across the way; Shimura marched boldly between the buildings, sixshooters blasting, killing with every bullet. Totally unscathed, he joined us in the prison, reeking of gunsmoke, the blue of his kimono greyed over with powder residue.

"'Where's El Pacino?' he asked me.

174

"'Over there,' I said, pointing to the building opposite.

"'Let's go,' he replied.

"But a throng of retreating samurai temporarily blocked the way, and hard behind them came one of Lone Wolf's paper dragons, an especially ornate and fiery one. Waiting until this particular parade passed by, we started outside, only to find another crowd of samurai coming our way, Curtis ripping into them from above, every gun on his wings spewing flame. Columns of dust and chopped meat marched towards us, erupting amid the press of fleeing bodies. For a moment it looked like we were about to be chopped to pieces as well. Then Curtis broke off the attack, climbing and veering off to the left. Only a single Mexican was left on his feet, and he was rotating and swaying and like a bowling-pin about to heel over.

"The fire from the house across the way had ceased; chainsaw-blade running with scarlet, Toru met us at the door.

"'Came in from the other side,' he said.

"'Did you see El Pacino?' Shimura asked.

"'No,' Toru replied.

"We passed through the house. Looking out the door, we saw Lone Wolf's dragon pursuing the same crowd of samurai, the throng reduced by at least half.

"'Have to find El Pacino,' Shimura gritted.

"Little did we know that Curtis already had.

"Trying to rally his troops, El Pacino was standing in the middle of the common; having recognized him by his extra-large bandit-chief sombrero, Curtis circled once, then commenced a steep dive, intending to take out the whole mob with a two-hundred pound bomb.

"But El Pacino wasn't easily intimidated. Even as his men dived for cover, he snatched a Blowpipe SAM launcher from one, set it to his lips, and PUFFED.

"The missile slanted up under Curtis's fuselage and exploded. Shrapnel tore through the cockpit, not to mention Curtis.

"*Oh blissful death!*' he thought, pushing forward on the throttle, aiming the Zero's nose at El Pacino.

"Macho as he was, El Pacino felt compelled to back off at last, chucking the emptied launcher and holding on to his hat as he dashed away.

"Curtis struck the ground behind with such force that his plane dug a full ten feet into the earth before exploding. A fist of hot air hurled El Pacino onto his face.

"Dirt raining over him, he got to his feet, jolted but unhurt---then flinched as forty guns spoke at once.

"He whirled to see twoscore of his men collapsing, and beyond their slumping bodies, a smoking fresh-fired baby cart complete with Lone Wolf and Sue.

`"Smile!" the midget cried, looking down the barrel of his Sharps-Creedmore at El Pacino. The muzzle belched flame.

"'Tell jur gun it's not polite to belch!' the bandit cried, staggering as the slug tore through his left lung.

"Reloading, Sue answered with a burp of his own, grander and more majestic than any midget's eructation had a right to be.

"'What's an eructation?' El Pacino demanded, spotting a Volcanic rifle lying beside one of his slaughtered troops.

"'It's obvious from the context!' Sue answered, cocking the hammer on his Sharps.

"But El Pacino scooped the Volcanic up and put a slug into Sue before the little guy could pull the trigger. Sue jerked backwards out of the baby-cart, knocking Lone Wolf over.

"'You killed Sue!' Origami Ito shouted, bounding back up. 'Where'll I find another midget sidekick who'll want to ride around in a baby-carriage all day?'

"'Not my problem,' answered El Pacino, chambering another shell.

"Lone Wolf folded himself a quick Cheiftain tank. But as he was working on the Brits to man it, El Pacino potted him.

"'Should've made an Abrams,' Origami Ito gasped. 'Americans are easier to fold---'

"El Pacino gave him two more, then went round to the other side of the crater to see what the rest of his men were up to.

"They weren't up to much, as it turned out. Cuisinarted quite to Hell, they were strewn all over the ground, arranged in a rough circle around Saito, who, apparently just for variety's sake, was lying stomach-down this time, like Laura Petrie on the walnuts, hands folded under his chin.

"'Your move,' he said.

"El Pacino cocked his rifle---and felt a dull blow beside his neck. Suddenly he was aware of Saito standing right in front of him, staring at his sword. It was looted of course, nowhere near as fine a piece of steel as his own sword, and he'd slashed so many guys in the last fifteen minutes that it was completely blunted.

"'Lose jur edge?' asked El Pacino, and shot him.

"'Stinky-poo,' said Saito.

"'Are ju referring to my joke, or the way jur dying?''

"Saito slumped without answering, whereupon El Pacino spotted Shimura, Toru and me standing on the edge of the common.

"'Prepare to die!' Toru cried.

"'*Senor* Chainsaw!' El Pacino replied. 'The peasants told me something about ju!'

"'Complimentary, I hope,' Toru gritted.

"'They said the author's wife didn't think ju should croak till the end of the story!'

"'So?'

"'This *is* the end of the story!'

"Toru keeled over dead.

"'This isn't the end!' I cried. 'This is just the climax!'

"'Close enough, evidently!' El Pacino replied. 'Are ju and jur brother going to gang up on me, or are ju going to settle this honorably?'

"'It's just you and me, El,' said Shimura.

177

"'Choot-out?' the bandit asked.

"Shimura nodded.

"El Pacino dropped his Volcanic, hands drifting towards the Colt at his hip. From out of nowhere came swell of Ennio Morricone music, complete with a chorus of guys going `Ah-ah-ah' in Italian. After an eternity of sweaty faces in close-up, Shimura pulled his pieces, completely getting the drop on El Pacino.

"But in a hideous replay of what had happened to Saito, Shimura's bullets merely bounced from El Pacino's chest. Shimura had shot so many guys in the last fifteen minutes that his pistols were completely blunted.

"Nonetheless, El Pacino was badly jarred by the impacts; he fired two slugs, but missed clean with one shot, putting the other into Shimura's thigh. Shimura toppled.

"Shrieking, I dashed towards El Pacino as he fought back to his feet.

"'This is for my brother, Toru, Saito, Kamikaze Curtis, Origami Ito, Sue, Hanbei, and Tatsuya!' I cried.

"El Pacino flashed a devilish smile, asking:

"'I am a formidible villain, aren't I?'

"But as he stood there basking in his own deadliness, he committed a classic blunder--- he allowed me to get some paper from Lone Wolf's Body, fold a quick little Trojan horse, and pedal right up to him. By the time he realized his danger I was climbing back out, right in front of him…never before did I carve an enemy with so many strokes, and I doubt I ever will again. Heaven itself was dripping salsa by the time I finished with him.

"But the battle for Anytown wasn't over yet. Fully a third of El Pacino's army remained alive, and even as I went to kneel by Shimura's side, they entered the common from the east.

"'Surrender, and we'll kill you!' they roared.

"'Don't you mean, "Surrender, *or* we'll kill you?"' I demanded.

"'That would be lying!' they answered, and charged.

at back their first attack with ease. Properly employed, E's can very deadly, deadlier even P's and Z's, though they're not as ethal as Paula Abdul or Right Said Fred.

"Then the survivors received a vast number of reinforcements; unbeknownst to me, El Pacino had hired a second group of samurai, this bunch from Paraguay. And these fellows were a much tougher lot than the Mexicans. Even five hundred to one, they were still no match for me; but there were more than that.

"At least twelve and a half more.

"Things were looking pretty grim when an Iroquois helicopter hove into view, rocket-pods and Gatling tearing into my close-packed enemies. A few samurai managed to flee; the rest wound up as the chief ingredient in the pulpy swamp that the chopper set down in.

"Out of the chopper came Shiro, Tototo, the tin man, the Branded-a-Cowardly-Lion, and last but least, the scarecrow.

"'Uncle-*san*!' Shiro cried.

"'What are you doing here?' I cried, mystified. 'You haven't even been born yet!'

"'You bailed us out at the end of the last story,' Shiro replied. 'Just thought we'd return the favor! See you!'

"They got back in the whirlybird and took off---"

Looking at Shiro, Hanako interrupted: "How did you accomplish that?"

"I'm not sure," the kitten replied.

"Ahem," said Tomokato.

Hanako answered: "Forgive us, brother-in-law *san*."

Tomokato went on:

180

"Putting a shoulder under Shimura, I went back to the Maximum Security Structure and informed Watanabe that the battle was won. The peasants poured outside, and there was a tremendous celebration followed by a tremendous cleanup. But serendipitously, a representative from a Kyoto medical supply company happened to be passing by, and he paid the peasants handsomely for the remains of El Pacino's more intact followers.

"Shimura and I lingered in Anytown until his leg healed up; the peasants treated us like gods in the flesh, and when it was time for us to leave, the whole village turned out to see us off.

"'*Sayonara*,' said Watanabe. 'And once again, a thousand thanks.'

"'Thanks for the trees,' we answered, kimonos nigh to bursting. A last wave to the crowd, and we headed down the road."

"Have you ever been back, uncle-*san*?" Huki asked.

"How could I go back?" said Tomokato.

"Was the village destroyed?" Duki asked.

"Was it swallowed in an earthquake?" Luki inquired.

"Covered by lava?" Agamemnon asked.

"No," said Tomokato. "I made the whole thing up."

"You *didn't*," said all the kittens at once, appalled.

"It would be much more satisfying if it were all true!" Huki added.

Tomokato nodded. "I stand refuted," he said, and held his cup out to Hanako. "Might I have some more *sake*, please?"

The kittens turned to Shimura, asking: "He *didn't* make it up, did he?"

"Only the end," Shimura said. "Regrettably, we were both killed."

"What?" the kittens cried.

"But the author's wife intervened."

The kittens sighed and settled back, very much relieved.

ALIENATED

While browsing through one of Shimura's magazines, the October issue of Third World Drawbacks, Tomokato ran across a Guatemalan legend that told of an invisible demon who took human trophies. This sounded very much like one of Nobunaga's slayers, an alien who had run off with the warlord's shoulderblades and gallbladder; therefore, upon concluding their visit to Japan, Tomokato and Shiro headed to Central America, soon finding themselves in a running battle with the thing...

From: *Cat Out of Hell*

"He doesn't know we can see him, uncle-san," Shiro whispered.

Tomokato nodded---he could think of no other explanation for the alien hunter's behavior.

Tippytoeing in plain sight, face concealed behind a white-metal mask, the creature was sneaking towards them through the jungle clearing, clawed hands clutching a huge spear. Between his swinging dreadlocks and downright comic movements, he looked rather like a Rastafarian ballet-dancer from Hell.

"My sword must've shorted his invisibility device," Tomokato said. "Don't let him know we can see him."

Shiro asked: "Should I whistle non-chalantly?"

"That would be good," Tomokato said. Taking out an emery-board, he commenced filing his nails, every few seconds fetching a sidelong glance at the alien. Shiro was whistling *Shiny Happy People*, a tune that Tomokato knew he detested; from somewhere the kitten had produced an Ed Roth Model kit, and was painting some finishing touches on Mr. Gasser.

The alien got quite close, and pausing, drew himself up to his full height, staring at the felines. The metallic mask bobbed as if he were laughing silently to himself.

Slowly the thing crouched, then tweaked Tomokato's nose. Tomokato didn't react.

The alien scratched the side of his head, obviously puzzled by this lack of response. He pinched the cat's nose again. Tomokato kept filing his nails, asking Shiro:

"I wonder where that alien is?"

"Beats me, unc," Shiro replied.

The alien picked up a bit of twig and bounced it off Shiro's head. Shiro didn't bat an eye.

The alien stood, staring down at them, and leaning his spear against his chest, clapped loudly. They paid no attention.

"WooWooWoo!" he shouted.

They yawned.

The alien lit a cherry bomb and tossed it behind them; when the explosion failed to produce the slightest twitch, he took out a large bass drum, attached cymbals to his legs, and began marching up and back, blowing on a bugle, thumping the drum, and banging the cymbals, doing the damnedest imitation of Dick Van Dyke in *Mary Poppins*.

Unable to restrain himself any longer, Shiro looked at Tomokato, asking: "Silly, isn't he?"

The alien dropped the bugle and halted, knees knocking together with a clang.

"Duh...*say!*" he said, voice muted by the metal mask. Then, cymbals banging, he turned and raced back across the clearing, still beating the drum for reasons that remain murky even for yours truly.

Tossing Mr. Gasser aside, Shiro unslung a Bergmann *Kugelspritz* submachine gun and began emptying its snail clip in the alien's direction. The alien staggered, but kept on running.

"Come on!" Tomokato cried, unsheathing his sword.

"What do you bet he'll lead us back to his ship?" Shiro asked.

The guess proved prescient; they hadn't chased the alien far through the steaming Guatemalan forest when they came to another clearing, in which a small-to-middling alien spacecraft either sat, rested, or lay.

The creature dashed into a circular opening in the ship's side. Tomokato heard him shedding his one-man-band appurtenances; then came a loud hum, and the entrance began to contract like the pupil of a huge eye.

Utilizing the intensely difficult *Benihana Rodan*, or *Suck the Gut Ridiculously Far In*, Tomokato leaped through the shrinking aperture. Hardly had he struck the floor when Shiro landed atop him.

The alien was still in the process of taking off his bass-drum. Bounding up, Tomokato rushed towards the monstrosity, launching a whistling *Katana* blow even as the drum dropped away.

The alien jumped backwards, pointing an angry claw at the cat and crying:

"Uhh...Hey! Watch it with that thing!"

Tomokato took the thing's hand off. The alien stared at the stump, pointing it directly at his own face-mask. Yellow-green gore spurted onto the eye-pieces. The creature stumbled away, trying to wipe the the stuff off with his free hand.

Tomokato took another couple of whacks at him, and the alien sprawled forward onto the glowing buttons of a control-panel; Tomokato was just about to give him another slash when there came a mighty roar, and the spacecraft lifted off. The cat fell, pinned to the deck by g-forces.

The ship accelerated for what seemed an eternity. Tomokato began to feel as if he were spreading out along the deck, and was just on the verge of unconsciousness when the craft began to slow.

He struggled up to one knee. Shiro did likewise, sliding a new clip into the Bergmann.

Prying himself up off the console, the alien dashed for an adjoining compartment, disappearing just as Shiro popped the bolt back on the *Kugelspritz*. The kitten and his uncle leaped in pursuit.

The other compartment seemed to be a combination armory and trophy room; two of the walls were covered with all manner of weapons, the other two hung with mounted skulls from various extraterrestrial species.

One of the skulls caught Tomokato's attention, looking rather like something from a movie he'd seen; if the author wasn't so chicken about copyright violations, the cat might even have thought it was a skull from one of those aliens from *Alien*. As it was, it was long and biomechanical and extremely H.R. Gigeresque, and you can damn well envision it any way you choose.

Except as Minnie Mouse, perhaps.

"*I* think it looks like Minnie Mouse!" the hunter-alien cried, pulling something that looked like a ray-blaster down from a wall.

"No!" cried Shiro. "*That* looks like Minnie Mouse!"

He pointed. The alien turned, staring at Minnie's skull; complete with ears, it hung between Mickey's and Jiminy Cricket's.

"Well," the alien said, "I knew I had her skull here somewhere."

He fired the blaster.

Shiro laced the creature with Bergmann bullets--- and laced him and laced him. The alien crashed sideways into a transparent case containing a large leathery-looking egg-sac. The case shattered, the egg-sac toppling near the alien's face-mask.

Suddenly the end of the sac nearest the alien blossomed, springing open, and a shape like a small stingray shot out and landed splat on the alien's mask. Smoke burst from underneath it, and moments later, the stingray-critter vanished into a hole eaten in the mask. Tomokato heard a series of really obscene sucky-hickey noises.

He and Shiro moved cautiously towards the hunter-alien. The creature had fallen completely motionless.

Tomokato eyed the hole in the hunter's face-mask. It was still smoking, but he thought he could see something moving inside. Had he been a character in the sort of flick I'm satirizing, he'd probably have gone right up and stuck his mug directly into the opening, but as he wasn't, he didn't.

"No further," the cat said, holding Shiro back. "Please fire a burst into that hole."

"Can't unc," Shiro said. "Out of ammo."

"Back into the control-room," Tomokato said.

Once they retreated across the threshold, Tomokato eyed a control-panel beside the door. Much to his surprise, the alien words for *open* and *close* were identical to their Japanese counterparts.

"Can that truly be the result of mere chance?" Shiro asked.

"I don't know," Tomokato said, pressing the *close* button. "It *is* worth noting that we were able to understand that alien."

"Yeah, but he was speaking English," Shiro pointed out. "As a matter of fact, *we* seem to be speaking English right at this moment."

"You're right," Tomokato said, puzzled. "Now that you mention it, I think I've been speaking English all my life. And I thought it was Japanese!"

"Isn't life strange?" Shiro said.

They went over to the main console. A viewing-screen showed another spacecraft approaching, standing out boldly against the disc of a huge yellow gas giant. Apparently composed of two enormous flashlights and a couple of colossal dinner-plates, it somehow left the cat with the distinct impression that it must be filled with aging character actors who all wanted a chance to direct. The ship was silhouetted by the thickest, bluest matte-line that Tomokato had ever seen, except perhaps for the ones that used to surround George Reeves on the old *Superman* show.

"Doesn't look quite real, does it?" Shiro said.

"We're suspending our disbelief," Tomokato answered.

"Yeah, but why?" Shiro asked sourly.

Tomokato didn't reply. Hearing an ineptly-recorded humming sound-effect, he turned.

Four columns of light had appeared in the middle of the room, filled with small glittering ascending flecks that looked suspiciously like alka-seltzer bubbles. Ghostly figures took shape, swiftly growing opaque. The light-columns faded, leaving four men in tacky velveteen uniforms.

One was a late-middle aged fellow with a sizeable spare tire and a curly toupee riding halfway up his forehead. Shiro told Tomokato:

"Looks like the guy who spotted the gremlin on the plane."

"Gremlin?" Tomokato asked, but before Shiro could answer, the fellow wearing the rug said:

"Life-form readings, Mr. Spocky."

Tall and pointy-eared and slightly greenish, all dolled up in Ming the Merciless makeup, Mr. Spocky aimed a beepy flashy thing at Tomokato and Shiro.

"Cats of above-average size, Captain," he said, somehow divining this by looking at a little blinking red lightbulb.

"Who are you people?" Tomokato asked.

"My name is Captain James T. Paunch," the leader replied. "I'm the commander of the Starship *Eisenhower*. That is my Science officer, Mr. Spocky, and that----" He directed Tomokato's attention to a spindly-looking old fart with manically upswept eyebrows---"Is our ship's doctor, DeTrees."

"DeForrest," the doctor corrected.

"DeTrees," said Paunch.

"DeForrest," the doctor insisted.

"DeTrees," Paunch answered stubbornly.

The doctor sighed resignedly and told the cat: "Can't have DeForrest without DeTrees."

"And that," Paunch continued, indicating the last member of the party, the cutest little comedy relief person Tomokato had ever seen, "Is Ensign Tolstoy."

"Tolstoy?" Tomokato said.

"The scriptwriter only knew three Russian names," Tolstoy replied. "It was either Tolstoy, Stolichnaya, or Popov."

"What about Chekhov?" Tomokato asked.

"Who?" Paunch asked.

"Chekhov."

"*Gesundheit*," said Paunch, whereupon he, DeForrest, and Tolstoy burst out laughing, freeze-framing for a second.

Tomokato eyed them narrowly.

"Little outer-space humor there," Paunch told the cat. "Who are *you*, by the way?"

"My Name is Miaowara Tomokato. That's my nephew, Miaowara Shiro."

"Is this your ship?"

"No. It belongs to the alien we were pursuing. He was involved in the murder of my Lord."

"Where is this creature?"

"The next chamber. He's been parasitized by another alien, and---"

"Mr. Spocky?" Paunch interrupted.

"Logic would dictate that we march right on in there and put ourselves in the greatest danger possible," Mr. Spocky replied.

"The greatest danger---possible?" Captain Paunch asked.

"Under the circumstances, Captain."

"Now wait a minute, smarty-pants!" DeForrest growled in a curmudgeonish but nonetheless loveable way. "I'm sick and tired of logic dictating this and logic dictating that!"

Mr. Spocky arched a wry eyebrow at him. "What would you prefer?"

"Going into that room for a totally worthless reason!"

"Like following the dictates of logic?"

"Exactly!" DeForrest cried. "What are we waiting for?"

Mr. Tolstoy went to the hatch, looking at the control panel.

"Wery peculiar," he said, "Everything's in Japanese!"

Tomokato and Shiro exchanged glances.

The hatch opened, and there stood the hunter-alien, *sans* mask, holding the stingray-parasite by the tail.

"Duh," he said, crustacean face displaying an outre but eloquent sea-sickish look. Dropping the stingray, he rubbed his stomach. "Ticky Tummy!"

"Phasers on stun!" cried Paunch.

"What does *phaser* stand for, by the way?" Shiro asked.

"Phony Amplification and Stimulation of Emitted Radiation," Spocky answered. "It shoots cartoon animation."

"What good is it?"

"While the enemy's admiring the animation, we pistol-whip him."

"Stun's the only setting, huh?" Shiro asked.

"That would seem to be a logical deduction---"

"If you hit me," the hunter warned, "I'm gonna barf."

"You're bluffing," Paunch answered.

"But what if he isn't, Captain?" Spocky asked. "Remember our experience on Ipecac IV?"

"I hate to admit it, but Spocky's right," said DeForrest. "Took forever to get the stains out. Our uniforms look crappy enough as it is."

"What would you recommend?" Paunch asked Spocky.

Spocky replied: "Inviting him aboard the Eisenhower would probably be the most logical course."

"Nonsense!" Tomokato cried. "That thing is dangerous! He goes from planet to planet, hunting rational-life forms! Look at those trophies in the other room!"

"Duh," said the alien, "They were on the ship when I bought it."

"Standard...package?" Paunch asked.

"Yeah."

"Enough of this!" said Tomokato, advancing upon the hunter, sword raised.

"Neck-pinch, Spocky!" said Paunch.

Spocky pinched Paunch on the neck.

"Not...*me*!" gasped Paunch, collapsing.

"Very well, Captain," said Spocky, and pinched *himself* on the neck.

Astonished by this behavior, the cat had paused just long enough for DeForrest to shoot him up with twenty cc's of vaporized sedative; Tomokato dropped to his knees.

"Unc!" cried Shiro. "Unc!"

The kitten stepped towards Tomokato. Spocky was still pinching his own neck; evidently, by virtue of his non-human physiognamy, he was somewhat resistant to himself. But at last he crumpled, landing on top of Shiro.

That was the last Tomokato saw, except for the floor rushing up at him....as from a great distance, he heard the hunter-alien say:

"Thanks, doc. I feel much better now."

Then Tomokato was out.

"Yoo-hoo," came a gravelly voice. "Wake up! Rise and shine---!"

The cat suffered through a good deal more of this before recognizing the voice as DeForrest's.

"Where am I?" the cat asked, vision blurred.

"Sick-bay on the *Eisenhower*," said the doctor. "You're just coming out from under that sedative."

okato realized he was lying on a supremely uncomfortable quite cheap-feeling surface. Vision coming slowly into focus, looked groggily about.

The sick-bay was a blue-pastel fiberboard room with an eye-chart on one side and a glassed-in case holding a bedpan and some cotton balls on the other. The walls showed brackets where some obviously advanced medical equipment (or at least some obviously advanced-looking *bogus* medical equipment) had once been attached.

"You're staring at the brackets," DeForrest said. "All the good stuff was taken out. Cutbacks."

"Cutbacks?"

"Yep. Third season. You know."

Tomokato was about to say he knew nothing of the sort when Shiro came in.

"Uncle-*san!*" the kitten said. "You're awake."

Tomokato swung his legs over the side of the slab.

"Everything's cool," said Shiro. "They're not going to hurt us."

"As a matter of fact," DeForrest told Tomokato, "You're invited to dinner."

"With that alien?" the cat demanded.

"It *is* a stupid idea, isn't it?" the doctor asked.

"Yes."

DeForrest beamed. "Persuaded the Captain myself. Spocky was arguing for the same thing, but my reasons were much worse than his, I'm proud to say."

"Why do you hate logic so much?" Tomokato asked.

"A boiling pot of it dropped on me when I was a kid."

"A boiling pot of logic?"

"Yeah. Mom was delousing her jammies in the *Principia Mathematica.*"

"That *would* delouse her jammies, all right," Tomokato acknowledged.

"No," DeForrest replied. "My jammies were just as lousy as ever. But I was burned something awful. And I've been totally put out by any form of rationality ever since."

"Medecine's a rational pursuit."

"Not the way I do it."

"Isn't it based on deduction and induction?"

"Nope. Special effects and props. This is the future, after all."

"This is the present," Shiro said.

Deforrest laughed. "Well, shucks. As my old grandaddy used to say, suckin' on his mint julep in some southern state, 'Kelly, the future *is* the present, only later.' Never knew what he meant till now, though." He checked his watch. "Time for dinner."

They went out into a chintzy fiberboard hallway uttterly devoid of crewpersons.

"First season, we actually had a half-dozen extras wandering around," DeForrest said. "Second season, we were cut down to one or two. Now, we don't have anybody. Not that it matters, though. Not anymore. Had an SFD installed..."

"SFD?" Shiro asked.

"Stock-Footage Drive," DeForrest explained. "We just keep going to the places we went first season, only we change the names."

"That's terrible," Shiro said.

"Could be worse," DeForrest answered. "It's not like we've had to tangle with Space Hippies or Yangs and Cooms or stupid shit like that." He paused, scratching his head. "At least, not yet. Of course, even thinking about Space Hippies causes brain damage, so I suppose I might have forgot."

They came to an elevator, and as they waited for the doors to open, he began singing softly, something about "Headin' out to Eden." Mercifully, the lift arrived before he got very far into the song.

They entered; he hit the button for b-deck. The doors closed, but Tomokato had no sense of motion at all. After a short but embarrassing period, the doors opened again, and the doctor and felines stepped out into the same hallway.

201

.e's only one corridor left on the ship now," DeForrest said.

.ird season?" Shiro asked.

.he doctor nodded sheepishly.

They walked back along the corridor, past the sick-bay, entering a dining-hall decorated in late-sixties dormitory rec-room. At a long table sat Captain Paunch, Mr. Spocky, Ensign Tolstoy, the hunter-alien, and several characters you haven't heard about yet.

Seeing the alien, Tomokato reached for his sword, only to discover that it had been removed from its scabbard. As he was rather hungry---not to mention disarmed--- he elected not to make a scene for the time being.

Paunch and his crew rose, the Captain motioning the felines towards two empty places, some distance away from the alien.

"Some more introductions," Paunch said, indicating a voluptuous black woman in a very military-looking miniskirt. "This is my Chief Cleavage Officer, Lieutenant O'Hara. Lieutenant O'Hara, Miaowara Tomokato."

"O'Hara?" Tomokato asked.

"I'm black Irish," O'Hara replied.

"What a lame joke," Shiro said.

"Sorry," the author answered, and meant it.

"Aren't you going to introduce *me* to her?" Shiro asked Paunch.

"Please don't, Captain," O'Hara begged.

"What did I ever do to you?" Shiro demanded.

She leaned across the table and whispered in his ear.

"Oh, that," Shiro said.

Paunch pointed to a little terrier wearing a space-uniform. Balanced most precariously on its hind legs and played by the same pooch who played Tototo in story number two, the doggie wagged its tongue at Tomokato.

"And that's my engineering officer," Paunch said.

"Scotty?" Tomokato ventured.

"Arf!" Scotty affirmed happily, barely drooling.

"And this," said Paunch, nodding towards an Oriental man, "Is my Chief of Staff, Mister Sununu."

Tomokato asked: "Just what Oriental country are you from, by the way?"

"Damned if I know," Sununu replied. "New Hampshire, perhaps?"

"What's that east of?"

"Vermont?"

"Anyway," Paunch said, "To dinner."

The meal had already been served, each plate heaped with a charming selection of multicolored cosmic pastes. The glasses

ıst futuristically square, and filled with delicious-looking
ıluid. Shiro lifted his glass, asking:

ıat is this stuff?"

Arf," Scotty answered.

"I'll translate," Sunnunu told Shiro. "He said, `Lime Kool-Aid,
shades of Jonestown, don't drink it, tastes like piss, yucch.'"

"All that with one *arf?*" Shiro asked. "How would he say,
`Tomorrow and tomorrow and tomorrow creeps in this petty
pace, from day to day, unto the last syllable of recorded time, and
all our yesterdays have lighted fools the way to dusty death?'"

"Arf," Scotty said.

Shiro was suitably awestruck.

Paunch said: "I was just telling this hunter-alien here---"

"Duh, call me Bobby," the alien said.

"Bobby it is. Well, as I was just telling Bobby here, this whole
situation is curiously reminiscent of the time the *Eisenhower* visited
Ringling III---"

"Arf!" said Scotty.

"Mr. Sununu?" Paunch asked.

Sununu answered: "Scotty says, excuse me sir, this situation isn't
very much like that one at all."

"I'm well aware of that," Paunch said, with precisely the sort of
gravitas that Tomokato had always associated with Canadian ex-
Shakespearean actors.

"Arf!" said Scotty, Sununu translating:

"Very good, sir!"

"In any case," Paunch resumed, "there we were on Ringling III. I'd
led the landing-party onto the planet, just as any prudent
commander would do. Without a spacesuit, of course; no point
letting the atmosphere know you're afraid of it. Well, as we were
standing there coughing our lungs out, Ensign Tolstoy noticed
these huge footprints.

"'Mister Spocky,' I said. 'Analysis?'

204

"Spocky looked at his beepy-flashy thing.

"'Two possibilities, Captain,' he said. 'The first is that this planet is inhabited by giants...'

"'And the second?'

"'By clowns.'

"'Clowns?" I asked. 'Is it...*possible*?'

"'If we can imagine a universe where English is the language of every alien race that we encounter....I suppose so, Captain.'

"But the question was definitively answered moments later, when an army of clowns swept into the clearing, caught us in butterfly-nets, loaded us into cars in which there wasn't nearly enough room, and drove us off to their circus.

"There we learned that the planet had once been visited by a *travelling* circus; a great big circus *book* had been left behind, and had become the natives's very own bible. This tome contained the formula of a gas that turned people into clowns; under the influence of the vapor, I developed a big red nose, Mister Spocky grew a line of fluffy yellow buttons down the front of his uniform, and Ensign Tolstoy got even more like he is now.

"But before the transformation process was complete, I hit upon a daring plan: overpower the guards. Of course, there were no guards, but we didn't let that stop us. We found our comunicators in a convenient location, and beamed back up to the ship. There I decided that this clown-business was more than enough reason for violating the Prime Directive and completely destroying the culture on Ringling III.

"But how to do it? Spocky suggested we contact the clowns' main computer and hit it with the Liars' Paradox, thus causing it to explode.

"'Nah,' I answered, for no particular reason, then asked: 'What about...*Anti-Clown?*'

"'Arf!' said Scotty.

"Sununu immediately translated: 'Aye Captain, they couldna swalla that!'

"Luckily, the hold was full of the stuff. Me and Spocky and Tolstoy sniffed enough to reverse our clown-symptoms, then dumped three hundred boxes out the starboard porthole and left."

"You didn't stick around to see if it worked?" Shiro asked.

"Nope," Paunch said. "We were under attack by a Remulan U-Boat."

"A U-Boat in outer space?"

"How else could we rip off the plot of *The Enemy Below*?"

"You have a point," Shiro said.

"They had this cloaking technique," Paunch said. "Insidious. Called us up, ship-to-ship. An instant later, we were blind."

"What did they say?" Tomokato asked.

"Close your eyes."

With that, everyone at the table, with the exception of Tomokato and Shiro, closed their eyes.

"Duh...I can't see!" Bobby cried.

"The Remulans just about tore us to pieces," Paunch said. "To this day, I don't know how we survived. But Dr. Deforrest came to the rescue. Being a doctor, he knows about eyes, and eyelids, and stuff like that...

"'Open your eyes!' he said, charging onto the bridge."

Paunch and his crew and the alien all opened their eyes.

"The Remulans were just about to finish us," Paunch went on. "But very cleverly, I phoned *them*.

"'Close *your* eyes!' I said."

Paunch and the others shut theirs again.

"And the shitheads fell for it!" he crowed. "Of course, my crew closed theirs too...we collided with the Remulans, limped away with 'em stuck in that big dinner-plate item on the top of the ship...Eventually, though, it occurred to Dr. DeForrest to say 'Open your eyes' again...We reached Portsmouth Harbor and were all knighted. Two years later, we were sent to Tahiti for breadfruit...Native dancing....Total breakdown of discipline...Mr.

Christian accused me of stealing the strawberries myself, but I proved with geometric logic..."

Tomokato began to hear something that sounded like ball bearings clicking together.

"Captain," said Mr. Spocky. "Captain..."

"Excuse me," said Paunch. "Where was I? Ah yes, Ca-Ca Time..."

"Ca-Ca time?" Tomokato asked.

"As you may or may not know, Mister Spocky is from the planet Hephaestus---"

"Captain, please," Mister Spocky interrupted.

"---And Hephaestians have a number of notable peculiarities, even besides pointy ears and girly eye makeup---"

"Sir, I implore you..." Spocky groaned.

Paunch patted him on the hand, said, "Quiet, dear," then plowed right ahead: "Perhaps the most remarkable thing about them is the fact they only have to go to the bathroom every seven years. This period is known as the Squattondapottaphee, or Ca-Ca Time. The Hephaestians, logical folks that they are, are deeply ashamed of the fact that they have to take a dump once in a while. And so they've shrouded the whole business in layers of mystery and ritual, burning incense, opening the bathroom window, stuff like that.

"In any case, during the Squattondapottaphee, or Squat for short, they visit Thundermug V, a moon that's been designated as a ceremonial crapper. This satellite is ruled over by the twin priestesses T'poo and T'Pee. According to the ritual of Ca-Ca, a Hephaestian who intends to relieve himself must bring two special assistants with him, one to hold the toilet paper and one to wipe. Spocky told DeForrest that it was a very great honor, but frankly, I didn't quite know what to say---"

Bobby began to snort and sneeze, working his very weird facial structures.

DeForrest stood up, leaning forward over the table. "What's wrong?"

"Uh..." said Bobby. "Ka-choo! Something's crawling around in my nose!"

"Can't help you," DeForrest declared, sitting back down.

"Ka-Choo!" said Bobby again. Inserting a long hooked claw into one of his nostrils, he turned his face sideways, towards Ensign Tolstoy, and was about to commence some no-doubt stupendous feat of alien nosemining when the whole center of his face exploded in a splash of extraterrestrial snot, every little shiny globule spinning in slow-motion. Tolstoy caught the full brunt of it, and by look of things, he was lubricated bone-deep and beyond.

"*Gesundheit*," said Shiro.

Tomokato was just about to inform him that this jape was in dubious taste when a little rope-ladder dropped from the cavity in Bobby's face, unrolling swiftly. Bobby's head twitched round, and he emitted what sounded to Tomokato like some kind of death-rattle. The corpse remained upright just long enough for a small slithery rubber thing covered with what appeared to be K-Y jelly to climb down the ladder and rear up briefly on the table, making snarl-snarl at the onlookers, who were rather startled, to say the least.

Bobby's body slumped forward. Dodging, the Noseburster said, "Nah-nah, wussies!" to those staring at it, bounded from the table, and skidded out the door on a trail of slime.

"What in tarnation?" DeForrest cried.

"I told you!" Tomokato said. "Bobby was parasitized, back on his ship."

"And now there's a critter loose here!" said DeForrest. "And Tolstoy's all covered with snot!"

"I don't mind, really," said Tolstoy, glistening cherubically.

"Why not?" said Shiro, nauseated.

"I am a comedy relief guy after all. Also the number one spear-carrier, since the rest of the crew was laid off."

"He's right, Captain," said Mister Spocky. "Logic dictates that we send him out all by his lonesome to look for that creature."

"Logic dictates nothing of the sort!" cried Tomokato.

A look of doubt registered on Paunch's face; he scratched briefly under his toupee.

"Captain," said Spocky. "I think he's got me. But *surely* logic dictates that you shouldn't take advice from cats. It's silly enough even talking to them."

"You've been talking to me all along!" Tomokato answered.

"Which means it's high time we stopped."

"No need to stop being polite," said Paunch, shaking his head. "Nevertheless..." He turned to Tolstoy. "Go on out there and get yourself killed."

Tolstoy beamed. "Wery good, Kiptain," he said, whipping his arm up in a salute, dousing Mister Sununu with a whole sleeveful of glutinous noseblow. As Tolstoy strode proudly from the room, Paunch chuckled:

"What a putz."

"We could always go with him, unc," Shiro suggested to Tomokato.

"*I'm* the Captain of this ship," said Paunch. "And I'm commanding you to stay right here. Besides: do you really care if that little butterball buys it?"

Tomokato wanted to say that he did, but he couldn't quite justify putting his life or Shiro's on the line for a man with such an achingly phony Russian accent; as though a tape-loop were running in his head, he kept hearing Tolstoy's saying "Wery."

At length, when Tomokato failed to respond, Paunch said, "That's that," and cupped his hands beside his mouth, crying, "Found anything yet, Ensign?"

"Not yet!" Tolstoy answered, his voice muted by as much distance as you could get in one single not-very long corridor.

"Such suspense!" breathed Lieutenant O'Hara.

"Where?" Shiro asked.

But even though Shiro was not feeling much in the way of apprehension, Ensign Tolstoy was; his initial flush of pride at being chosen for this suicide mission had worn off soon after he left the dining-hall, and with each step he took, the cold invisible hand of fear hitched his jockey shorts one notch higher twixt his chubby little cheeks. Heart in his mouth, he reached the end of the corridor, where the alien's slime-trail vanished into an open floor-level vent.

"Anything to report?" called Captain Paunch.

"The creature went into a went, sir!" Tolstoy answered.

"A what?"

"A went, Kiptain!" Tolstoy cried.

"Yes, I know it went. But where?"

"The went!" Tolstoy answered.

"The *what* went?"

"No, this went right here," Tolstoy said.

"What went right there?"

"Yes."

"Yes what?" Paunch demanded.

"Yes, the what went in the went."

"The *what* went in *what* went?" Paunch cried.

"What?"

"What?" Paunch shouted.

"Can't you make yourself a bit clearer, Kiptain?" Tolstoy replied, bending to stick his mug directly into the opening.

Right in front of him crouched the Noseburster, which had, inexplicably, grown quite a bit larger in the brief span since it left the dining-hall.

"Kiptain!" Tolstoy cried. "I've fou---"

"Shhh!" the noseburster hissed.

Tolstoy lowered his voice to a whisper. "But I've got to warn the Kiptain!" he explained.

Shaking its head, the Noseburster opened its jaws, its backup jaws, and its backup backup jaws.

"Tolstoy!" Paunch cried. "Tolstoy, are you dead yet?"

No answer.

Paunch looked to Spocky. "Does that mean he's dead, or that he's *not* dead?"

"Yes, Captain," Spocky said.

"Go out and look for him, Sununu," Paunch said.

The Chief of Staff rose apprehensively from the table, gulping.

"Arf!" barked Scotty.

"It was good knowing you too," Sununu answered, and marched from the dining-hall.

"Och," said Scotty mournfully. "Who's ginna translate for me noo?"

Phaser on MA, or Maximum Animation, Sununu followed the slime-trail just as Tolstoy had done. Rounding a bend in the corridor, he sighted the end of the hallway, where a large cocoon hung in a corner of the ceiling.

But even as he approached, the eggsac dropped, pulling a ceiling panel with it. That came as no surprise--- indeed, he was amazed the cocoon had stayed up long enough to fall. He'd once hung a pinup of Nancy Kwan from the bulkhead in his cabin, and the photograph had pulled the whole wall down on him.

Reaching the coccoon, he nudged the ceiling-panel off with his foot. A gaping hole in his forehead, Ensign Tolstoy gazed up at him through the sac's gauzy side, not looking wery wiable...his nose began to bulge. Sununu thought it strange that a noseburster was already about to emerge, seeing as how the gestation period for the one that killed Bobby had been much longer. Sununu also thought it peculiar that a creature bent on parasitizing its prey would ream out the brains of its victims. But given near instanteous maturization of the parasite, he supposed it made a certain amount of sense, provided he didn't think about it for more than two seconds at a time.

Determined, apparently, to keep him from worrying himself too much about the sheer awfulness of the science here, a Noseburster did indeed erupt into view, although, in keeping with the general level of consistency in the material I'm making fun of, it came lunging out of Tolstoy's ear, slipping down into the depths of the cocoon.

Hardly had Sununu recovered from this shock when he heard a loud crash behind him, and spinning, saw that the first noseburster, fully grown now into something like a basketball player designed by Robert Mapplethorpe, had fallen through the ceiling, above which it had no doubt been squatting nefariously.

"Sununu!" came Captain Paunch's voice. "Are you all right?"

"Sure, Captain, fine," said Sununu, so frightened that he felt compelled to lie about his situation. Needless to say, the thought of fleeing never even entered his mind, even though the alien gave him plenty of time. The thing appeared to have sprained its ankle, and seemed unable to get off the floor...at length it extended a hand to him. Sununu hesitated to aid the creature, whereupon it huffed impatiently; maddened by terror, he helped it up.

The alien went to the coccoon, fished the ear-noseburster out, and squirted it from between its hands as though it had been a bar of black mucusy soap, straight towards Sununu's face.

Sununu considered shooting the parasite in midair with his phaser, but judgement severely impaired by dread, decided not to, and also opened his mouth real wide. The parasite slid down his throat with a loud "Whee!," and for an instant Sununu was reminded of his cousin Suzie Lu Sununu, who was one totally prehensile French Kisser. Then the aftertaste---rather like that of peanut-butter Slim-fast bars---struck him, and his mind foundered in oblivion.

"Okay then," said Paunch, after Sununu failed to respond to his latest cry. "Who do we send next?"

"What have you accomplished with all this?" Tomokato demanded.

"I got them both killed, didn't I?"

"If we're going to hunt down that alien," Tomokato replied, "We'd do much better to stick together!"

"Captain," said Spocky, "The deaths of Tolstoy and Sununu *were* long overdue. But we're out of spear carriers now, and---"

"What about Scotty?" Paunch asked.

"He's more like a spear carrier than you or I, sir..."

"Then wouldn't it be better if he died first?"

"...But I think it would be unfair to lump him in with Sununu and Tolstoy," Spock continued.

"What about O'Hara there?" Paunch asked.

"Remember the Second Prime Directive, Captain: good looking women don't get killed on spear carrier duty. And O'Hara's better looking than most of the women in the Fleet. For one thing, she has a chin."

"So that leaves you, me, and DeForrest," Paunch said.

"Except for those cats," Spocky pointed out.

"Seeing as how my nephew and I will be endangered in any case," Tomokato said, "And rather more so if we rely on any of you, we'll hunt the thing down."

Spocky gave him his sword back.

"What about my machine-gun?" Shiro asked.

Spocky handed Shiro his Bergmann.

"You wouldn't have ammo for this, would you?" Shiro asked.

"For a Bergmann *Kugelspritz*?" Spocky asked. "You'd have better luck capturing some from the alien."

"I see," said Shiro.

"Nephew, let's go," Tomokato said.

They went out into the corridor, proceeding along the slime-trail. Rounding the corner, they saw an alien on a step-ladder, busily trying to affix a large cocoon to the ceiling, and just as Spocky had suggested, it had several clips for the Bergmann, hanging from a biomechanical web-belt around its waspy waist.

Farther on was a second cocoon, lying on the floor, a second, smaller alien in the process of working its way free of the silk.

The creature on the stepladder noticed the approaching pair, but continued trying to attach the cocoon to the ceiling. When at length the sac finally stuck, it just pulled the panel down, and the alien stamped once in annoyance, then slunk down off the ladder and crouched in a very odd pose, apparently in the belief that this rendered it invisible.

"We see you," Tomokato said.

The alien stood, grabbing one of its legs and putting its ankle behind its head.

"We can *still* see you," said the cat.

The alien assumed a sitting lotus position, head cocked at an unusual angle. Amazingly, this did cause the thing to blend right into the background---almost.

The second alien, having wriggled free of the coccoon, had performed a similar trick, taking on the semblence of a stretch of cheap baseboard. But Tomokato was still able to discern the thing---just barely.

"Shiro, wait here," he said, moving towards the first alien. Deciding not to close with it, he hurled his sword through its all-but invisible head, intending to pluck the blade from the corpse and proceed towards the other creature.

Yet even as he withdrew the weapon from the slumping body, he saw that the blade was smoking and pitted, the creature's blood eating it away. Seeing his dilemma, the second alien straightened and advanced upon him.

Tomokato threw the rapidly-disintegrating sword. The weapon shattered against the creature's gleaming elongated black head.

Shiro rushed up beside the cat, inserting a clip---taken from the dead alien, no doubt---into his Bergmann. He pulled back the bolt and hosed the second alien down.

Squealing, it shattered in a burst of acid and black chitin, its corrosive blood swiftly eating a hole in the floor, the remains

214

dropping through. The felines rushed up to the opening, looking down into starshot blackness.

"Why isn't the vacuum sucking all the air out?" Shiro asked.

"Vacuum?" said Tomokato. "That's a travelling matte."

As if to prove Tomokato's point, George Reeves went drifting by below, lying on his back with both hands behind his head, one leg crossed over the other. He paused directly beneath them.

"Did you really kill yourself?" Shiro cried.

"Nope," Reeves replied. "Ernest Hemingway got me."

"I thought he killed *himself*."

"Not the first time. He was so drunk he put the shotgun in *my* mouth instead. Go figure, huh?"

Cape spread out to left and right, George slid from sight like Ophelia going downstream.

Hearing a preliminary nosebursting noise, Tomokato and Shiro looked back at the cocoon that the alien had been trying to attach to the ceiling. Sununu was visible inside; suddenly two Nosebursters came ooshing out of his face, vanishing from sight inside the silky sphere.

Tomokato immediately moved to push the cocoon out into the travelling matte, but after the sac dropped down through the opening in the hull, he saw the two Nosebursters, having escaped from the sac, hanging for dear life from the lip of the hole. Shiro aimed his Bergmann at them, but the critters boosted themselves over the edge and zig-zagged swiftly into the vent at the end of the hall, Shiro's bullets bringing up the rear.

"This bites," said the kitten.

"Isn't that an obscene expression?" Tomokato asked.

"Nope," Shiro answered. "As a matter of fact, I picked it up from you."

"You did not."

"Yes I did. Remember, you were holding up this poisonous snake, and---"

"Enough," said Tomokato.

215

They returned to the dining-hall.

"We killed two, but two more escaped," Tomokato reported.

"There were four in all?" Paunch asked. "How is it...*possible*? So little time has elapsed."

"Sir," said Spocky, "We are either dealing with a species that reproduces extremely rapidly, magic, a stupid scriptwriter, or all three."

"Granted," said Paunch. "But what should we do next?"

Scotty looked at his watch. "Well, Captain, it's time to toss some more coal on the SFD."

"You're going down to engineering?" DeForrest asked.

Scottie clapped on an engineer's cap. "Aye."

"Will you be all right?"

"I dinna know," said Scotty bravely. "But there's only one way to find out."

Claws ticking against the battered linoleum, he trotted from the room.

"So," said Paunch. "There are two aliens on the loose, and Scotty's gone off to certain death. Any suggestions---?"

There came a muffled thumping from the kitchen.

"Sounds like something's in one of the food-lockers," O'Hara said.

"Aren't those compartments hermetically sealed?" Paunch asked. "Could those aliens get in there?"

Spocky answered: "Not unless they knew the access code---"

More thumping.

"You know," said Paunch, "If we went trooping in there, and stuck our mugs into the locker, I bet we could *all* get ourselves parasitized."

"Not if there are only two aliens, Captain," Spocky pointed out.

"Still, it's worth a try," Paunch replied.

With that, he, Spocky, Deforrest and O'Hara went into the kitchen, Tomokato following at some remove. Reaching the locker where the noises where coming from, Spocky tapped in the access code. The door swung slowly inwards.

"Okay right," said Paunch. "When it opens all the way, we shove our faces right in."

Tomokato watched them lunge forward, then turned to Shiro, saying: "Those idiots---"

But Shiro wasn't there.

Paunch and his crew loosed a loud gasp; Tomokato looked round once more. They'd all entered the locker, and were standing around Shiro, who was sitting on the floor with a big lamb chop in one paw.

"Shiro!" Tomokato cried.

"Uncle!" Shiro replied.

"How's that lamb-chop?" DeForrest asked.

"Better than multicolored cosmic pastes, that's for sure," Shiro said. "But I think I'd like it more if it were re-hydrated."

Two doors down from the dining-hall, just past the sick-bay, was engineering. Floor covered with egg-cases, ceiling hung with huge curtains of web, it showed every sign of having been visited by at least one of the critters that had gotten away from the cats. The egg-cases bulged and gurgled as Scotty drew near, but he wasn't about to be kept from his beloved furnace; nonetheless, when he heard something knocking around *inside* it, that gave him a certain amount of pause. There was no firelight visible through the bars in the door; had he actually allowed the fire to go out? Or had, horror of horrors, one of the creatures gone inside and doused his coals, for some inscrutable alien reason?

Phaser at the ready, he crept up to the handle and swung the door wide. Sitting amid the ashes was a little kitty basket, in which Shiro was curled up, fast asleep!

But didn't you just leave him, back in the dining-hall? Scotty thought, astonished.

"What're you dewn' in there?" he demanded.

Shiro looked at him groggily, asking: "Isn't this a food-locker?"

217

Something cleared its throat loudly. Scotty whirled to see a huge and very fancy-looking mother-alien ceasing to pretend to be a complex of steam-pipes. Scotty was sure he could've dazzled her with Phaser-animation, but pistol-whipping her successfully seemed out of the question.

"Di' ya have your gun?" he asked Shiro.

"Are you kidding?" Shiro asked, leaping from the furnace, Bergmann blazing, punching a score of acid-squirting holes in Big Mama. She recoiled against the wall, shrieking.

Shiro and Scotty dashed for the door. The kitten reached the threshold in plenty of time, but Scotty was distracted by an egg-case even then in the process of springing open, and shouting, "Excuse me!" he rushed over and stuck his face in. All warmed up and with someplace to go now, the thing within got romantic with him in no time.

Love at last? Scotty wondered.

Shiro looked over his shoulder to see the terrier up on his hind legs, wearing the egg-case and staggering about like Shemp Howard with a paint-can jammed over his head.

"Take it off!" Shiro cried.

Scotty didn't seem to hear; he began waltzing dreamily about, as though with an invisible partner.

Against his better instincts, Shiro started to go back for him, but stingray-critters were popping like jack-in the boxes from every eggcase in sight, and worse yet, the mother-alien, having affixed a last band-aid to one last bullet-hole, came stomping his way. Firing a burst to cover his retreat, he skeedaddled.

Hearing the rattle of Shiro's gun, Tomokato and the others rushed from the food locker, back into the dining-hall.

"Let's just be glad we're not dealing with Remulans!" said Paunch as they made for the corridor outside.

"Why?" Tomokato asked.

"Just think what would happen if one of them told us to close our eyes!" Paunch answered.

He was almost to the threshold when a raspy non-human voice rang out:

"Close your eyes!"

Glazzies shut, Paunch whirled, crying:

"I can't see!"

Skidding, Spocky butted him on the brow with a crack like a Nashville Slugger connecting with a hellacious fastball; then came a soggier impact as DeForrest whammed his skull into the back of Spocky's. The trio sagged down, knocked cold.

Meanwhile, O'Hara had collided with Tomokato; both had toppled.

"Open your eyes!" he snarled, wrestling out from under her. Looking at the rear wall, he saw a full-grown alien climbing out of an aperture marked *Alien Use Only*.

"Didn't you hear me?" the creature asked the cat. "I said, `Close your eyes!'"

"Close yours!" Tomokato answered.

"Ask nice!" the thing responded.

"Close yours *please!*"

"*Pretty* please!"

"Pretty please, with sugar on it!"

"All right, but just this once," the alien said.

Tomokato couldn't quite tell what it had shut, but it began to stumble about blindly, soon staggering through a wall. Looking into the hole, Tomokato saw the alien go through another wall, then another, finally crashing out into the travelling matte and dropping from sight.

"Neatly done, unc," said Shiro.

Tomokato turned to see him standing beside O'Hara.

"Where were you?" the cat asked.

"The readers already know, uncle-*san*," said Shiro.

"What was that shooting?"

"My gun," Shiro answered.

"Just as I thought," the cat said, nodding. "Did you see Scotty?"

"The aliens got him. There was this great big mother-alien too---"

"Don't the readers know that as well?" Tomokato asked.

"Got me, unc," Shiro said. "On the other hand, they also knew what happened to Scotty, so subtract one point."

"Which leaves me---"

"One point behind *me*."

"Do the readers know how far the mother followed you?"

"Nope."

"Why don't you tell me, then?"

"I don't think she followed me very far at all," Shiro said.

"That's a lie," she said, sticking her head into the dining-hall. "You know perfectly well that I chased you all the way here."

"Nope," said Shiro. "That whole segment was cut out of the manuscript. So you'd just better go on back to engineering, and deduct five points."

"Five?" Big Mama protested.

"*Ten,* if you don't get going this instant!"

She spat on the floor and withdrew.

"I win," Shiro said.

"Does this mean we can repeat information the readers already know?" Tomokato answered.

"For a half an hour," Shiro said, looking at his watch. "Starting--- *now*."

Paunch, Spocky and DeForrest regained consciousness, rising to their feet.

"Open your eyes," said Tomokato.

They complied.

"Captain," said O'Hara, "I don't mean to be alarming, but I think we're in serious trouble."

Shiro elaborated: "Scotty's been parasitized, engineering's full of alien egg-cases, and the queen-mother's just gone back to lay some more."

"Then we'll just have to go down there and exterminate the whole lot," said Paunch.

"I suspect we'll need something stronger than Phasers, Captain," said Spocky.

"Something that..*works*?"

"Precisely. The problem is, we don't have anything like that."

"What about Anti-Clown?"

"These things aren't clowns."

Paunch snapped his fingers. "Not...*yet*."

"What do you have in mind, Jim?" asked DeForrest.

"Remember the sample I brought back from Ringling III?"

"The clown-transformation gas! Right!"

Paunch went into a walk-in closet, got the cannister that contained the vapor, handed a box of Anti-Clown to Spocky, and parcelled out a bunch of gas-masks.

"Let's boldly go," he said, and they all trooped down to engineering, slipping the masks on before entering.

The Mother was bottle feeding one of her brood; several dozen other young'uns were pushing toy trucks around the floor, going "Vroom! Vroom! Vroom!" amid bits and pieces of Scotty--- apparently he'd been parasitized by every parasite available, and they'd blown considerably more than his nose. But just to make sure, DeForrest picked up one of the Terrier's little bloody detached paws, felt for a pulse, and declared:

"He's dead, Jim."

221

"Paunch howled in rage, spraying the aliens with the clown-vapor. Instantly, every single one of them sprouted a huge shock of orange hair.

"Now, Spocky!" Paunch cried. "The Anti-Clown!"

Ripping open the box, Spocky began sowing handfuls in the direction of the creatures, who very considerately had made no attempt to attack. Within moments, the Bozo-hair on the aliens receded into their chitonous pates.

"Hah!" said Paunch, folding his arms on his chest.

"Captain," said Spocky apprehensively, tugging on Paunch's sleeve.

"Showed *them*," said Paunch.

Big Mama gently burped the infant she'd been bottle-feeding.

"Showed them what?" Tomokato asked Paunch.

Big Mama laid the infant down.

"That we're not to be trifled with," Paunch told the cat.

Big Momma crossed her arms over her chest, then bellowed, "Trifle with them!"

Her young jumped up, hurling their playthings. A storm of sturdy Tonka-Toys bowled Paunch, Spocky, and DeForrest to the floor. Shiro tried to blast the oncoming aliens back with his Bergmann, but it was useless, and he retreated into the corridor withTomokato and O'Hara.

"If only we had some more guns!" Tomokato cried.

"Follow me!" O'Hara answered, leading them to her cabin, which proved to be a veritable treasure-trove of firepower.

"What are you doing with all this stuff?" Shiro asked, admiring a rack full of double-barrelled elephant guns.

O'Hara shrugged, taking down an M-16 with a grenade-launcher. "I'm a gun nut."

Tomokato began shoving shells into a Stryker-12 rotary-feed shotgun.

"I hear them coming," he said. "Shiro, cover the corridor."

Reloading his Bergmann, Shiro went to the door and fired several bursts.

"Mommie, boo-boo!" cried a wounded alien outside. "Need kissies---"

Shiro fired once more, cutting the little feller off and sneering: "Kissies."

Slinging two bandoliers of shotgun-shells across his chest, Tomokato joined him at the door, leaning out into the hall.

Leaking like acid-filled seives, the creatures Shiro had shot were swiftly melting their way through the floor, but that still left enough deck for a considerable army of aliens to proceed along the corridor, holding the limp forms of Spocky, Paunch and DeForrest as shields.

"Go ahead, shoot!" the monsters cried.

"Okay, tough guys!" Shiro yelled. But Tomokato said:

"Don't you dare!"

"They're dead men anyway," Shiro answered.

"Doesn't matter. O'Hara, how's the fan-mail running?"

"Right at this instant?" O'Hara asked. Tomokato heard papers shuffling. "Four to one against snuffing the old fools."

"There you have it, nephew," Tomokato said.

"But what are we going to do?" Shiro demanded, as the aliens drew closer and closer.

"If only we had some more Clown-Transformation Vapor!" Tomokato said.

"The first grenade in my launcher is full of CTV!" O'Hara said.

"What good did it do the last time?" Shiro asked.

"My theory is, if you're going to fight, fight clowns," Tomokato said, then told O'Hara, "fire it into the ceiling, above the aliens!"

She did just that. A fog of CTV covered the creatures, who immediately began to transform.

224

"Now," said Tomokato, "If my theory is correct..."

The cab of one of the Tonka-trucks had become tangled in the various doo-dads and pointynesses with complicated Japanese names that covered his helmet. Pulling it loose, he hurled it towards the aliens.

"Bet you can't all fit in that!" Tomokato cried.

Plainly affronted, the aliens demonstrated their clownitude by squeezing into the little vehicle, every last one, leaving Paunch, Spocky and DeForrest lying on the floor. Blasting a hole through the linoleum, Tomokato ran up and kicked the truck through the opening, out into the travelling-matte.

Quite clownish now themselves, the Captain and his two goombahs sat up, rubbing their stomachs.

"What happened?" Paunch asked Tomokato.

The cat told him.

"Doesn't that mean that we're about to be killed by the Nosebursters inside us?" Paunch asked.

"I'm afraid so."

"Then why didn't you just *shoot* us?"

"The mail was running four to one against that," said O'Hara.

"Well," said DeForrest, "At least it's nice to know we're still so beloved."

"No, that wasn't it, sir," the Chief Cleavage Officer replied. "The audience wants to see your leathery old faces explode in a blast of blood and snot."

Paunch asked: "Can it be that we've actually worn out our welcome at last?"

"Logic would dictate that it had to happen sometime," Spocky said. "Or not."

"Logic shmogic," said DeForrest. "Logic is a bunch of pretty flowers that smell *bad*."

"In spite of the fact that such a pronouncement would be totally out of character for me," Spocky said, "I somehow feel that that was *my* line, and not yours."

"Put 'er there, pal," said DeForrest. The two shook hands heartily, thus symbolizing the triumphant synthesis of reason and intuition; an instant later, their heads shattered in twin cloudbursts of parasites and glop.

"Shoot me!" Paunch begged O'Hara.

"Sorry," said O'Hara, waving the mail. "Demographics."

Several toupee-bursters reamed their way through Paunch's rug.

"Come on!" cried the other aliens, waiting some distance up the hall. The parasites that had just exited Paunch slithered to join them, and the whole bunch slipped from view around the corner, undoubtedly bent on finding a nice place to grow for two or three minutes.

"They'll be back," Shiro said.

"And they'll probably bring Big Mama too," O'Hara said.

"Is there any way off this ship?" Tomokato asked.

"A shuttle-craft. But the landing-bay is past engineering."

"We're going to have to fight Big Mama no matter what," Tomokato said. "Let's get going."

They started cautiously up the corridor, sidestepping the acid-holes in the floor. As they approached engineering, they discovered the aliens had erected a toll-barrier across the hallway, attended by the Queen Mother and a whole shitload of her young.

Tomokato and his companions paused.

"What's the plan, Unc?" Shiro asked.

The cat pondered the situation.

"Pay the toll," he said.

Shiro fished out some change, deposited it in the basket, and the gate went up; Big Mama and her brood stepped aside, obviously very frustrated.

Once he thought he was out of earshot, Shiro said:

"Good thing their machine can't detect slugs."

"Good thing they can't hear us," Tomokato answered.

A large Gigeresque voice answered from behind: "Good thing I followed you."

Tomokato spun to see the Queen looming over him.

"Good thing you alerted us to your presence," he said, and began emptying the Stryker into her, dodging back from the splashing acid-blood, Shiro and O'Hara joining in with their weapons.

"Good thing I can stand an incredible amount of punishment," Big Mama said.

Tomokato almost said *Good thing we've got a vast amount of ammunition*, but decided that particular joke had been beaten to death, if indeed it had ever been funny to begin with. Ego badly bruised, the author tried furiously to force him to say it, even thrusting a pistol in Tomokato's face; but in so doing, he made the mistake of getting between the cat and Big Mama, who promptly seized him and chucked him over her shoulder to her advancing young-uns, who reamed his brains out most gleefully, thus turning the rest of the story over to the author's twin brother Vhong.

But Vhong was suffering a writer's block; ultimately he had to bail himself out by resurrecting his brother, who was now very chastened and most unwilling to force Tomokato to utter any more 'good thing' lines.

"Good thing, too," said Shiro, quite of his own volition. He, his uncle, and O'Hara had utilized Vhong's writer's block to put some distance between themselves and the aliens; once inside the landing-bay, they activated the waferboard sliding-door.

"That won't hold them for long," said O'Hara.

"Or at all," said Shiro. "Where's that shuttle?"

Aside from a few oil-spots on the floor, there was no sign of it.

"Must've been repossessed," said O'Hara. "This *is* the---"

"Third season," said Tomokato and Shiro at once.

There came a series of crispy-crunchy sounds, and several long spidery black arms busted through the door. Tomokato and the others poured a hail of fire into the waferboard, blowing the entire barrier away.

As they reloaded, Tomokato squinted through the gunsmoke into the corridor beyond, where a midden-heap of Big Mama's kiddies was sinking through the floor.

Yet more of her whelps were on the way, inexplicably large numbers of them, carrying long poles. Looking like refugees from a *very* special olympics, they tried to vault the gap in the floor, only to be met in midair by a wall of shotgun pellets and bullets, which dismembered them most spectacularly and satisfactorily.

Stymied at the doorway, some tried to get in through the vents, but met the same fate. Others came crashing through the ceiling, although half went crashing through the floor as well. Those that didn't were blasted into steaming goo.

In the lull that followed, Shiro said:

"I only have two bullets left."

"How can you tell?" Tomokato asked.

"I count my shots."

"Even full-auto?"

"Yes. I'm very proud of myself."

"A remarkable skill," Tomokato had to admit. He snatched up one of the vaulting-poles that had come hurtling into the bay.

"Would you please cut this to a good quarter-staff length?" he asked.

Shiro blasted it through.

"You're expecting to hold them back with that?" O'Hara demanded.

"Not for long," said Tomokato. "I'm afraid our only hope is a *deus ex machina.*"

As if to lend weight to this analysis, Big Mama appeared in the corridor outside, her whole body covered with clinging young. Stretching her long alien gams, she stepped over the hole at the threshold in a single mighty stride. Leaping down, her offspring charged the cat, who rushed to meet them, cracking a good half-dozen elongated skulls before the splashing acid ate through his staff.

Backpedalling swiftly, he rejoined Shiro and O'Hara.

"That *deus ex machina* is sure biding its time," said O'Hara, as the aliens drew near.

Shiro asked: "What does *deus ex machina mean*, by the way?"

"The Mussolini from the machine," said O'Hara.

"No," said Tomokato. "That's *Duce ex machina*."

Nonetheless, *Duce ex machina* is what saved them, at least for the time being; through one of the walls burst Mussolini *and* his mistress, pursued by a bunch of partisans with Beretta submachine-guns.

"I toll you we maka the wrong turn," said Mussolini to his squeeze, sounding remarkably like Kevin Kline in *I Love You to Death*.

Apparently incensed by this ethnic stereotype, the partisans cut loose with their guns, and quite unlike those sharpshooters in that famous Italian joke, they put a great deal of lead into *Il Duce* and his babe, so much so that they had nothing left over for the aliens, who, pretending to be Germans, quickly scared them back the way they had come.

"What craven incompetents!" O'Hara cried. "And I thought the author was part Italian!"

"Yes, but he likes to pass himself off as a WASP," said Shiro. "Pretty despicable, huh?"

"Yep," said Big Mama, her brood advancing on the felines and O'Hara once more.

But just before the situation got terminally sticky, the real *deus ex machina* arrived--- demolishing the bay doors, a spaceship skidded to a stop just short of our protagonists. Startled, the aliens leaped back, and who can blame 'em?

The vessel's front end lifted with a whir. Out stepped the Terminationer, carrying an Oerlikon 35 millimeter anti-aircraft cannon.

Tomokato, Shiro, and O'Hara all ducked. Big Mama's troops surged forward. The Terminationer chopped the creatures up with the Oerlikon while the kitties and the Cleavage Officer---sounds like the title of a fifties sex-farce, doesn't it?---snuck round him, diving into his ship.

"Do you know how to pilot a craft like this?" Tomokato asked O'Hara.

"Nope," she replied. "But how much can there be to it?"

Going to the only console in evidence, she started pushing the plastic buttons, being very careful not to break her dynamite long red nails.

The ship's front end swung down; moments later, the engines cut in with a roar, and the vessel lurched into motion.

Looking through the forward view-plates, Tomokato saw the Terminationer spraying the Queen Mother, who appeared to be the only alien left alive. The rapidly-accelerating spaceship smashed into the robot, knocking him from sight, then struck Big Mama, pinning her against its nose as it butted its way through bulkhead after flimsy bulkhead.

At last the craft exploded out into the travelling matte. The mother began smashing her fanged tongue against the view-plates, which soon cracked.

But as one might have expected, the Terminationer's very own spaceship was full of weapons, making O'Hara's stash seem downright paltry by comparison. Even as the Queen forced her head through the glass, Tomokato and Shiro rolled Big Bertha right up to the alien's snout. The railway gun gave the alien pause at last.

"You know, you never really made any attempt to reason with me," she said.

"How's this for an argument?" Shiro asked, and pulled the lanyard, blowing her---or rather, several thousand shiny black pieces of her---clear into the next star-date.

Yet hardly had she made her exit when the Terminationer came crawling up from under the ship and took her place at the hole in the view-plate.

Tomokato loaded another shell into the cannon.

"Don't shoot!" the Terminationer cried.

"Why not?" Shiro demanded.

"Because no matter vhat ridiculous amount of trauma you inflict on my combat chassis, you know perfectly vell dot I'll be back."

Tomokato sighed wearily. "That does indeed seem to be the way of it. But if we let you kill us now, all that supreme toughness and resiliency of yours will actually have proved to be in excess of function. And how would you feel then? It's for you own good, really. Shiro?"

The kitten fired the round. The Terminationer vanished in the blast, but when the smoke and flames cleared, Tomokato saw him, already tiny with distance, hurtling towards the Horsehead Nebula.

"Supreme toughness and resiliency or no," said O'Hara, "I bet that's the last you'll see of him for a while."

"But not a very long while," Tomokato answered.

"He's trying to kill you?"

"My nephew."

"Why?"

"We're not sure, exactly."

"Is the reason ever going to be explained?"

"Later on in the book, I expect."

"Hey unc," said Shiro. "Wouldn't it be a hoot if the readers got all the way to the end and never found out?"

"Actually, yes," Tomokato replied. "But our continued existence depends on their goodwill. O'Hara---how's the mail running?"

She made a quick tally. "Ten to two in favor of tying up all the loose ends."

"There you have it, Shiro," Tomokato said.

"I suppose continuing to exist is preferable after all," Shiro answered resignedly.

"Well," O'Hara said, "As Mr. Spocky used to say, I suppose so, Captain, I suppose so... Or was it, 'Fascinating, Captain, fascinating'?"

To which Shiro responded. "Did anyone ever answer, 'Redundant, Spocky, redundant'?"

"Why would they?" O'Hara asked, seemingly in dead earnest. Then she cracked a smile, and she and Shiro burst out laughing, freeze-framing while Tomokato looked on in distaste.

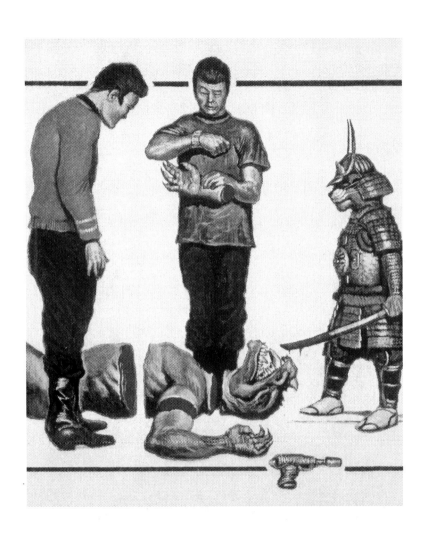

IT'S A TERMINATED LIFE

Tomokato decided that he and Shiro needed a bit of sharpening up. Upon returning to earth, they set out for their secret training facility at Mt. Wheaton, a volcano located in one of the more remote regions of Wheaton, Illinois. Much to their surprise, they discovered a delegation from the press waiting at the mouth of the access-tunnel....

From: *Cat Out of Hell*

Cameras whirred and clicked.

"Miaowara Shiro?" the reporters asked.

"What are you doing here?" Tomokato demanded. "This is a secret facility!"

They laughed through their noses.

"But seriously," said one, "We'd like to speak with your nephew."

"About what?" Shiro asked.

"Your involvement in the Awfli Choklati scandal."

Tomokato wasn't much interested in popular music, but he *had* heard of Awfli Choklati, two very peculiar French-German-Negro singers sporting dreadlocks and very fey nickers; Shiro was always making fun of them, and their music had impressed Tomokato as particularly atrocious. He'd been mildly gratified when their career came to a screeching halt--- an astute critic had pointed out that the recordings for which they had supposedly done the vocals were all instrumentals.

"Unc," Shiro said. "You know how much I hate those guys."

Tomokato believed him, but Shiro typically had a low opinion of his partners in crime.

"Are you denying that you've worked for Aristophanes Records?" a second reporter asked the kitten.

"No..."

"Isn't it true that you invented the whole Awfli Choklati scam?"

"Certainly not!" Shiro cried. "I was simply a consultant for Aristophanes."

"What kind of consultant?" a third reporter inquired.

"I brought them offensive packaging concepts---"

"Enough," Tomokato broke in. "Nephew, come with me."

Taking Shiro by the paw, the cat dragged him up to the cunningly-concealed panel which controlled the door to the access tunnel. Using all his speed so that the reporters wouldn't catch the code, he punched in a 9-digit sequence. The door slid open. Snatching the mail from his mailbox, he pulled Shiro into the tunnel, then shooed several of the reporters back outside before the door closed. The tunnel's lights had lit when the sequence was punched; Tomokato noticed a letter to Shiro atop the sheaf of mail.

It was from Aristophanes records.

The cat opened it, finding a check for a million five.

"What's this?" Tomokato asked.

"A check," Shiro said. "Sheesh."

"They paid you a million and a half dollars?"

"I came up with some *really* offensive concepts."

Tomokato looked at the notation on the check. "Payment, Awfli Choklati."

"I worked on their follow-up album. Did everything I could to torpedo it. The cover shows a maggot looking at their first album and barfing."

"And the people at Aristophanes bought that?"

"No, but they had to pay me anyway. It was in the contract..."

"So you destroyed your consulting career just to cause problems for Awfli Choklati?"

"Nah. I reworked the concept and sold it to this Thrash group called Schnott. You know, the one where their fans call themselves Schnottzis? Used to be known as Elephantiasis....."

"You're lying," Tomokato said, walking away from him.

"I'm not!" Shiro cried, running up alongside.

"You cheated all those people that bought those records. And worse yet, *you* invented Awfli Choklati..."

"No I didn't," Shiro answered. "But even if I had, it's not like it was Marxism-Leninism or Hello There Kitty or something like that..."

"You're just as crooked as you ever were," Tomokato said.

"Have I been indicted?" Shiro asked. "Have I been charged with anything?"

"Be quiet," said Tomokato, stepping from the tunnel into the training facility, which took up the whole bottom of the volcano crater. A huge glass bubble overarched the crater floor, which was covered with padding; weapons from every land and historical period lined dozens of racks. The entire setup had been paid for by a grant from the U.S. Federal Government, Divison of Cat Secret Training Facilities; if you have a cat and would like to write them, their address is 1442 Connecticut avenue,. Washington, D.C. 40402, attention Liz Sperling, and include a 12 by 16 manilla S.A.S.E. Allow six weeks for return.

But whatever.

"Your crimes are a terrible blot on our family's honor," Tomokato said. "On *my* honor, because I've taken responsibility for you. As I've said, Shiro, you make me wish I'd never been born."

Taking off his armor, he knelt, placing his scabbarded shortsword across his lap.

Shiro seemed to recall seeing the cat in a similar posture.

He's going to kill himself again, he thought, feeling a surge of panic. But before he completely lost control of himself, it occurred to him that there must be something defective about his memories, seeing as how his uncle could hardly kill himself twice.

On the other hand, he reminded himself, *Cats* do *have nine lives...*

That did seem to render the situation less urgent. Still, he was in no mood to watch Tomokato's intestines come slurping out on the floor, and he was in even less of a mood to help uncle on his way by slicing his head off, even though, generally, slicing people's heads off and watching their guts come slithering out appealed to him.

He decided to pray. Totally lacking in religion as he was, he wasn't quite sure who he was praying to, but evidently his supplications were floating up to the right spot, seeing as how an obviously angelic little fellow with bushy white brows and a long dark overcoat appeared out of nowhere, carrying a copy of The Mysterious Stranger. Noticing Shiro looking at the book, he said:

"It's really quite an awful piece of work, but we find it absolutely hilarious where I come from."

"Who are you?" Tomokato asked.

"My name is Henry. I'm your guardian angel."

Tomokato looked at him incredulously.

"The answer to your prayer," Henry went on.

"I wasn't praying," Tomokato replied.

"Shame on you," Henry said. "You should pray more often."

"*I'm* the one who was praying," said Shiro.

"As if anyone would listen to *you*," Henry answered. "You'll notice *your* Guardian Angel isn't here. I know him very well. He doesn't like you."

"My Guardian Angel doesn't like me?"

"He's putting in for a transfer."

"To who?" Shiro asked.

"Charles Manson," Henry replied.

"Anyway," Tomokato said, "What are you doing here?"

"I came to help you," Henry answered. "You musn't let Shiro's awfulness get you down."

"Mustn't I?"

"You can't go around wishing you'd never been born."

"Why not?"

"For one thing, it's too late."

Tomokato grunted, nodding.

"For another," Henry said, "You've done more good---particularly for Shiro---than you know."

Tomokato laughed bitterly. "His Guardian Angel would rather work for Charles Manson."

"Does sound bad, doesn't it?" Henry admitted. "But if you'll indulge me for a while, I think I can make my case."

"How?"

"By showing you what the universe would be like if you'd never existed."

"You can do that?"

"You mean *you* can't?" the angel asked.

"You're making fun of me," Tomokato said.

"Yep."

"Is that an angelic thing to do?"

"Obviously," Henry answered. "Now then---"

"Wait," Tomokato said, noticing a shadow on the floor. Looking up through the dome, he saw a figure drifting downwards on a parachute, with what appeared to be a Leopard 2 tank clutched under one arm.

"It's that robot again!" the cat cried.

The Terminationer alighted on the dome, the parachute settling over him and the tank. There was a crackling sound, the dome gave, and the automaton and his panzer dropped to the floor in a hail of broken crystal.

"Can you get rid of the robot for me?" Tomokato asked the angel.

"Sure," the angel answered--- and did nothing whatsoever.

"Will you get rid of the robot for me?" Tomokato asked.

"Nope," Henry replied. "I like watching great big fights. Why do you think I became your guardian angel?"

The Terminationer was still in the process of untangling himself from the parachute; Tomokato ran over to one of his TOW missile launchers. Flinging the parachute aside, the robot jerked back the Leopard 2's bolt, clapped his hand to the forward pistol grip, and was just about to fire when Tomokato loosed the TOW. The automaton tried to dodge; the missile struck the tank in his arms. White flame blossomed, billowing towards the broken ceiling.

"Can I proceed now?" Henry asked the cat, ducking a piece of shrapnel.

Tomokato looked at the tangled fiery mass that had been the tank, but was unable to make out anything that might've been the Terminationer.

"Am I going to need my armor?" he asked the angel.

"Boy are you," Henry replied.

Using the *Hitachi Fujitsu*, or *ancient samurai technique for quickly putting on armor*, Tomokato slipped back into his gear in a matter of seconds.

"Okay," he said.

"Wait, wait!" Shiro shouted, pulling a Suomi submachine gun out of a rack and stuffing three drum clips into his kimono. Rejoining Tomokato and the angel, he said:

"Let's book."

Henry snapped his fingers. "Julie Andrews!" he cried.

Wind swept over them, heavy with a hideous sour stench, and the fire from the burning tank sputtered out...the sky had gone from blue to black.

"Hey!" Shiro cried. "How come it's night all of a sudden?"

"The sun blew up last Tuesday," said Henry. "It's always dark now, except for the novas."

"Novas?"

"Just wait," Henry said. There were several bursts of light, in different parts of the sky...before long the vault of heaven seemed to be full of flashbulbs. In the strobing glare, Tomokato saw that his facility was no longer furnished. The access tunnel appeared to be gone as well.

"All that government money went to some other cat," Henry explained.

But the remains of the tank were still smoking in the middle of the crater-floor, and even as the cat looked, the robot rose slowly out of them.

"Well what do you know?" Henry said. "He was sucked into this alternate future with us."

"You're an angel," Tomokato said. "Can't you forsee things like that?"

"It would seem not," Henry replied, with a cheerful laugh.

"Up the crater wall!" Tomokato cried.

There was no dome now. Picking their way by the light of the exploding stars, they ascended the jagged incline.

Glancing below, Tomokato saw the Terminationer trying to disentangle what looked like a small spare tank out of the wreckage of the Leopard...the cat and his companions reached the rim of crater before the robot was done.

There was no trace of Wheaton, if indeed it had ever existed in this alternate reality. Riven with red-glowing cracks, a desolate plain stretched eastward, huge shapes like theropod dinosaurs patrolling the grim tableland, running at great speed with their tails straight out behind.

"What happened?" Tomokato asked, horrified.

"I told you," said Henry. "You haven't been born."

Silhouetted against the light of the exploding stars, a vast black city loomed in the east like an obsidian mountain range, the light of the novas gleaming intermittently from its many towers. Sharklike spacecraft hovered about, or rose from innumerable platforms.

"Where's Chicago?" Shiro asked.

"That *is* Chicago," the angel replied. "Or rather, Shi-town, as it's known now."

"No it's not," Shiro said. "I spent some time there. It couldn't have changed so much."

"Think so?"

"Are the Cubs still losing?" Shiro asked.

"Is God omnipotent, omnipresent and ominiscient?"

"Hmm," said Shiro. "Maybe it is Chicago after all."

Tomokato looked up at the moon. Without sunlight to reflect, it was a dark mass, dimly fringe-lit from time to time by the bursting stars. Abruptly it dropped from orbit, and, landing some distance north of Shi-Town with a very loud noise, rolled over the horizon into Wisconsin.

"Why did it fall?" Shiro asked.

"The Eye must have decreed it," Henry said.

"The Eye?"

"He Who Could Only See More If He Had *Two* Eyes," Henry answered. "He really hates celestial bodies."

"Why?"

"They ignore him. He was unusually patient with the moon as it was."

Tomokato heard movement, and peered back down into the crater. The robot was racing up towards them, carrying that much littler tank.

"Let's go!" the cat cried.

They rushed down the slope. Reaching the bottom, Tomokato saw that the plain's surface was entirely covered with skulls--- most of them human, but many from alien species.

Cannon-fire shattered the crunchy shingle off the right, sending bone-chips flying. Tomokato and the others raced farther out onto the plain.

Apparently attracted by the noise, a theropod patrol came sprinting towards them; from the south, a small shark-ship flew near, emitting a high-pitched whine, small orange lights like eyes glowing all along its polished surface. A beam blazed from the craft's snout; Tomokato froze in place, paralyzed.

On the fringe of sight he saw Shiro and the angel, likewise motionless. Whether or not Henry was actually paralyzed, or merely standing still for fellowship's sake, (or for laughs, for that matter) Tomokato had no way of telling.

249

The theropods closed in. Tomokato was appalled to see that they were clad in black S.S. uniforms, although he soon noticed that one of the runic S's was missing from their collars, and that their armbands sported black pawprints rather than swastikas. The pawprints were very similar to the Miaowara *mon*, except for one thing--- a red eye directly in the middle of the palm.

The cannonfire had stopped. One of the tyrannosaurs snagged Tomokato with a little meathook arm and carried him off; another ran up alongside, carrying the Terminationer, minus the spare tank. Tomokato wondered why the robot had been affected by the paralysis-beam, ultimately deciding that the ray must be of some very ingenious all-purpose sort. He *was* in an alternate universe after all, and generally, that explained just about anything.

Clawed feet pounding, crunching bone with every step, the dinosaurs sped across the plain of skulls to the black gate of Shi-Town. Spotlights illuminated a vast inscription on the arch: *I WON'T GROW UP.*

A single smooth iron sheet, sixty feet tall, the gate slid downwards into the earth. The dinosaurs entered a huge courtyard dominated by a collossal statue. Tomokato guessed the figure was a cat, although it was difficult to tell, given the preposterous muscularity of the figure. It sported an eyepatch, and held a Thompson submachine gun in one paw, a large dumbbell in the other. The cat was in the process of doing a very vicious-looking curl.

DER FURRY read a tablet on the pedestal.

The tyrannosaurs proceeded across the courtyard, passing a long scaffold strung with all manner of bodies. To his horror, Tomokato discerned Colonel Claus, Wisconsin Platt, Wisconsin Solo, and the W.O.B.L. hanging from the scaffold. Beside the W.O.B.L. Will Rogers dangled, lynched with one of his own lariats, apparently. On his chest was a sign that read:

But not everyone liked me.

Next to Will Rogers swung St. Francis of Assisi, and next to St. Francis, half a forest full of the saint's little animal buddies, like something out of some grim and ill-thought out cross between *Bambi* and *The Killing Fields*.

The dinosaurs entered a vast torchlit corridor; along either wall were lines of guards, alien and human, standing stiffly at attention, looking very smart in crisp black uniforms and horned helmets, every other inch of them adorned with some kind of gun. Officers strutted up and down in front of the sentries; with awful regularity one would shout "You've failed us for the last time!" and shoot a sentry in the head. Once the body slumped backwards into an opening which opened to receive it, another guard would rise up out of the floor in precisely the same spot the fallen one had occupied, as though he'd been spring-fed from a clip. The system seemed to function like clockwork, even if it was hard to see exactly what the point was.

Deep inside the mammoth structure, the theropods went to a dino-sized office and inquired if the "Security Director" was in. Told that he was with the High Priest, they swiftly brought the prisoners to a hallway roughly the length of Long Island, its walls hung with black paw-print banners and quotes from Der Furry. At one end was a dais with an altar upon it; over the altar hung a hundred-yard long flag setting forth what might well have been Der's whole program:

A full clip in every gun, a drain in every floor, and Me.

The tyrannosaur captain went through an archway on the left, spoke with someone, then came back out. Presently a man in long black vestments appeared, accompanied by a particularly large tyrannosaur in a superbly-fitted tux.

Tomokato's jaw dropped.

The cleric was Hasdrubal Lectern.

And more unpleasant still, the Chief of Security was Ubersaurus Rex. He squinted at the Terminationer, then asked the captain:

"You say they were being pursued by this robot?"

"Yes sir," the captain answered.

"Is he the one the rebels sent back?"

"To assassinate the God-Emperor? I believe so, sir."

"Hmm," said Rex. "Dismissed."

The captain and his troops marched out.

"Who are you?" Lectern asked the prisoners.

"We'd better co-operate," Henry told the felines.

"Why?" Tomokato asked.

"Because there's a bunch of exposition that depends on it."

"Ah," said the cat. "My name is Miaowara Tomokato."

"And mine is Miaowara Shiro," said the kitten.

Lectern and Ubersaurus Rex smiled gruesomely at each other, *both* of them shining flashlights up under their chins.

"The robot must have blundered into an alternate past," Rex said.

"But the angel brought them all here," Lectern said.

"To teach some particular moral lesson, no doubt..."

"Excuse me," said Tomokato. "How did you know my companion there is an angel?"

Rex replied: "You might as well ask me how I know his name is Henry."

"Very well. How do you know his name is Henry?"

Lectern spun Henry round. *Henry the Angel* read a nametag on Henry's overcoat.

"Miaowara Shiro," mused Ubersaurus Rex.

"It *is* a tempting thought," said Lectern.

"What is?" Shiro asked.

"Putting you on the throne," said Rex. "Subject to our guidance, of course."

"Henry," Tomokato said. "Why did you do this? If you hadn't brought us here, Shiro would *never* have become the Malevolent God-Emperor of the universe!"

"Thank you, Henry!" Shiro crowed.

"Shiro!" Tomokato cried. "You *can't* go along with this!"

"He can and he will," said Rex.

"You understand why we want you in the post, of course," said Lectern to Shiro.

"Yeah, sure," Shiro answered. "We had a chat with the robot."

"And what did he tell you?"

"That he was trying to prevent me from becoming the God-Emperor. I guess it's just my destiny. I always knew I'd find myself a real good job."

"Shiro," Tomokato said. "Never in my wildest dreams did I imagine you could sink so low..."

"Unc," the kitten answered, "When I saw that plain of skulls, I knew I was *home*."

"Miaowara Shiro," said Lectern, "God-Emperor of the Universe."

"I feel comfortable with it already," Rex added. "It almost has a familiar ring."

He and Lectern laughed.

"I take it you have no desire to help us," said Lectern to Tomokato.

"Are you kidding?" Shiro asked. "He's Moral-Rectitude-*san*, and it's gotten real old, believe me."

"You have no objection then, Emperor-to-Be, if I eat his liver?"

"Hell no," Shiro said. "Just save some for me. How about freeing me from this paralysis, by the way?"

Lectern produced a small silvery device and clicked it at Shiro.

"What about the robot?" Shiro asked, flexing his limbs.

"He's already programmed to kill a God-Emperor," Lectern said. "We won't have to tinker with him too much."

"And the angel?" Shiro inquired.

"Would you like to join us?" Ubersaurus Rex asked Henry.

"Oh, why not?" Henry replied.

Tomokato demanded: "What kind of an angel *are* you?"

"Angel second class," Henry replied. "I haven't gotten my wings yet. Which means I have to be kind of sneaky."

"Sneaky, eh?" Ubersaurus Rex asked. "Then why should we trust you?"

"Do you trust Dr. Lectern?" Henry replied.

"I'm not a fool," the dinosaur said.

"I wouldn't ask him to," Lectern put in. "He'd insist that I trust *him*, and where would it all end?"

"There you have it, the slippery slope," said Henry.

"Free him, doctor," said the dinosaur.

Lectern clicked the de-paralyzer at Henry, then summoned a group of blackclad temple guards.

"Take the cat to my quarters and marinate him," Lectern commanded.

Tomokato's eyes darted toward Shiro.

"Will the marinade kill him?" Shiro asked Lectern.

"Not for a few days, Emperor-to-Be," Lectern said.

"Good and slow," Shiro said, nodding...he eyed Tomokato. "Yep, Uncle-*san*. I really *am* going to let them do it."

As the guards carried Tomokato away, he heard Shiro saying: "I had a gun with me when I was captured...a Suomi Model 1931. It's a classic, one of my favorites..."

"It shall be returned to you, Emperor-to-Be," Ubersaurus Rex replied.

"Can that to-Be stuff and just call me Emperor," Shiro answered.

"Certainly, Emperor."

"I *love* it!" Shiro cried.

You little monster, Tomokato thought.

The guards hustled the cat to a large darksome apartment decorated in early chainsaw massacre. The air was thick and sour with dubious aromas. There were photographs of Lectern playing femora stick-ball with Ted Bundy, human-head polo with John Wayne Gacy, and solitaire with Henry Lee Lucas; from one wall hung a Wisconsin state flag autographed by Jeffrey Dahmer and Ed Gein.

The guards took the cat into the kitchen, where a huge iron pot rested on the floor, two-thirds full of black fluid. The cat smelled Teriyaki sauce and several other less mentionable things. The guards hoisted him onto the rim of the vessel; what appeared to be a thoroughly soggy Liberace gazed sightlessly up at him with a heavily marinaded smile.

Hell is upon me, Tomokato thought, and had just begun to tip when four squat felines, bodies bursting with muscles, faces badly scarred, came leaping out of somewhere, drawing SIG-Sauer pistols from the myriad holsters spaced at regular intervals over their bodies.

"Pull him back!" one growled, in a voice that Tomokato found curiously familiar.

"Set him on the floor!" said another, his voice even more curiously---even *maddeningly*--- familiar.

The guards laid Tomokato beside the pot.

"The Emperor's mother wants to see him," said the first intruder.

"The High Priest shall hear of this!" said a guard.

"Maybe. But not from you guys."

Skillfully and swiftly slipping sound-suppressors onto their SIG-Sauers (sufferin' succotash!), the cats treated the guards to an exuberant display of close-in silenced rapid fire, manually re-priming their pistols after each discharge; but the guards, being steadily riddled with bullets as they were, seemed quite oblivious to the marvellousness of the felines' technique. One by one, they bounced over the side of the pot, joining Liberace in the marinade, so weighed down with lead that they sank immediately from sight in the black pungent-smelling juice.

One of the cats clicked a de-paralyzer at Tomokato and said, "Come with us."

Tomokato narrowed his eyes.

"It's entirely to your advantage," the other answered.

"Who are you?" Tomokato asked.

"The God-Emperor's brothers."

Tomokato thought he detected the remains of a Japanese accent.

256

"You're taking me to see your mother?" he asked.

"Come on. We've wasted enough time here."

They led him through a series of secret passages to a suite that made the cat---who was certainly no Neoplatonist, Christian or otherwise--- wonder if he were contemplating the idea of bad taste in the mind of God. Tigerskins covered the floor; virtually every inch of wallspace was taken up with huge black velvet paintings in spray painted gold bamboo frames. Clouds of incense hung near the ceiling, and *I Wanna Marry a Lightouse Keeper* was playing on the stereo; the TV, sound muted, was displaying a particularly inane-looking bit of Nipponese animated porn involving unicorns and big-breasted blonde nymphs with no feet to speak of.

"Sons, you may leave," said a sultry feminine voice.

"You think you'll be safe, mama-*san*?" they asked.

A voluptuous female cat appeared in a doorway, balanced weightlessly on the highest thinnest spike heels Tomokato had ever seen. She was wearing a tight *cheongsam* with a very high slit and a circular area cut out of the bodice to reveal an expanse of superb pneumatic cleavage. Her stockings were black, embroidered with dragons that coiled round her long muscular legs, which truly went *all* the way up.

"I'll be all right," she replied.

Her sons left.

She strode up to Tomokato, admiring him brazenly, exquisitely-slanted eyes dark and lovely in a white haughty face.

"I like you a lot," she said huskily.

"You don't even know me," he answered.

"You're male, I'm female. What else is there to know?"

"Knowing how to paint with inks is nice," Tomokato replied. "Also calligraphy."

She bit her lower lip. "Say that again."

"Also calligraphy."

She moaned, rubbing her hands up and down her thighs.

"Excuse me," he said, disturbed by this display. "I didn't mean to encourage you."

"You remind me of my husband," she breathed.

"Does he know that you carry on like this?" Tomokato asked.

"He can hardly blame me. He hasn't touched me since I killed him."

"Perhaps that's just as well," Tomokato said.

"I *had* to do it. He didn't want me to have a career."

"What sort of career?"

She screamed. "That's what he kept asking me! After the second or third time, I just couldn't take it anymore. Of course, I developed a very short temper after I came down with that fever..." she sat down on a black leather sofa, crossing those glorious legs and patting the leather beside her. "Come over here, you dray bid putty-tat you."

"I'd rather stay here, if you don't mind."

"Mind?" she asked, exhaling sharply through her nostrils, squeezing her legs powerfully together. "Mind?"

"Yes," he said. "Mind."

"Do you know who I am?" she screeched, then said immediately: "Don't answer that. No one knows the *real* me." She pouted at him, then waved a hand towards the black-velvet paintings. "I did all of them myself, you know...which is your favorite?"

"The one with the Mexican Girl in the clown makeup."

"That's my favorite too. Can't you see what I'm trying to tell you? I love you!"

"Is that why you had me brought here?"

"Yes---in part. I have secret cameras mounted in the altar chamber. I saw you with Ubersaurus Rex and Lectern, and knew that I simply *must* have you. But I couldn't hear what was being said----the audio was on the fritz. You wouldn't like to tell me, would you?"

Tomokato realized he'd be signing Shiro's death-warrant, and while the little criminal obviously deserved anything that was coming to him, Tomokato hadn't decided what to do about him.

"We were discussing golf," he said at last.

Her eyes greyed over at the mere mention of the ostensible sport, and she blinked dizzily.

"Surely you'd like to change the subject," he said.

Rubbing her forehead, she asked: "Who are you, anyway?"

"Samurai Cat."

"Goofy name."

"It's not my fault."

"But really," she said, "Who are you?"

"My nephew's uncle."

"If I had a nephew, I could say the very same thing."

"Not truthfully," Tomokato answered.

She weighed his point. "You're right," she said, cupping her full breasts with her red-nailed paws. "I'm no one's uncle." Reclining, she lifted her legs high, said "la-la," and kicked her shoes off. "Just breathing your air makes me feel like a woman."

"You still *look* like a cat," Tomokato said.

"A big savage jungle cat," she said, sliding to the floor and coming towards him on all fours. "A lioness in heat."

"Lions live in the savanna."

"Ooh," she said. "Correct me again."

"You'll have to make another mistake."

She looked at him lustfully, sighing:

"I've always thought that the Smoot-Hawley Tarriff prolonged the Great Depression."

"Sorry," he said. "I'm afraid I agree with you."

She rose, clasping him about the waist. "Kiss me."

In truth, he was sorely tempted, but he was deeply committed to a life of harsh asceticism. Also, attractive as her mouth was, he was certain it had been some obnoxious places.

"What's the matter?" she asked. "Is it my face?"

"You're very beautiful," he answered.

"Took me quite a while to get something I could live with," she said. "Went through a dozen plastic surgeons."

"Plastic surgeons?"

"After the bomb-blast...it was the rebels, of course. There was nothing much that could be done for my sons; they were *so* ripped up. To tell you the truth, I think they enjoy being so scarred. But I think I look---and sound--- as good as new. Better, in fact." She pinched him on the cheek. "So what's it going to be? I'm telling you, if you can't smelt my ore, we're going to have to kill you."

"What's that rocket over there?" Tomokato asked, deftly changing the subject.

She looked over her shoulder at the missile, which was visible through a huge plate-glass window.

"That's one of my son's projects," she said.

"Which son?"

"The Emperor," she said, leading him over to the window by the paw. "The missile was built to test a certain theory. Have you ever heard of Solaronite?"

"No," he answered.

"That's what the warhead is made of. Solaronite's existence was first postulated by one Edward D. Wood Jr,. He was once a laughing-stock, but now, thanks to my son, he's recognized as what he truly was---the greatest genius of the twentieth century---"

"But what does Solaronite *do*?" Tomokato asked.

"It will enable us to explode the very particles of sunlight," she replied.

"I don't understand," he said.

261

"I'll explain it simply," she said, adopting her best Dudley Manlove. "Take a can of gasoline. Say this gasoline is the sun. Spread a thin line of it to a ball representing the earth. The gasoline represents the sunlight, the sun particles. Here we saturate the ball with the gasoline or sunlight. Then put a flame to the ball. The flame will travel speedily around the earth, back along the line of gasoline, sun particles, to the can, or the sun itself. It will explode this source and spread to every place that gasoline, our sunlight, touches. Explode the sunlight here, and a chain reaction will occur direct to the sun itself, and to all the planets the sunlight touches---to every planet in the universe---"

She swayed as though she'd been overcome by the sheer weight of the thoughts she'd just expressed.

"But what if the test is successful, and the universe is destroyed?" Tomokato asked.

"We can't concern ourselves with questions like that," she replied.

"Why not?"

"We just *can't*."

"Of course," Tomokato said, "I might point out that your offspring has *already* blown the sun up..."

She smiled maternally. "I'm *so* proud of him. He dedicated the explosion to me."

"Oh?"

"He says he thinks of me every time he blows something up."

"Hmm."

"Anyway, all we need is light from some other star."

"Then why was it necessary to mount the warhead on a missile?"

"Visual excitement."

"What about that insignia on the booster?" Tomokato asked.

"The pawprint was the device of my husband's clan," she answered. "The eye is for the God-Emperor, who only has one since the explosion."

"You know," Tomokato said, "The *mon* of my clan looks remarkably similar..."

"How very interesting," she yawned. "Are you going to boff me or not?"

"I'm sorry," he said. "I find you extremely attractive, but I've renounced boffing."

"And I though you were a stud."

Tomokato replied: "Most people think that. And I suppose, if it comes right down to it, that I *am* a stud. But in a completely un-studlike way."

She stepped back from him, calling: "Oh, boys."

Her sons charged into the room, Sigs and paralyzers in paw...Tomokato backflipped high into the air, landing behind their mother. Four paralysis-beams struck her, freezing her solid.

"Mama-*san*!" her boys cried in unison, so stunned by their mistake that they paused momentarily, giving Tomokato time to reach one of the black-velvet paintings, the Mexican-clown-girl. While the cat had a deep visceral detestation for such art, he also possessed a keen appreciation of its sheer deadliness, and had spent many gruelling hours mastering the esoteric forms---unknown even in the East, or anywhere else, for that matter---through which its devastating potential could be unleashed in combat.

But his opponents were also versed in *Shi-tart-do*, or *The Way of Crap Art*. Holstering their pistols, they chose to meet him in kind, seizing particularly egregious paintings and advancing slowly towards him, plainly expecting him to put his back to the wall.

He hurled himself toward the cat furthest on the right, slashing.

His chosen victim parried the stroke with a wondrously inept copy of one of Frank Frazetta's Conan covers, then launched a blow of his own. Tomokato's painting rose in answer, and he managed to disarm his antagonist. But even in that brief exchange, it had been obvious that the youngster was a talented and powerful fighter. Tomokato downed him with a kick to the jaw.

The other brothers were racing up behind; Tomokato spun. A hurricane of tacky images flashed before his eyes, Boris Bimbos on Pegasuses, a group portrait of Abraham, Martin and John, a copy of the Last Supper in which all the participants appeared about to barf...frenziedly defending himself, Tomokato had no doubt that he could've taken any of one of the brothers, or perhaps even two at the a time; but three were too much.

I wonder who their father was? he thought.

He sent one of them crashing to the floor, then caught the corner of a bamboo frame straight upside the snout; he brought his Mexican girl down on the skull of the cat who'd struck him, destroying the painting, then felt a tremendous impact in the back of the head. He realized that the brother he'd disarmed must have found himself a new weapon: only an imitation Rembrandt, probably *Man in the Golden Helmet*, one with a more than slightly greenish tinge, could have struck with such force.

"Actually," he gasped, sagging towards the floor, "Didn't it turn out that the original was a forgery?"

"How can an original be a forgery?" his antagonists answered angrily in unison.

Tomokato stayed conscious just long enough to say, "If you pass it off as someone else's work…"

Then conked.

The brothers de-paralyzed their mother. Looking down at Tomokato, she said:

"Think I'll give him a second chance. Take him to my private dungeon."

"What about the kitten who was with him?" one asked. "Did you get a good look at him?"

"Yes," she replied.

"Amazing, eh?"

"To say the least," she answered. "Get moving."

"Run through it again," said Shiro to Ubersaurus Rex.

"We'll arrange an audience with the God-Emperor," the dinosaur said. "It's reasonable to think he'll find you intriguing, and he'll certainly want to get a good look at an intact Terminationer. We'll tell him the robot has been re-programmed and disarmed; in

264

reality, the Terminationer will be carrying a hidden weapon---someone made a regrettable error in searching him. When I give the secret command, he'll kill the Emperor. The audience-hall will be sealed off by my troops, and we'll put out the story that the Emperor was wounded in the attack. After a few weeks, you'll make your appearance."

"And no one will notice the difference?" Shiro asked.

Lectern answered: "We have super-steroids that will compensate for the differences in your anatomy; other drugs and surgery will do the rest. Believe me, you'll be very convincing."

Shiro rubbed his paws. "And then I'll be able to act as rotten as I want to?"

"I'm afraid you'll have to," Ubersarus Rex said. "Just to maintain the illusion that you're the God-Emperor."

"Doesn't have much in the way of a conscience, huh?" Shiro asked.

"Let's put it this way," Henry put in, "*his* guardian angel shot himself after two weeks."

"Whoa," said Shiro. "Sounds like a *very* bad boy."

"He is," Henry said.

"Still can't figure out why you decided to join us."

"Angels are pure intellect," Henry said. "My reasons are very complicated. It would take me at least fifty thousand years to explain them---by which time you'd have lost interest in the original question, I think."

"What exactly is the true extent of your power?" Lectern asked.

"Let's put it this way," said Henry. "If power were penguins, I'd be Antarctica."

"Could you make me an angel?"

"What would you want with him?"

"*Angel* food," Lectern replied.

"Hasdrubal," Ubersaurus Rex asked, "Weren't you talking about being *transformed* into an angel?"

"I suppose I was at that," Lectern said, smiling unwholesomely at Henry. "*Could* you change me into an angel?"

"Sure," Henry said. "Poof!"

"I don't feel any different," Lectern answered.

"It'll take a while," Henry said. "Drink lots of fluids." He indicated a paralyzer hanging at Lectern's belt. "I'd really like one of *those* things, by the way. I used to be able to paralyze folks, but I'm on probation."

"For what?" asked Ubersaurus Rex.

"Flirting with the idea of joining Satan's Rebellion," Henry replied. "The Archangel Michael had written this really vicious review of my first novel, see? I was all bent out of shape."

"But you didn't go along with Satan?" Lectern asked.

"He didn't like my book either," Henry replied. "Actually, I went and reread it, and they were both right. Good thing I never asked the Big Man what he thought of it. He can be very frank, you know. Really puts you in your place."

Shiro said, "But aren't you siding with Satan--- "

"By siding with you guys?" Henry looked about apprehensively. "Just don't tell God."

"God is all-knowing," said Ubersaurus Rex.

"Yeah, so *don't tell him*," Henry said. "He *hates* that."

"He's coming round," said one of the brothers. "Put him down, and we'll paralyze him."

Tomokato felt himself being lowered to the floor. Through slitted eyes, he saw one of his captors aiming a paralyzer at him; he heard a click, but no beam emerged from the device. A second try fetched one, but the ray seemed a tad more watery than the ones Tomokato had seen, and it had no effect. Plainly the paralyzer was malfunctioning.

Nonetheless, he held himself absolutely rigid, and the brothers picked him up once more, eventually depositing him before a tall iron door. Keys jingling at his belt, a cat in a guard's uniform came up.

"Our mother has plans for him," one of the brothers said.

"Is he immobilized, My Lords?" the jailer-cat asked.

"You could surf on him."

"Why would I *want* to surf on him?" the jailer asked.

"You forgot your board."

"I don't have a board."

"Then you'd damn well *better* surf on him, hey?"

Laughing, they made off.

Opening the cell, the jailer dragged Tomokato in and stood him up in a corner, asking:

"Like your accomodations?"

The room was quite bare, except for a small "Robo-bar" refrigerator, stocked, no doubt, with preposterously expensive snacks and drinks.

"I wouldn't take anything out of there, if I were you," the jailer said.

"I'm going to be *billed* for this?" Tomokato asked.

"What alternate dimension are *you* from?" the other cat laughed.

Tomokato laughed too---and snatched a paralyzer from the man's web belt.

"Hey, that's mine!" the jailer cried indignantly, just before Tomokato immobilized him. Deftly Tomokato divested him of his uniform and put it on, pleasantly surprised by the way the horned helmet fit over his own headgear.

"*All* that stuff is mine!" the jailer shouted. "They made me pay for it!"

Tomokato looked at him skeptically.

"I had to go to this uniform shop," the jailer continued. "I was the only jailer there that day. It was just me, and all these male nurses and male cheerleaders and flight attendants... I couldn't take it. I'll never go back there again, never, I tell you---!"

Tomokato knocked him cold, then locked him in the cell. Leaving the dungeon-complex, he wandered through cavernous hallways, at last taking an elevator up to the ground floor.

As the lift's doors opened, Ubersaurus Rex stalked past with Lectern and Henry. The tyrannosaur, in full Gruppenfuehrer regalia, was carrying the Terminationer in his foreclaws. Tomokato couldn't see Shiro, but guessed he must be tucked away in one of the Big Ube's pockets.

Five dino storm troopers brought up the rear. No one in the group seemed to notice the cat; he fell in behind them. But he hadn't gone very far when one of the tyrannosaurs looked back.

"Are you *sure* we're going the right way?" Tomokato asked.

The dinosaur snorted disdainfully.

The procession soon came to the God-Emperor's audience-hall. Tomokato was reluctant to follow the others inside; they seemed to be walking on thin air, suspended above an artificial lake, held aloft by what he decided must be a vast invisible force-field.

Gingerly he stepped out onto the unseen floor. Beneath him the water seethed with sharks, titanic crocodiles, krakens, hundred-foot long serpents, giant two-headed killies, great big crappies, mutant sea-squirts, demonically-possessed flounder (already breaded), popcorn shrimp, and Charlie the Tuna, who seemed even more bent out of shape than ever.

Across the lake stood an artificial rock formation; stairs led to a dais and a throne, behind which stood a brace of Tyrannosaurs in red.

Different uniforms, Tomokato noted. *Are they under Rex's command?*

Beside the throne stood the God-Emperor's mother; before it his brothers sat. Upon it was the Emperor himself, or so Tomokato guessed, a monstrously squat grey cat wearing an eyepatch and more handguns and machine pistols than could possibly be strung on a single body. Slowly pumping a two-hundred pound dumbbell with his right arm, the God-Emperor looked out balefully and single-orbedly at the newcomers.

Tomokato heard a powerful rumbling. Visible through a crystal wall behind the God-Emperor and his tyrannosaur guards, a dark round silhouette rolled mountainously along---undoubtedly it was the moon, still rolling round the earth. Novas flared, fringe-lighting the vast object, briefly illumining the purple night.

"All bow!" cried the Emperor's mother. "Bow down before He Who Will Make Damn Sure You're All Killed If You Don't Bow, He Who Could Only See More If He Had two Eyes, Everyone's Favorite, the God-Emperor of the Universe (and Canada!), *Miaowara Shiro!*"

Tomokato felt as though he had been kneed in the stomach.

Shiro? he thought, almost forgetting to bow with the others.

"Come on, Mama-*san,*" the God-Emperor said, glaring at her. "I told you to leave Canada out of it."

"You own it, whether you like it or not," she replied.

Tomokato looked up, squinting at her.

Hanako? he thought, mind reeling.

"Just blow it up, Shiro," said one of the brothers---Agamemnon, Tomokato guessed, going by the color of his fur.

"What *have* I been waiting for?" Shiro agreed, and pulled a microphone from the arm of his throne, commanding, "Toast Canada!"

Beyond the window, a missile lifted off, trailing flame. Moments later, there came a loud blast, and back bacon rained over the chamber's transparent roof.

"Power corrupts, eh?" he asked.

His guards and brothers erupted in furious laughter. Hanako appeared annoyed at first, then shook her head and began to laugh too, pinching him on the cheek. He flinched backwards at her touch.

"All rise," said the God-Emperor.

Tomokato straightened, then realized that Henry was standing beside him.

"Now you see my point, don't you?" Henry inquired.

"Point?" Tomokato asked.

"You said Shiro's rotten behavior made you wish you'd never been born. And I said you'd done him more good than you knew. Well, there's the proof---" Henry nodded towards the throne. "This is a universe where you've never been born. After your mother had Shimura, she refused to have any more kittens---"

"Why?"

"So she could play golf."

"*Golf?*" Tomokato asked.

"And she wasn't even good at it," Henry went on. "Your brother met Hanako anyway, and they fell in love; but when she was wounded by those ninjas---the ones who haven't been mentioned in any Samurai Cat book till now--- you weren't there to tend her, and the fever made her a little funny. She shot your brother one hundred and thirty times. Signed her name on his chest.

"Needless to say, her sons grew up a little funny as well. Do you think Lee Harvey Oswald acted alone?"

"What does that have to do with anything?" Tomokato demanded.

"You've heard of the grassy knoll, haven't you?"

"Those were my *nephews* in there?"

"Except for Shiro. He was the one in the book depository. And he was barely out of diapers. Oswald was totally innocent. Cubans sent him to assassinate someone else entirely."

"This is terrible," Tomokato said.

"Just getting started!" Henry said. "You know when Shiro came to Chicago to study economics?"

"He became a gangster," Tomokato said numbly.

"Absolutely. Only in *this* universe, he *remained* a gangster. You never took him under your wing. He rubbed out Moran and Capone and took over the city. That's where it got the name Shi-Town."

"Shiro-town," Tomokato said.

"After that, he set his sights on the Governer's mansion, then the White-House. He spread around enough simoleons to buy himself a tied election against FDR--- and as you know, in the event of a tie, the issue's decided through single combat. Roosevelt was a mean hand with a spiked crutch, but he didn't stand a chance. Shiro took him apart. And then it was World War Two.

"Shiro signed a nonagression pact with Stalin *and* Hitler, provoked a war between them, and stood back while they fought. Aterwards he picked up the pieces, acquiring those SS dinos in the process, as well as a pack of Nazi rocket scientists, who made it possible for him to carry his program to the rest of the universe. So now he's blown up half the stars in the cosmos, and getting ready to blow up the rest---"

"The Solaronite bomb will work?" Tomokato asked.

"Are you kidding me?" Henry replied. "What do you think Ed Wood Jr. was? A talentless moron?"

"I'm not sure..."

"Not only was he a greater genius than Shakespeare, Dante, Einstein and Newton rolled together, he looked real foxy in an Angora sweater."

"Angels approve of tranvestitism?"

"Of course not," Henry answered. "But a fact's a fact---"

He broke off, for the first time appearing to notice that everyone, the dinosaurs, Lectern, the evil Shiro and his mother and brothers, plus the Terminationer and the real Shiro (who was looking out of one of Ubersaurus Rex's pockets) were all staring at him and Tomokato.

"Is there anything else you'd like to say to him?" the evil Shiro asked Henry.

"As a matter of fact," Henry said, "I'd like to ask him if he wants to split."

"Go ahead," said the God-Emperor.

"Now that you've learned your lesson," said Henry to the cat, "*would* you like to split?"

"And leave these maniacs in charge of this alternate universe?" Tomokato asked, taking off his stolen uniform.

Henry smiled. "We thought you might want to clean this up."

"*We?*" Tomokato said. "I thought you joined the bad guys."

"Nah," said Henry. "Just wanted to get my hands on one of these." He pointed to a paralyzer attached to his belt. "Also, to give the story a creepier feel."

"Marinaded Liberace wasn't creepy enough?" Tomokato demanded.

Henry considered the question. "Maybe me apparently going over to the enemy was a bit gratuitous after all..."

"Are you quite finished?" the God-Emperor cried.

"I think so," said Henry.

"So, Gruppenfuehrer," said the evil Shiro to Ubersaurus Rex. "You intended to replace me with my alternate self, eh?"

"*Moi?*" the Tyrannosaur asked.

"Don't look so surprised, Cretaceous-breath," said Hanako. "I have cameras in the temple. Saw you and Lectern with the little bastard. Couldn't hear the conversation, but it was easy enough to guess what you were up to..."

"Little bastard?" Ubersaruus Rex replied.

"Is that an alternate Shiro in your pocket, or should I make an off-color joke?"

"Secret command!" cried Ubersaurus Rex to the Terminationer.

"About effingk time," the robot replied, but removing the Aegis cruiser he'd secreted in his jacket proved to be a rather laborious process...aiming a sinister black clicker at the force field beneath the robot, the evil Shiro disrupted the patch the robot was standing upon, dumping him and his big macho boat into the beastie tank beneath.

The God-Emperor pointed to Ubersaurus Rex. "Arrest the traitor!" he cried.

"Us?" answered Rex's troops, cocking their helmetted heads to the left *en masse*.

Up till then, Tomokato had assumed that Rex must have brought them into the plan, and that they'd side with the Gruppenfuehrer against the Emperor; but they were plainly confused by this turn of events.

Apparently reading their hesitation as allegiance to Rex, the Emperor turned to *his* tyrannosaur bodyguards, crying:

"Shoot them!"

Unlimbering oversized Sturmgewehr assault-rifles, the redclad dinos trained them on U Rex's troops, opening fire. U Rex's gunsels responded in kind. The guards swiftly slaughtered each other to a saur.

Only Ubersaurus Rex survived the intratheropod carnage; opening one hole after another in the floor, the evil Shiro had kept the dinosaur hopping furiously about, and not a single bullet had struck the monster as a result. Having taken cover behind a dead tyrannosaur's tail, Tomokato and Henry watched the Gruppenfuhrer's leapings in silent awe; the brute was sure light on his feet.

I wonder why he doesn't try to work his way up onto the steps? Tomokato puzzled.

"Just what I was thinking," the dinosaur said, and bounded onto the stairs.

The cat realized that the volume on his mind was turned up way too high, and as the dinosaur charged towards the God-Emperor, Tomokato twirled the dial down.

The evil Shiro and his brothers drew one pistol after another, tearing into the oncoming behemoth. The top of the steps became a veritable volcano of shell-casings; blood rained from the dinosaur, pouring in rivers down the stairs.

But the big Ube continued towards the throne.

"Oh, for heaven's sake," cried the Emperor's mother. "Use your light-fifties!"

Huki, Duki, Luki and Agamemnon all had Barretts strapped over their shoulders; snapping their fingers in disgust at their own stupidity, they unslung the rifles and commenced drilling the tyrannosaur with fifty-caliber slugs.

Exit-wounds splashing bright scarlet blood through his black uniform, Ubersaurus Rex got almost to the top, but the Barretts took him down at last. He rolled to the bottom of the steps, whereupon the Emperor opened the floor beneath him, dropping him into the drink. A vast red cloud widened as the underwater monsters rushed to the feast.

"Thanks for ridding me of the bastard!" cried Dr. Lectern, standing up from behind a dead tyrannosaurs, lobbing a grenade. The explosion kicked the Emperor back over his throne; Hanako bounced away to the side, while Huki, Duki, Luki, and Agamemnon came tumbling to the bottom.

"So, Emperor!" said Lectern to the non-alternate-Shiro, who'd leaped out of Ubersaurus Rex's pocket at some point. "The universe is all ours now." He leveled a Skorpion machine-pistol at Tomokato.

Shiro leveled his Suomi at the Cannibal. "Should I wax 'im, unc?"

"Don't you want to be God-Emperor?" Tomokato asked.

"Nope, never did," Shiro said. "Just decided to do some infiltrating. Also, it made the story creepier---"

"How do I know you're not lying now?"

"Why would I? Because I'm frightened of you? I could've shot you a long time ago."

"He's telling the truth," Henry said.

"And I was telling the truth about Awfli Choklati, too," Shiro insisted.

"Bullshit," Henry coughed.

Tomokato caught sight of the evil Shiro climbing back over the throne.

"Mom fed us shrapnel every day when we were kids," the Emperor announced. "I'm immune."

Hanako appeared at his side; Huki, Duki, Luki and Agamemnon rose to their feet.

The God-Emperor thrust his disrupter towards Lectern and gave it a click.

Lectern loosed a cry, dropping through the floor.

But Hasdrubal the Horrible never struck the water.

Through the surface burst the bloodied head of Ubersaurus Rex, jaws gaping, and Lectern dropped inside the gigantic maw even as the dinosaur thrust his head up into the hole the disrupter had made...Lectern tried to climb out, but the hole pinched shut around the tyrannosaur's snout, closing his jaws, cutting Lectern in half.

Even with the hole locked around his schnozzola, Ubersaurus Rex managed to lunge farther upwards; Tomokato felt the forcefield lift beneath him, and rolled to the foot of the steps. Climbing onto the stairs with Henry and Shiro, he looked back at the dinosaur.

The monster was working his snout back and forth, frenziedly widening the hole. Within moments, he succeeded in hooking his tiny foreclaws on either side of the aperture, and stretched it open further.

The Emperor's brothers rushed up the steps towards their fallen Barretts. Ubersaurus Rex climbed up onto the floor, greedily gobbling Lectern's top half. The tyrannosaur was in shreds, serpents and sharks still clinging to him in places. Before the evil Shiro could dump him through another hole, the Big Ube seized one of the serpents in his jaws and snapped it like an immense towel, flicking the control from the Emperor's paw, smashing it.

"Now *that's* something I've never seen before," Shiro told his uncle.

"What about this?" Ubersaurus Rex asked, donning a pair of huge skates and throwing the serpent about his neck like a huge scarf; gracefully skimming across the force-field floor, he traced out a gargantuan figure-eight, finishing with a flawless triple spin, looking rather like Tai Babylonia on a really large and ugly night.

"Nope, never seen that either," Shiro answered.

"I've never seen you strangle yourself with a giant snake!" the evil Shiro cried.

"And you're not going to!" Ubersaurus Rex replied, kicking off his skates and charging the steps once more, whirling his serpent, flicking the light-fifties away from the Emperor's brethren.

Suddenly two hundred tenor voices rang out in unison: "Heeeere we come to save the day!"

Tomokato looked back towards the main entrance.

A huge crowd of guards had arrived; they cut loose with every firearm at their disposal. Slugs whistled over Tomokato's head, small caliber, but quite sufficiently numerous. Turning, he saw Ubersaurus Rex twitching furiously, whirling, going "Oooh! EEE! Owww! Akkk!" and clutching at himself with his tweezery forelegs, footing a clattery mazurka of morbidity.

"Got me," he announced at last. Sitting down carefully on the steps, he took his boots off, wiggled his clawed toes, and laid his head on his chest, closing his eyes.

"Just a tad on the late side, aren't you?" the Emperor cried to the guards, stamping.

"We've failed you for the last time, Your Implacable Crabbiness!" they agreed, put pistols to their heads, and blew their brains out in perfect unison.

The God-Emperor eyed Tomokato, Shiro, and Henry, saying: "As for you---"

Another five hundred guards came rushing into the chamber.

Shiro shouted: "Just a tad on the late side, aren't you?"

Understandably mistaking his voice for the God Emperor's, they replied, "We've failed you for the last time, Your Implacable Crabbiness!" and dutifully shot themselves.

"Pretty good," the evil Shiro was forced to admit, reloading a Tech-9.

"Thank you," Shiro answered.

But before they could start in on each other, Henry clicked his paralyzer at the God-Emperor.

Huki, Duki, Luki and Agamemnon popped clips into their Sigs; Henry froze them each in turn.

Hanako hosed him down with a burst with one of those fallen tyranno-Sturmgewehrs. But even though the bullets passed harmlessly through Henry's angelic non-substance, his clicker went the way of all mortal devices.

Shiro trained his Suomi on Hanako; yet for some reason he hesitated.

"Some reason Hell," said Hanako triumphantly, looking directly into the camera. "It's because I'm his mother, ha-ha!"

"Not really my mother," he gritted. "Only my mother in this alternate universe!"

"Oh, I guess," she replied, swinging the Sturmgewehr towards him. But she too hesitated.

Shiro looked into the camera. "Could it be that I remind her too much of her son?"

Henry thrust his face between Shiro and the lens, asking: "Aren't emotions mysterious things?"

"Yep," said Shiro and the evil Hanako together, and started to party.

Remarkably, every single one of their bullets met each other in midair, tip to tip.

"I'll be doggone," said Shiro.

Another mob of guards poured into the audience-chamber.

"Just a tad on the late side, aren't you?" Shiro yelled.

"You're not the God-Emperor!" they replied.

"Yeah, but you're still late!" Shiro answered.

"Dammit," they muttered, shoved their pistols against their temples, and bowed collectively to reason.

But this little interlude had given Hanako enough time to lay her paws on a paralyzer of her own; moments later, Shiro, Tomokato and Henry were all frozen, and her sons were moving about with all the mobility of those capable of motion. The God-Emperor and his family came partway down the steps.

"So," said the evil Shiro to Tomokato. "You're the uncle I never had."

"No," Tomokato spat, "You're the nephew *I* never had."

"No," said the Emperor, pointing to Shiro, "In this universe, *he's* the nephew you never had."

"How do you account for his presence, then?" Tomokato asked.

"I've never gotten any presents from him," the evil Shiro said. "Undoubtedly, that's because you never had him. Which is another bone I'd like to pick with you."

"Perhaps we could make it up to you," said Shiro. "What would you like?"

"Something to blow the universe up."

"You've already got that."

"Suppose it's a dud?" the Emperor asked. "For that matter, suppose the one you give me is *also* a dud?"

"Then you'll have to use the first one," Shiro answered.

"I like the way you think," the Emperor replied. He turned to Tomokato. "You expressed some doubts earlier about my Solaronite bomb."

"It sounds like a pretty stupid idea," Tomokato admitted.

"Then we'll just have to give you a demonstration," the Emperor said. "By the way, have you noticed that you've been fairly passive in this story so far?"

"Actually, I hadn't," Tomokato said. "But now that you mention it..."

He broke off as a fresh infusion of guards thundered in.

"Late, late, late!" the Emperor screamed.

Tomokato heard a host of guns being unholstered.

"But before you pop yourselves," the Emperor said, "Take these wretches to the launch-pad." He indicated the prisoners.

"Shiro, my love," said Hanako, extending her paw to him, apparently expecting him to assist her to the bottom of the steps.

"You know, last time I looked, you had your own legs, Bitch-*san*," he replied, and started down with his brothers, all of them chortling mightily.

Hanako looked at Tomokato. "A mother's heart is made to be broken," she sighed. "Sure you don't want to boff me? After all, this is probably your last chance to boff anyone."

"I had my last chance some time ago," he replied, just as the guards laid hands on him.

Hanako waved them back, seized the cat's chin, and pressed her lips against his. But, icy in his iron zen self-control, he refused to respond, blunting her tongue against the adamantine fence of his steely warrior's teeth.

"What an adamantine fence of steely warrior's teeth you just blunted my tongue against," she said, stepping back, eyes desperate with frustrated longing.

"What can I say?" he asked.

"Say you'll surrender."

"You'll surrender."

She hissed a short, sharp breath. "No, say *I'll* surrender."

"You'll have to say that for yourself," he replied.

"Great Buddha, I hate pronouns," she said, and motioned the guards to bear him off.

Tomokato looked down through the force-field floor as he was carried away. The water was clearing, the blood being filtered out, and to his astonishment, he saw what he guessed was the Terminationer, totally denuded of clothes or flesh, lugging his waterlogged Aegis Cruiser across the bottom of the tank, towards one of the filtration apertures…now that he was no longer covered in meat, the water monsters were paying him no nevermind.

The Emperor's party soon came to the huge courtyard from which his missiles were launched. Looming like a prop in a movie with a budget that Ed Wood could only have wet-dreamed about, the Solaronite Special stood beside its derrick, three hundred feet of stainless steel, gleaming in the beams of a dozen searchlights.

The evil Shiro led the way into a command-booth along the base of one of the walls; except for the men carrying the prisoners, the guards stayed outside.

"Really, my son's going to launch the damn thing," Hanako whispered to Tomokato. "I think we've still got time for a quickie---"

"We'd have time for a lot more if you *kept* him from launching it," Tomokato answered.

"You mean you'd---"

"I didn't say that. But we *would* have a lot more time, wouldn't we?"

Wriggling in indecision, she bit one of her nails and said, "Oooh, oooh, oooh."

"Your Emperorhood," cried the guard holding Tomokato. "Your mother's contemplating putting a stop to these proceedings."

"Really?" asked the evil Shiro.

"She's got the hots for your non-uncle, and wants the universe to continue."

"Who are you going to believe, my love?" Hanako asked the Emperor. "That spear-carrier, or your very own mother?"

"Eat lead, mom!" cried the evil Shiro, and gave her half a magazine from his Tech-9.

Falling, she de-paralyzed Tomokato with her clicker, saying: "Kill that little snake, My Love."

With a swift *Hokkaido Honshu Kyushu*, or *Embarass the Goyim Utterly Move*, Tomokato whirled free of the guards, pulling two fourteen-shot Berettas from them.

The evil Shiro let fly a wild burst of slugs, emptying his clip, killing the guards; but Tomokato had already ducked. Keeping low, the cat shot the men holding Shiro and Henry.

Huki, Duki, Luki and Agamemnon got into the act. Tomokato felt a bullet glance off his left shoulder-guard, then three rapid, violent impacts as three more caught him in various unessential parts of the body. Blasting away brutally and boldly with both Berettas (boy!), he traded fire with the Emperor's brothers. Bullets ripped half the armor from his body, slipped between the lobes of his brain, zipped through those nine or ten spots in the heart where a slug can pass without doing any serious damage; he, on the other hand, tended to be just a few milimeters luckier with his marksmanship, as he was the hero. The brethren backflipped, somersaulted, and died in various gymnastic ways, decorating the command post with numerous splattery colors, all of them red.

The Emperor rushed over to a big lever on the wall with a board above it marked *Launch Rocket With This*. Dropping his now-empty Berettas, Tomokato picked up one of the many *katanas* scattered at random throughout the command post and charged towards the evil Shiro.

The Emperor laughed at him, crowing: "One more step, and I launch the rocket!"

"You'll launch it anyway, won't you?" Tomokato asked.

"Yes," the Emperor replied, "But not as soon, ha-ha!"

Tomokato hurled his sword.

The blade passed through the evil Shiro's paw, jerking it from the lever.

"Luckily, though, I have a *second* paw!" the Emperor cried, and pulled the lever with it.

There was a loud *bzzzt!* and sparks flew from any of the many spark-exits in the wall. Tomokato looked out the window at the rocket. There was no sign of ignition.

"Oh well," said the Emperor, plucking the sword from his wounded mitt and tossing it away. "That's what cigarette-lighters are for!"

Producing one, he sped through one of the exits, making for the rocket's emergency fuse.

Tomokato picked up another sword and chucked it through the door, straight into the Emperor's back. The evil Shiro halted. Turning, he looked down at his chest; the point of the blade had emerged from his ribcage.

"Neat!" he said, smiling.

Picking up yet a third sword, Tomokato went to finish him.

"Guards" the Emperor cried, fetching no response...The ones who'd remained outside the bunker were all way off to the right now, milling around, shouting and shooting and dodging. Tomokato saw the bloodied bow of an Aegis cruiser rising again and again, trailing crushed soldiers. With all the guards between him and ship, he couldn't see who was wielding it, but knew it must be the Terminationer.

He looked back at the evil Shiro---not a second too soon.

Having pulled the sword from his body, the Emperor was standing right in front of him, blade raised.

"Sayonara, Alternate Father's Brother-*san!*" he cried, drooling blood.

Coughing, the Emperor's mother dragged herself over to Shiro and Henry, who had toppled to the floor; she de-paralyzed them.

"I wish *you'd* been my son," she told Shiro.

Shiro tried to comfort her. "I wish you'd been my son too. Sorry I can't stick around, though. Got to help uncle."

"Tell him farewell for me," she answered.

"You'll get to tell him yourself," Henry said. "You have exactly that much time left."

"To crawl out and meet him?"

"He'll be back. Just stay put. You are, after all, quite a mess."

"Sure feels like it," she answered.

Taking pistols from a dead guard, Shiro rushed out.

"Aren't you going to help his uncle?" Hanako asked Henry.

"Nope. As I'm an angel, I thought I'd stay here and comfort you." He pulled out a harmonica. "Do you have any favorites?"

Hanako thought a bit. "'Red River Valley.'"

He patted her soothingly on the head. "'Red River Valley it is.'"

The Emperor laid on a storm of blows; to his extreme discomfort, Tomokato found himself very evenly matched. The kid had clearly inherited the Miaowara martial genius, and the fact that Tomokato was riddled with bullets didn't help much either.

But abruptly the Emperor broke off the attack, retreating swiftly. Shiro rushed up beside Tomokato, blazing away with a brace of Heckler and Koch VP-70's.

The evil Shiro deflected each shot with such skill that Tomokato couldn't repress a surge of familial pride; then, once the good (?) Shiro's pistols went dry, the Emperor dashed for the rocket once more. Reaching the fuse, he began flicking his lighter.

"Guards!" he cried. "Guards!"

Preoccupied as they were with not being squished by the Terminationer, the majority didn't hear, but the minority did, and they got off some rounds before the Aegis came knocking on their skulls. Just about to slice the Emperor, Tomokato caught a couple more slugs, nothing to worry about, but enough to put him down temporarily. Shiro snatched the sword as it fell from his paw.

The evil Shiro looked back over his shoulder, flicking away madly.

"Just think!" the Emperor said. "The whole universe blown to bits!"

"A charming prospect," Shiro answered, "but it's not as if I could claim any credit."

"Ah, but you could," said the Emperor. "I won't be able to do it if you kill me."

"Of course," Shiro said, "If I killed you, then I could light the fuse myself..." He broke off, considering this possiblity.

"Plagiarist!" the Emperor huffed.

"On second thought---" Shiro said, bringing the *katana* down, splitting the evil Shiro's head like a melon, that is to say, *most* gorily, as melons are rather blunt.

But the lighter had already lit the fuse.

Shiro tried to cut it, but it was burning too fast, the flame racing up the side of the rocket, out of reach.

Tomokato staggered to his feet. Shiro helped him back toward the comand post.

A tremendous blast knocked them on their faces. Tomokato turned over, watching the missile lift skywards.

But other missiles were converging on the Solaronite rocket.Tomokato recognized the make--- they were Standards, ordnance from an Aegis. The Terminationer, having finished with the guards, had turned his attention to the Emperor's demented toy.

The sky went red as the Standards connected. The Solaronite rocket traced out a huge fiery DAMN I'M HIT! and dipsy-doodled from view.

Tomokato turned. There stood the Terminationer, a shining skeleton, his smoking ship trailing under one arm.

"Are you still going to try and kill my nephew?" Tomokato asked.

"Wrong Shiro," the robot acknowledged.

A vast scarlet mass came lumbering from a doorway behind him; the robot pivotted, but U Rex, or what was left of him, swapped him hard with his colossal head, knocking him and his boat clear through the side of the courtyard.

"Wasn't he working for you?" Tomokato asked the dinosaur.

"As far as killing the Emperor was concerned," Rex replied. "That was similar enough to his original program. But we couldn't go further than that." He glanced over at the Evil Shiro's corpse. "I see his Imperial Highness is dead. I suppose I have you to thank."

"My nephew," Tomokato replied. "Are you grateful?"

"After my fashion," the tyrannosaur answered, jaws swinging wide.

Tomokato heard a loud rumbling; the wall aft of Ubersaurus Rex crumbled forward.

"Excuse me," cried the cat to the Gruppenfuehrer, just as the dinosaur began to look round. "But you're about to be crushed by the moon."

The Big Ube fixed his eyes on Tomokato once more. "That old one," he snorted contemptuously---just before the fallen satellite mashed him into mesozoic wallpaper, squeezing Hasdrubal the Horrible up from his guts as it did so.

"Still without a spoon," said the cannibal, landing with a vile plop quite close to Shiro and Tomokato, who were even then sidestepping old Luna. Needless to say, the moon made even shorter (or flatter?) work of Lectern than it had of Ubersaurus Rex.

Tomokato and Shiro went back into the command booth.

Henry was just finishing a rendition of "Snoopy and the Red Baron." Tomokato knelt beside Hanako.

"The stars were against us," Hanako gasped. "Will you miss me?"

"I really shouldn't lie," Tomokato said. "But I will just this once. Of course I'll miss you."

"Kiss me, please."

"Very well, but no tongue."

He leaned forward. She kissed him chastely on the lips, whistled the damnedest bluebird imitation he'd ever heard, and died.

The Terminationer came limping into the command post.

"What will you do now?" Tomokato asked, rising.

"Notify ze rebels," the robot answered. "We'ff vun."

"There's not going to be much of a future around here, with the sun blown up and everything," Shiro said.

"Oh, that," said Henry, and snapped his fingers.

Sunlight flooded the courtyard.

"Could you have done that all along?" Tomokato asked.

"Apparently," Henry replied.

"You're a very peculiar angel, you know that?"

"And what would you expect angels to be like?"

"Could you take us back to own universe now?" Tomokato asked.

"Absolutely."

The Terminationer waved goodbye. "Sanks," he said.

Henry snapped his fingers again. "Julie Andrews!"

Tomokato and Shiro found themselves in a dark gallery, staring at a huge fishtank containing an alligator snapping turtle.

"Where are we?" Shiro asked.

"Chicago, of course," Tomokato replied.

"The Shedd Aquarium, right."

Tomokato looked at him sidelong. "So. You really *were* behind that Awfli Choklati business."

"Yeah," Shiro admitted. "But you've got to put it in perspective, uncle-*san*. Consider what I've done in the past. Or how bad I *might* have turned out."

"Are you ever going to go *genuinely* straight?" Tomokato asked wearily.

"Just going to have to wait and see, unc," Shiro replied.

Tomokato nodded, knowing he was in for the long haul. He slipped a finger into a particularly runny bullet-wound in his chest.

"I'd better get to a doctor," he said.

Shiro nodded, walking along beside him, helpfully sticking a digit into a hole in the cat's side. In spite of everything, the cat was deeply touched.

Born in 1952, author-illustrator Mark E. Rogers is best known for the Samurai Cat books: *The Adventures of Samurai Cat, More Adventures of Samurai Cat, Samurai Cat in the Real World, The Sword of Samurai Cat,* and *Samurai Cat Goes to the Movies.* The sixth and final installment in the series is *Samurai Cat Goes to Hell.*

His other books include the Zancharthus trilogy(*Blood + Pearls, Jagutai and Lilitu* and *Night of the Long Knives*),*The Dead, Zorachus, The Nightmare of God, The Expected One, The Devouring Void,* and *The Riddled Man.* One of his novellas, *The Runestone,* was made into a movie; and *The Dead* is presently under development as a feature film---with a screenplay by Mark---at KNB-EFX.

Mark's work has been adapted by Marvel comics, and has appeared on the cover of Cricket Magazine; he's published three art portfolios, and a collection of his pin-up paintings, *Nothing But A Smile,* is available from Xenophile Books. www.XXXenophile.com   Some of Mark's illustrations may be found at www.merogers.com

Mark lives in Newark, Delaware, with his wife Kate---a philosophy professor at the U of D---and their four lovely kids, Sophie, Jeannie, Patrick, and Nick.